KT-221-640

'Somewhere for a woman like me, Mr Evernden?' The cool tone from behind him held the slightest trace of a French accent.

Hell. Apparently the impertinent Mademoiselle Boisette had no qualms about eavesdropping. So be it. Beating around the bush only led to disappointed expectations, as he well knew from his business dealings. Christopher swung around to face her.

His breath hooked in his throat. She had the face of an angel. By God, he'd seen many lovely women in the salons of London, but beautiful did not begin to describe this vision.

As if she read his thoughts, her mouth curved in a smile. She was no seraph. Pure devilment gleamed in the cerulean gaze locked with his.

Placing her gloved fingertip between her teeth, she glanced at him. Her lashes lowered and then swept up again. A lingering question lurked in her eyes.

Eve biting the apple.

He enjoyed the warmth of a willing woman, but had no need of a professional courtesan. And, no matter how beautiful or sensual, he had no interest in a woman who had brought scandal to the name of Evernden.

Author Note

I adored Christopher the moment he walked onto the page, because I knew only a strong, determined woman like Sylvia could lead him on a merry chase. The story is set in places dear to my heart: Dover, where my father was born; Tunbridge Wells, where I downed a few pints with my husband in our courting years; and France, which brought back memories of crossing the channel by ferry one summer. And then, of course, there is Regency London. I love poking around in St James and Mayfair, where you can find traces of the Regency in the buildings if you look very carefully.

I had so much fun writing Sylvia and Christopher's story. I do hope you enjoy it. I love to hear from readers, so please visit me at my website, www.annlethbridge.com, where you can find all my latest news and where you can reach me directly.

THE RAKE'S
INIIERITED
COURTESAN

Ann Lethbridge

⊙™ MILLS & BOON®

Pure reading pleasure™

DID YOU PURCHASE THIS BOOK WITHOUT A COVER?

If you did, you should be aware it is **stolen property** as it was reported *unsold and destroyed* by a retailer. Neither the author nor the publisher has received any payment for this book.

All the characters in this book have no existence outside the imagination of the author, and have no relation whatsoever to anyone bearing the same name or names. They are not even distantly inspired by any individual known or unknown to the author, and all the incidents are pure invention.

All Rights Reserved including the right of reproduction in whole or in part in any form. This edition is published by arrangement with Harlequin Enterprises II BV/S.à.r.l. The text of this publication or any part thereof may not be reproduced or transmitted in any form or by any means, electronic or mechanical, including photocopying, recording, storage in an information retrieval system, or otherwise, without the written permission of the publisher.

This book is sold subject to the condition that it shall not, by way of trade or otherwise, be lent, resold, hired out or otherwise circulated without the prior consent of the publisher in any form of binding or cover other than that in which it is published and without a similar condition including this condition being imposed on the subsequent purchaser.

® and TM are trademarks owned and used by the trademark owner and/or its licensee. Trademarks marked with ® are registered with the United Kingdom Patent Office and/or the Office for Harmonisation in the Internal Market and in other countries.

First published in Great Britain 2009
Harlequin Mills & Boon Limited,
Eton House, 18-24 Paradise Road, Richmond, Surrey TW9 1SR

© Michèle Ann Young 2009

ISBN: 978 0 263 86784 8

Set in Times Roman 10½ on 12 pt.
04-0609-78508

Printed and bound in Spain
by Litografia Rosés S.A., Barcelona

*I dedicate this first book
for Harlequin Mills & Boon
to my two beautiful daughters, Angela and Fiona.
Their support of my writing
means the world to me.*

Ann Lethbridge has been reading Regency novels for as long as she can remember. She always imagined herself as Lizzie Bennet or one of Georgette Heyer's heroines, and would often recreate the stories in her head with different outcomes or scenes. When she sat down to write her own novel, it was no wonder that she returned to her first love: the Regency.

Ann grew up roaming England with her military father. Her family lived in many towns and villages across the country, from the Outer Hebrides to Hampshire. She spent many memorable family holidays in the West Country and in Dover, where her father was born. She now lives in Canada, with her husband, two beautiful daughters, and a Maltese terrier named Teaser, who spends his days on a chair beside the computer, making sure she doesn't slack off.

Ann visits Britain every year, to undertake research and also to visit family members who are very understanding about her need to poke around old buildings and visit every antiquity within a hundred miles. If you would like to know more about Ann and her research, or to contact her, visit her website at www.annlethbridge.com. She loves to hear from readers.

THE RAKE'S INHERITED COURTESAN
is the first novel by Ann Lethbridge
for Mills & Boon® Historical Romance

Chapter One

Dover, Kent—1816

Safe behind her black veil, Sylvia Boisette steeled herself to confront those who, because of her birth, were a part of her world, but who would never accept her as part of theirs.

Dusty fingers of gold streamed through the bank of windows along the library's west wall, highlighting the room's comfortable shabbiness. On the threshold behind her, the eager servants murmured in anticipation of the reading of the will.

'I believe Mr Tripp wishes you to sit there, *mademoiselle*,' the butler muttered over her shoulder. He gestured to the far end of the room.

In front of the bewigged, craggy-faced lawyer, ranged the backs of three seated figures, a black-clad bastion of stiff respectability, and beside them, one empty chair.

'Who are they?' Sylvia whispered to the butler. Isolated in painful solitude at the funeral, she could only guess the identity of the strangers in attendance and the servants always knew everything.

'Imogene Molesby, the master's sister, to the right,' Burbridge murmured. A large-boned woman, she wore an outdated black bonnet and sat closest to the windows. 'Her husband, George.' Molesby's bulk seemed to overflow his straight-backed chair.

Beside him sat the handsome young man whose height and breadth had overshadowed the pitifully small group of mourners at the graveside, his aloof, patrician countenance full of disapproval. She nodded towards him. 'And the other?'

'Mr Christopher Evernden, Lord Stanford's younger brother.'

A buzz of anger in her veins chased off the numbness that had held her in thrall all morning. Lord Stanford, the head of the Evernden family, hadn't even bothered to come to his uncle's funeral. And Monsieur Jean had always spoken so well of his nephew.

Pauvre Monsieur Jean. How she would miss reading to him in this very room, his smiling face lit by the glow of a fireplace now as cold and empty as her heart. Sometimes, moisture glinting in his tired eyes, he had told her how much she resembled her beloved mother. Icy fingers clenched in her stomach. She might carry the burden of her mother's beauty, but she would not follow her path to ruin.

A deep breath steadied the beat of her heart. With a solemn swish of black silk skirts, she trod the bars of light and shade on the faded Axminster rug as if they formed the rungs of a ladder to her future, or an escape from her past.

Mr Tripp acknowledged her presence with a nod.

Fighting the sudden trembling in her knees, she sank on to the empty chair beside Mr Evernden. His sharp, sideways glance projected his distaste with the sureness of an arrow, while a chill disapproval emanated from his companions. She forced her spine straight. From this moment on, she would forge her own destiny.

Behind the ancient walnut desk, the lawyer glanced down at his papers. 'That is everyone, I presume?'

The straight-backed chair beside her issued an impatient creak and, from behind her veil, she risked a glance at its occupant. Polished Hessian boots planted flat on the floor, his muscular thighs extended well beyond the chair seat. Gold glinted in his dark-honey, wind-tousled hair. Fair skinned, with a chiseled jaw and high forehead, he bore the stamp of English nobility. His expressive mouth, set in a straight line, spoke of firmness of purpose.

Her stomach tumbled over in a strangely pleasurable dance.

Caught midbreath, she froze. She never allowed herself to notice men. One glance and the lascivious greed in their eyes sent her diving for the cover of cold disdain. She tried not to see them at all. Her interest stemmed from curiosity, nothing else. She focused her gaze on the lawyer.

Mr Tripp began to read. 'Being of sound mind...'

Beyond the window, fleecy clouds scudded across a robin's-egg-blue sky, their shadows gambolling like lambs across the familiar green, rolling hills. She would miss walking those headlands between here and Folkestone.

Tripp droned on and she forced herself to listen. Monsieur Jean left small sums of money to his butler and the housekeeper. He left a guinea to each of the other servants. How like the gentle man to remember them. His prized books, already boxed and waiting for transportation, went to an old friend too ill to travel to the funeral.

'To my sister, Imogene, I leave the ormolu clock which belonged to our mother,' Tripp intoned.

The clock Mrs Molesby and monsieur had fought over for years. How he had chuckled over that tale. She repressed a smile.

'Cliff House will be sold to pay my debts,' Mr Tripp read.

Monsieur Jean had promised her something for her future. She needed very little. Sylvia held her breath.

Pausing, Mr Tripp looked over his pince-nez at the assembled company. He cleared his throat. 'I leave my ward, Miss Sylvia Boisette, in the charge of my nephew, Mr Christopher Evernden.'

Sylvia gasped at the same moment Christopher Evernden smothered a startled oath with a cough.

The lines etched in Tripp's face deepened. 'He will receive whatever funds remain from the sale of Cliff House for her future care. The balance, when she marries, is to be used for her dowry.'

The room rocked around Sylvia as if Cliff House had toppled from its chalky perch and now floated on the wave-tossed English Channel. Sylvia closed her eyes against a surge of nausea, holding her body rigid until her head ceased to spin. She would not let them see her distress.

What had Monsieur Jean done? The dagger of realisation stabbed through her whirling thoughts. By trying to protect her from beyond the grave, he had ruined her plans.

'Disgusting,' Imogene Molesby exploded. 'How dare he foist his ladybird on to a respectable member of this family? It's disgraceful. There ought to be a law against it.'

Heat scorched her face at the damning tone. She clamped her mouth shut against the desire to cry out against the woman's injustice. Not for her own sake, but for sullying her beloved Monsieur Jean's memory.

At the back of the room, the servants moved restlessly and low mutters broke out. She turned and shook her head to stem their loyal defence. She wanted no public outcry marring this day.

Mr Tripp mopped his brow with a large white handkerchief. 'That concludes the reading of the last will and testament of Mr John Christopher Evernden. A cold collation is offered to the family and mourners in the blue drawing room.'

The ormolu clock on the mantel ticked into the silence.

Hopelessly kind and a dreamer to his dying day, Monsieur Jean had buried her dream of starting a new, respectable life.

The chair arms solid beneath her shaking hands, Sylvia pushed to her feet.

Mr Evernden, shock and horror reflected in his hazel eyes, rose with her and executed a stiff bow. He wanted this as little as she. What English gentleman wouldn't be horrified at such a dreadful imposition? To be required to care for a woman of ill repute went beyond the pale of family duty.

Tears scalded the backs of her eyes and her mind unravelled at the speed of a spool of wool batted by a cat. She hadn't felt this lost since, at the age of eleven, she learned she would never see her mother again.

The tattered remnants of her composure her only shield against their censorious faces, she sketched a curtsy to Mr Evernden and the irate Molesbys. She nodded to Mr Tripp and, head held high, strode for the drawing room. The servants parted to allow her through the doorway. She acknowledged their murmured words of support as she passed.

She would not allow this to happen. There must be some way to be rid of this grim young Englishman.

Christopher, appalled and astonished, stalked towards the lawyer. He needed this error corrected immediately.

A hand clutched at his arm. 'I say, Evernden, we didn't expect to see you here today.'

Damn. The presence of the Molesbys added another layer of complication to the situation. He reined in his impatience. 'Mother insisted one of us had to attend. Unfortunately, Garth had another engagement.'

His chubby face shining and his gaze greedy with anticipation, Uncle George slid him a grin. 'That really is doing it rather too brown, don't you know. Leaving you saddled with his…' He coughed delicately into his hand and glanced at the affronted expression on his wife's horsy face. 'Well, I mean to say, his ward.' He winked. 'I hear she's ravishing.'

Christopher's heart sank. Garth's exploits, along with those of his infamous uncle John, were bad enough. When this news hit the clubs, Christopher's name would also be dragged through the Evernden mire. No doubt Uncle George would dine out on the story for weeks.

'Don't beat about the bush, George,' Aunt Imogene said with her habitual snort. 'We all know what sort of female she is.'

Knowing Aunt Imogene and her tendency to take the bit between her teeth, Christopher held his tongue. George stared at his boots, a penitent in purgatory.

In a travesty of a grimace, Imogene bared her protruding yellow teeth. 'And that is why your father banished him from the family. A young fool, he turned into an old fool. Can you imagine? He left all his money to her. All I got was the ormolu clock.' Her indignant voice rattled the ill-fitting windows.

Christopher kept his expression bland and his growing ire under firm control. No one could require him to inherit his uncle's mistress.

'Excuse me, Aunt Imogene, Uncle George. I need to speak to Tripp.' He bowed to the old couple and followed the lawyer into the drawing room.

While its cream walls and furnishings gave no indication of its designation as blue, at least this room looked more like a gentleman's home than the drab library.

At the window, stiff and forbidding in her deep mourning, Mademoiselle Boisette stared out across the English Channel. Outlined against the light, her high-collared black gown revealed shapely curves and a narrow waist. A deliberate ploy to display her charms to advantage, no doubt.

He wasn't interested.

Tripp hovered beside the sturdy Queen Anne sideboard piled high with pastries and platters of sliced roast beef, fruits and cheeses. Red tulips and sunny daffodils in a crystal centrepiece splashed colour into the muted room.

A glass of red wine in one hand and a fat meat pasty in the other, Tripp had the expression of a well-fed bloodhound. Apparently, reading wills sharpened the appetite.

'Help yourself,' Tripp said, spraying Christopher with crumbs. 'Oh, dear me. Excuse me, sir.' He dabbed at Christopher's coat front with his napkin.

Aware of the Molesbys' entrance into the room and their curious stares as they joined the vicar near the hearth, Christopher smiled and waved Tripp off. 'No, really. Don't be concerned.'

Tripp stopped flapping and gestured to the butler. 'Drink?'

For once, a drink sounded like a good idea. Perhaps several, after this got sorted out. Christopher selected a glass of burgundy from the butler's silver tray. He sent a swift glance towards Mademoiselle Boisette and turned his shoulder to the room at large. 'Now about this will,' he murmured. 'There's been a mistake.'

'I don't think so, sir,' Tripp replied. 'I helped Mr Evernden draw it up myself last month.'

'Last month?' Christopher reeled at the implication. Twelve years ago, Christopher's father had given his younger brother the cut direct and deemed him *persona non grata*. Christopher never saw him again.

Until six weeks ago.

He'd run into Uncle John in London and while he'd barely recognised the gaunt, old fellow, he didn't have the heart to cut a man whom he remembered for his generosity to him and Garth in their childhood.

Tripp took another bite of his pasty, chewed and swallowed. 'That's right. The moment he returned from London, he insisted I come right around to change his will.'

Dismay plunged Christopher's stomach to the floor. He recalled Uncle John leaning on his silver-headed walking stick on St. James's Street, his eyes twinkling as he asked after Garth and his mother. They'd chatted in a desultory way about Princess Charlotte's forthcoming wedding. The old man bemoaned the slump in trade since Waterloo and Christopher expressed concern about the Bridgeport riots. And that was it. Not a word of a personal nature crossed their lips and they had shaken hands and parted company. Apparently, simple common courtesy had landed him in a dreadful coil.

Christopher groaned inwardly. He suddenly wished he had cut off his right hand before allowing the old man to shake it. 'There must be some way to change it. Pay her off.'

'Mademoiselle Boisette, you mean?'

Who else would he mean? 'Yes.'

After a wishful glance at the sideboard, Tripp said, 'Perhaps we should discuss this in the study?'

Christopher glanced around the room where the smattering of local gentry paid their respects by eating everything in sight. In the far corner, Aunt Imogene held court, complaining loudly about the poor state of the ormolu clock to the vicar's plump wife and casting dark glances at Mademoiselle Boisette's rigid back. He nodded. 'Lead the way.'

Full of old, broken-down furniture and other rubbish, the crowded oak-panelled study smelled of camphor and dust. Moth-eaten feathered and furred trophies leaned against every available upright surface in the gloomy room. Boxes and papers spilled off the shabby desk and cluttered the chairs, leaving nowhere to sit.

'He used to hunt,' Tripp observed.

Ignoring the lawyer's attempt at delay, Christopher frowned. 'What can I do about this will?'

'Nothing.'

'Bloody hell. What do you mean, nothing?'

Tripp pursed his lips and lowered his brows.

'I'm sorry,' Christopher said. 'This all comes as rather a shock.' He took a swig of his burgundy. At least Uncle John had kept an excellent cellar.

'I imagine Mademoiselle Boisette is also surprised,' Tripp said, his jowls drooping to his cravat. 'A pleasant young woman. Always a very gracious hostess.'

The revelation of unsavoury secrets held no appeal and Christopher pressed on. 'Can I just sell the house and give her the money?'

Tripp appeared to consider the question carefully. 'Your uncle thought her too young. She needs a guardian.'

'Too young?' The words exploded from Christopher's mouth. His uncle must have been nigh on sixty. He wanted to throttle Tripp. 'How old is she?'

Tripp stiffened. 'Twenty-three. Your position of guardian is to continue until she's twenty-five.'

Dear God! Twenty-three and she had lived with his uncle for twelve years? No wonder the old man had locked himself away from society all these years. His stomach churned. The normally solid ground beneath him seemed to turn into a quagmire.

'I must decline,' Christopher said.

Tripp sighed. 'I feared as much. I told Mr Evernden the family wouldn't like it. He set great store by you, Mr Christopher. He would have been sorry to learn of his mistake.'

'At the risk of being rude, Mr Tripp, I must be brutally frank. I don't care what you think or what my uncle thought. I refuse to be imposed upon. I want it sorted out. Now.'

Tripp looked as affronted as Aunt Imogene. Christopher didn't care.

'The terms of the will are quite explicit, sir,' Tripp said.

'What about her mother's family, or her father?'

'She has no family of which I am aware. Her mother died in France. Mr Evernden did not reveal the name of her father. Anyway, since I gather her father refuses her recognition, it is of no consequence.'

The thin straw of rescue drifted out of Christopher's grasp. 'Then there must be something I can do with her. Some institution where she can learn a skill, somewhere a woman like—'

Tripp harrumphed. His eyebrows jumped on his crumpled forehead like rabbits on a ploughed field.

'Somewhere for a woman like me, Mr Evernden?'

The cool tone from behind him held the slightest trace of a French accent.

Hell. Apparently, the impertinent Mademoiselle Boisette had no qualms about eavesdropping. So be it. Beating around the bush only led to disappointed expectations, as he well knew from his business dealings. Christopher swung around to face her.

Mr Tripp rushed between them. 'Allow me to introduce Mademoiselle Boisette, Mr Evernden.'

Still veiled, Mademoiselle Boisette held out a small, black-gloved hand. She curtsied as he took it, a fluid movement with all the easy grace of a self-assured woman.

She turned to the lawyer. 'Would you be good enough to leave us to speak alone, Mr Tripp? We have some issues of mutual concern to address.'

To his relief, her tone sounded clipped and businesslike. No tears. At least, not yet.

Tripp rubbed his hands together. 'Certainly.'

He had food on his mind, Christopher could tell.

Tripp pulled out his calling card and handed it to Christopher with a flourish. 'Mr Evernden, if it would not be too much trouble, I would appreciate it if you would call at my office later today. I have some documents requiring your signature.'

Damned country solicitors. Why the hell hadn't he brought the documents with him? Christopher tamped down his irritation. First, he had to depress any hopes Mademoiselle Boisette might have about continuing the connection with his family.

The murmur of distant conversation and the clink of glasses briefly wafted through the open door as Tripp left and closed it behind him.

Mademoiselle Boisette glided to the desk. Her graceful movements, her calmness, reminded Christopher of a slow and gentle river. Her impenetrable veil skimmed delicate sloping shoulders and he ran his gaze over her straight back and trim waist. An altogether pleasing picture.

The wayward thought stilled him. He leaned his hip against a rickety table and sipped his wine. Nothing she could say would make him change his mind.

With her back to him, Mademoiselle Boisette set her wineglass amid the clutter of papers. A lioness's head leaned against one corner of the desk and her hand brushed reverently over its tufted ears.

She spoke over her shoulder. 'I feared these creatures so much when I first came to live here, I asked Monsieur Jean to remove them from the walls.' A breathy sigh, as light as a summer wind, shimmered the secretive veil. 'We both know there are far more dangerous creatures than these in the world, don't we?'

Reaching up, she pulled the pearl-headed pin from her bonnet. Her slender back stretched as she removed the hat in a fluid motion. She placed it on the desk.

A crown of braided gold encircled her head. Curling tendrils at the nape of her long neck brushed her collar.

As regal as a queen, she revolved to face him, her hands clasped in front of her. 'And that is why we need to talk.'

Christopher's breath hooked in his throat. She had the face of an angel.

Fringed by golden lashes, forget-me-not blue eyes gazed out of a heart-shaped face. Not a single blemish marred the perfection of her creamy complexion or peach-blushed cheeks. His mouth longed to taste the lushness of full ripe lips. A banquet offered to a starving man.

Like a callow youth faced with his first view of a woman's bare breast, his palms dampened. He resisted the temptation to wipe them on his pantaloons. By God, he'd seen many lovely women in the salons of London, but beautiful did not begin to describe this vision.

Since when did his appetites control his reactions?

As if reading his thoughts, her mouth curved in a smile, the small space in the centre of her pearl-white top teeth an enchanting fault amid celestial perfection.

She was no seraph. Pure devilment gleamed in the cerulean gaze locked with his.

Placing her gloved fingertip between her teeth, she glanced at him. Her lashes lowered and then swept up again. A lingering question lurked in her eyes.

Eve biting the apple.

He swallowed.

She tugged the tip of her glove free and then released it.

An indrawn breath lifted the swell of her bosom beneath her close-fitting gown. He imagined rose-tipped globes peaking to his touch.

His collar tightened. Sweat trickled down his spine.

Transfixed, he stared as she repeated the manoeuvre with each remaining slender finger. In all his years on the town, he'd never seen such wanton sensuality. Blood stirred and pulsed in his loins. He shifted, spreading his thighs to ease the burgeoning pressure.

Head tipped to one side, she focused her gaze on his mouth and licked her bottom lip with a moist, pink tongue.

An unendurable desire to echo that touch on his mouth, to trace the path of her glance, tingled his tongue.

As graceful as a ballet dancer and with agonising slowness, she drew off the glove, baring the white skin of her wrist, her knuckles, her slender fine-boned fingers.

Visions of white, naked flesh writhing beneath him shortened his breath. Sensations of silky skin, slick and wet and hot for him, closing around him as he drove them both to mindless bliss, tightened his groin. He fought the deep shimmer of pleasure.

She laid the wisp of black silk across the big cat's tawny muzzle.

He curled his lip. A brazen wanton indeed.

He enjoyed the warmth of a willing woman, but had no need of a professional courtesan. And no matter how beautiful or sensual, he had no interest in a woman who had brought scandal to the name of Evernden.

A dimple appeared at the corner of her curving mouth.

Taste her. Caress her full lips with his mouth, duel with her moist, soft tongue and press her slender form hard against him. Take what she offered with brazen abandon. Here. Now. The words matched the rhythm of his pulsing blood.

Damn. This little witch wouldn't play him for a fool as she had his dotard uncle. Lust never controlled him.

He slammed his glass amid the documents on the table, ignored the red stain spreading over the jumbled papers and folded his arms across his chest.

Seconds felt like minutes as, one finger at a time, she freed the other glove and slid it off. She ran the garment through her fingers, a torturous stroking of silk against bare skin. She dropped it beside its partner.

He remembered to breathe.

'Mr Evernden.' Her husky, accented voice caressed his skin the way a lioness rubbed in adoration against her mate. 'I have a proposition for you.'

Yes, his body roared in feral triumph.

Chapter Two

Disgust roiled in his gut, both at his unprecedented lack of control and the thought of his ancient uncle with his hands on this delicate creature. 'There is no proposal you could offer that would interest me, madam.'

Raising an eyebrow, she perused his person from heel to head, her gaze lingering on his chest before sliding up to meet his eyes. She smiled approval.

Molten lava coursed through his veins at the studied invitation.

Damn her impudence. Even the most audacious of the *demi-monde* made their desires known with more discretion. He didn't deal in money for flesh. The few women with whom he'd established mutually enjoyable relationships preferred gifts of jewellery, subtle tokens of appreciation and respect.

A seductive sway to her hips, she drifted to the centre of the room, her modestly cut gown intriguingly at odds with her aura of raw sensuality.

Once more, her gaze rested on his mouth and she moistened her lush lips. 'You sound quite sure of yourself.'

The only thing he knew for certain was his body's

demands in response to her blatant allure. He forced his expression to remain impassive. 'We are discussing you, not me.'

She inclined her head to one side. 'Really? What is it to be then, Mr Evernden? Not an orphanage, for I am too old. A parish workhouse, perhaps?'

Her husky, French-laced voice called to him like a siren's song. He clenched his jaw.

Tapping one slender, oval-nailed finger against her rather determined chin, she nodded slowly. 'You will take your uncle's money and leave me to the tender mercies of the town.'

Bloody hell. She made him sound like a thief. Only he had no need of his uncle's pitiful estate and no reason for guilt. He knew where his duty lay. It did not include taking his uncle's bit of muslin home. 'Nothing of the sort. You have to live somewhere suitable.'

Something hard and bright flashed in her eyes. Swept away by fair lashes, it was replaced by a mischievous gleam. 'Anywhere except your home, of course.'

The deuce. Could she read minds? 'Exactly.'

She dropped her bold stare to the floor and her imperfect top teeth nibbled her lower lip. 'Excuse me, Mr Evernden. I do not wish to be at odds with you, but I do request a fair hearing before you reach a final decision.'

'There is nothing to discuss.'

Her eyes flashed. 'There is your family name.'

A lump of lead settled on Christopher's chest. More scandal. His mother had enough misery to contend with as Garth debauched his way through life, without this female causing her anguish. 'My family is nothing to do with you.'

She turned and picked up her gloves and hat. 'Perhaps this is not the best place to discuss such a delicate matter.'

He followed the direction of her gaze around the cluttered, dirty room and shrugged.

'We would occasion far less remark in my private apartments, once the other guests have departed,' she urged.

Blast. He'd forgotten the reception. And Aunt Imogene. She would chew his ear off if she learned he'd been alone with this female. Not to mention what she would report to his poor, benighted mother. 'Very well.'

'I will ask the butler to bring you to my drawing room at the first possible opportunity.'

Christopher nodded.

Her hat clutched against her bosom, she peered out of the door, then slipped out.

Christopher raised his eyes to the smoke-grimed ceiling. He'd fallen into a madhouse.

He followed her into the hallway in time to see a swirl of black skirt disappear up the servants' narrow staircase at the other end of the passage. At least she showed a modicum of decorum.

Christopher straightened his shoulders and sauntered back to the reception. The company had thinned in his absence and Tripp was nowhere to be seen. Nursing his wine, Christopher wandered over to the window and glanced out. A privet hedge bordered the lane leading to the wrought-iron gates at the end of the sweeping drive where a knot of coachmen smoked pipes and chatted at the head of the four waiting carriages. Beyond them, a down-at-heel fellow in a battered black hat perused the front of the house. A prospective buyer?

The ramshackle condition of the property would not attract a wealthy purchaser despite the magnificent view of alabaster cliffs, the English Channel and, on a rare fine day like today, the faint smudge of the French coast on the horizon. Small vessels, their white sails billow-ing, scurried towards Dover harbour behind the headland. Mid-channel, larger ships plied their trade on white-tipped waves. No wonder his uncle had hermited himself away here with his *fille de joie*.

A picture of her face danced in his mind. He shook his head. No one could be that beautiful. The dim light had fooled him.

'Christopher?'

Damn it. What now? He swung around. 'Yes, Aunt?'

Excitement gleamed in his aunt's protuberant eyes. 'I am so glad George brought me today. Lord and Lady Caldwell were my brother's closest acquaintances.'

She motioned in the direction of the well-dressed couple engaged in conversation with chubby Uncle George. 'They have invited us to stay with them for a day or two.'

'How delightful for you both.'

Aunt Molesby dropped her penetrating voice to a whisper. 'Caldwell says that John actually used that woman as his hostess. Can you credit it?'

A veritable charger in the lists, nothing would stop his aunt at full tilt. Fortunately, she did not seem to expect an answer.

'Yes, indeed,' she continued. 'The shame of it. Lady Caldwell never attended, of course. Only men friends were invited for the gambling parties.' Her expression changed to disgruntlement. 'That woman didn't attend the gentlemen in any of their gambling pursuits. She always disappeared after dinner.'

Thank heaven for small mercies.

'You really should greet the Caldwells, you know,' she said, urging him in their direction. 'They were ac-quainted with your father.'

* * *

By the time Christopher had accepted the Caldwells'
words of sympathy, said farewell to the Molesbys and
spoken to the vicar, most of the food was gone and the
guests had departed.

The butler approached with a low bow. 'If you'll
follow me, sir, Mademoiselle Boisette will see you now.'

Quelling his irritation at the pompous tone, Christopher followed the butler up the curved staircase to the
second floor. Ushered into what was obviously an
antechamber, he surveyed the delicate furnishings and
the walls decorated with *trompe-l'oeil* scenes of what
he assumed to be the idyllic French countryside.

Rather than risk the single fragile, gilt chair collapsing
under him, Christopher declined the butler's offer of a seat.

'If you would wait here a moment, sir, I will inform
Mademoiselle Boisette you are here.'

Hell. Did she think he was here for an interview? He
would make his position clear from the outset.

The butler knocked on the white door beneath a
pediment carved with cherubs. It opened just enough for
him to enter.

More moments passed and Christopher paced around
the room. This situation became more tiresome by the
minute. Finally, the butler returned and gestured for him
to enter. 'This way, sir, if you please.'

A gaunt, middle-aged woman, her well-cut, severe
gown proclaiming her to be some sort of companion,
bobbed a curtsy as he passed and Christopher stepped
into the lady's bower, a room of light, with high ceilings
and pale rose walls. A white rug adorned the centre of
the highly polished light-oak planks. Mademoiselle
Boisette, seated on the sofa in front of an oval rosewood
table, glanced up from pouring tea from a silver teapot.

Stunned by the full effect of her glorious countenance, Christopher blinked. His mind had not played tricks downstairs. With hair of spun gold and small, perfectly formed features, she seemed even more beautiful than he remembered. Unfortunately, she had spoiled the effect by applying rouge to her cheeks and lips since their first meeting.

He took the hand she held out.

She smiled with practised brilliance. 'Mr Evernden, thank you for agreeing to talk to me. Denise, you may leave us. Mr Evernden and I have business to discuss.'

The woman twisted her hands together. 'I will be in the next room should you need me, *mademoiselle.*'

Mademoiselle Boisette inclined her head. *'Merci,* Denise.'

She indicated the striped rose-and-grey upholstered chair opposite her. 'Please, do be seated.'

Like the pieces in the antechamber, the delicate furniture seemed unsuited to the male frame. Careful to avoid knocking the table with his knees, he lowered himself onto the seat.

Despite the damned awkwardness of the situation, Mademoiselle Boisette seemed perfectly at ease. She might not have attended his uncle's card parties, but this young woman managed to hide her thoughts exceedingly well. Determined to remain impartial, he eyed her keenly. He would hear her out.

Pouring tea into a white, bone-china cup, she moved with innate grace. Her fine-boned fingers were as white and delicate as the saucer in her hand.

He didn't like tea. He never drank it, not even for his mother. He took the cup she held out. 'Thank you.'

She peeped at him through her lashes. 'What an

amusing situation to find ourselves in, Mr Evernden.' Her husky laugh curled around him with delicious warmth.

He steeled himself against her blandishments. 'I would hardly call it amusing, *mademoiselle*.'

After slowly stirring her tea, she replaced the spoon in the saucer without the slightest chink. She arched a brow. '*Mais non?* You do not find it entertaining? A farce. The son of a noble English milor' and a courtesan's daughter, trapped together by a dead man's will? My mother was *une salope*. A prostitute, I think you say in English?'

Startled, Christopher swallowed a mouthful of hot tea. Damn. It burned the back of his throat on the way down.

He struggled not to cough for several seconds. By God, he hadn't come here to listen to this. She might look like an angel, but she used the language of the Paris gutters. 'Your frankness, madam, is astonishing.'

To his satisfaction, she looked slightly nonplussed.

She tilted her head in enchanting puzzlement. 'I thought it would be better if we did not, how do you say it…mince our words?'

Did she think he would be taken in by such contrived gestures? Christopher glared at her. 'Very well, *mademoiselle*. If it is plain speaking you want, you shall have it. My uncle's will leaves me in a damnable position. I have no alternative but to place you somewhere you can do no further harm to my family's good name.'

'Do you have any idea what will happen to me in a workhouse or some other charitable institution?' Despite her smiling expression, desperation edged her voice. 'Oh, no, Mr Evernden. I will not allow it.'

Christopher glanced around the elegant drawing room. She was right. Wherever she ended up, it would not be like this. Her beauty would leave her vulnerable to all kinds of abuse. The thought sickened him.

Damn it. She'd been his uncle's mistress for years. What difference could it possibly make to a woman of her stamp? 'You have no choice. Cliff House must be sold to pay my uncle's debts. You must go somewhere you can learn a *respectable* occupation.'

A shadow darkened her eyes to fathomless blue. Fear? Anger? Golden lashes swept the expression away, leaving her gaze clear and untroubled. He was mistaken. Women like her did not know fear.

Except that looking at her, he couldn't quite give credence to the gossip. Or did he simply not want to believe something this beautiful could be so depraved?

She surged to her feet in a rustle of stiff silk and skirted the table between them. The heavy scent of roses wafted over him. He didn't recall her wearing so much perfume in the study.

As light as a butterfly, her hand rested on his upper arm. She slanted him a teasing glance. 'The key is re-spectable, *non*?'

Heat prickled up his arm. How would that hand feel in his? Soft? Warm? Before he could discover for himself, she floated to the window. A vague sense of loss swept him.

Her hair molten gold and the profile of her perfect face and figure haloed by the glow of the afternoon sun, she paused, looking out.

Another pose designed to drive a man to lustful madness. He tightened the rein on his self-control and waited in silence.

She pressed a hand to her throat, fingering the trinket suspended at her beautiful throat, then turned to face him full on.

He squinted against the light, straining to see her expression.

'Your uncle made no complaints,' she murmured. 'Are you sure you do not wish to take his place?'

Once more, unruly blood stirred at the suggestion in her husky voice. For a moment, he considered her blatant offer. Blast her. He was no cup-shot, idle rake like his brother. 'Quite sure.'

She remained silent for a moment, thoughtful, then smiled and raised one hand, palm up. 'Then give me two hundred pounds from the sale of Cliff House and I swear the Evernden family will never hear from me again. Nor will I ever mention my connection with your uncle.'

Blackmail. A brief pang of disappointment twisted in his chest, instantly obliterated by a flood of relief. Two hundred pounds was a pittance to rid his family of this blot on their good name. If he could only trust her word. 'Where will you go?'

The sultry coquette evaporated, leaving a haughty young woman staring down her nose. 'That, sir, is none of your concern.'

If she thought to bleed him dry a few hundred pounds at a time, she'd come to the wrong door. 'If you want money from me, I will make it my concern.'

She hesitated, then dropped her gaze. 'I am going to Tunbridge Wells.'

'Tunbridge Wells?' The nearest town of any significance to the Darbys' estate where he planned to spend the next fortnight. He'd arranged to pick up his curricle at the Sussex Hotel and send the town carriage back to London. 'And how do you intend to support yourself?'

While her face remained a blank page, storms swirled in the depths of her eyes. 'A friend owns a small, but exclusive, ladies' dress shop in the town. I plan to invest in her business.'

With short sharp steps, she returned to her seat. The

heavy scent of roses thickened the air. 'Would you care for some more tea?' She picked up the teapot. 'I have grown fond of the English *thé*.'

Christopher placed his cup on the tray. 'No. Thank you.'

She began to fill her cup.

A conniving woman of her sort needed careful handling. They lived by their wits and their bodies. Their stock in trade relied on a man's brain residing in his breeches. 'I will drive you to Tunbridge Wells.'

Tea splashed into the saucer and rattled the spoon. 'What?'

Not quite so self-assured, then.

'I want to see you safely delivered to your destination.'

She glared at him, then her lips curved in her sensuous smile.

God, his lungs ceased to work every time she did that.

'You wish to make sure I speak the truth?' she asked.

He inclined his head. 'As you say.'

She returned the teapot to the tray. Her low husky chuckle filled the silence and she cast him a sly glance. 'Are you sure that is your only reason for wishing to remain in my company?'

Smouldering annoyance flared to anger. The little hussy delighted in tormenting him. 'Mademoiselle Boisette, the sooner I wash my hands of you, the better I will like it.'

Her gaze dropped from his, her hand creeping to touch her gold locket. When she replied, her smile seemed forced. 'The feeling is mutual, Mr Evernden.'

She rose and he followed suit. The top of her golden head barely reached his shoulder.

'I assume we have nothing left to say to each other,' she said. 'I would like to leave for Tunbridge Wells in the morning.'

'I will let you know my decision after I have spoken to Mr Tripp.'

She hesitated, then narrowed her eyes. 'I am going to join my friend tomorrow, Mr Evornden, with or without your escort. I expect two hundred pounds to be delivered to me before I leave. If not, I will apply to Lord Stanford or perhaps your mother, Lady Stanford. Your uncle promised me that money.'

Next she'd be claiming a child by the poor old man. Well, Christopher would damned well make sure she never troubled any member of his family again. She might not yet realise it, but she had met her match.

Tripp had one more task this afternoon, drawing up a settlement. 'You will have my answer after dinner, *mademoiselle*. I wish you good day.'

He executed a courteous, shallow bow and headed for the door. An urgent craving to rid the cloying scent of roses from his lungs lengthened his stride.

From the arched window on the landing, Sylvia stared down at the athletic figure in the swirling great-coat as he climbed into a shiny black coach emblazoned with the Evernden coat of arms.

The sharp point of her locket dug into her palm. Relaxing her fingers, she tried to still her trembles and leaned her forehead against the cool glass. Had he believed her? Why would he not? The thought curdled in her stomach.

He seemed to be the solemn, honourable English-man described by Monsieur Jean on his return from London. The disgust curling his mobile mouth had poured venom through her veins. And yet, she'd seen the heat beneath his chill exterior, the stirring of interest reflected in glittering green shards deep in his forest-coloured eyes. If lust won out, she'd wrought her own disaster.

Since she had come to his house, Monsieur Jean had protected her from the outside world of brutal men, groping sweaty hands, hot fetid breath and stinking bodies. She closed her eyes and shuddered at the recollection.

She drew in a deep calming breath and watched the coachman flick his leaders with his long whip before he steadied his horses to pass through the wrought-iron gates. The coach turned towards the winding, cliff-top road to Dover.

A wry smile tugged at her lips. The young man's contempt hadn't left her trembling and as nauseous as the day she'd crossed the English Channel. It was the ease with which she'd played the strumpet that left her weak and sick. Like a well-worn mantle, she'd donned the cloak she thought she'd left in her past.

Non. The man might be one of the handsomest she'd ever met, but only necessity forced her to speak the words of a painted Jezebel and further destroy Monsieur Jean's reputation with her lies.

She had no choice. Beneath Christopher Evernden's reserved exterior, she sensed steel and a brain. A dangerous combination in a man. All she could do was wait and see if he would take the bait.

'Mademoiselle?' Denise's hand touched her shoulder.

With an effort, she pasted a smile on her lips and turned to face her old friend, the woman Monsieur Jean had brought from France to make her feel more at home in a strange country all those years ago.

'Come to France with me in the morning,' Denise said. 'My family will welcome you.'

An icy chill ran over her skin at the thought of returning to Paris. Memories of her childhood flashed raw and ugly into her mind. 'No, Denise,' she murmured, her heart eased by the tender look on the older woman's face. She smiled. 'You will see. With Mary's dressmaking skills and my designs, I will become a famous modiste, then I will call for you to come back to me.'

Tears welling in her brown eyes, Denise nodded. 'I will look forward to it, little one.'

A gut-wrenching smell assaulted Christopher's senses when he reached the quay a short distance from Tripp's office. Behind him, the town of Dover wound away from the docks. High on the cliffs, the ancient castle loomed over the harbour.

On the wharf, he skirted heaps of cargo, coils of old rope and clusters of merchants arguing in noisy groups. A group of seamen pushed past him with rolling gait, each brawny shoulder loaded with a barrel. Their curses rang in his ears. Nothing cleared the head like sea air, unless, like here, it was befouled with the smell of rotting fish and heated pitch. He grimaced. It really was a noisome, filthy place.

His long stride carried him swiftly past the waterfront where bare-masted ships speared the cloudy sky. The events of the day pounded at his mind in tune with the sea dashing itself against the cliffs.

Clear of the busy docks, Christopher strolled along the front, savouring the sharp breeze on his skin and the tang of salt on his tongue. Exposed by low tide, the yellow pebble beach sported seaweed and blackened spars. Nothing about Dover appealed to him.

Damn it all. It had been a simple task. Stay one night at the Bull, attend the funeral and the reading of the will, then be on his way to the Darbys' in Sussex by night-

fall. Only now, he had to deal with the problem of
Mademoiselle Boisette.

Why not give her the money and let her go her own
way? Because he hated to leave anything dangling.

He frowned. The interview with Tripp had confirmed
his fears that there was little to be had from the sale of
Cliff House. A half-pay naval officer had offered to
purchase it for a pittance and Uncle John's creditors
wanted a quick sale. Tripp thought there might be a few
pounds left, perhaps between ten and fifty, after the
creditors received their share. Mademoiselle Boisette
would be hard put to manage on so small a sum.

To top it all, Uncle John had reached out from the
grave and planted Christopher a facer. A letter, to be delivered if he refused to take Mademoiselle Boisette
under his wing.

Curse it. New rage flared up to heat his blood. He
dropped on to a wooden bench looking out over the
harbour. Sullen, foam-crested waves tumbled up the
beach and rattled the stones. On the horizon black
clouds heralding yet more rain. A dousing would make
a perfect end to the day.

He pulled the letter from his pocket and broke open
the red wax seal. Ripe with the smell of seaweed, the
stiff breeze fluttered the paper as he peered at the
spidery handwriting.

Dear Nephew,

*I write in haste, for I have little time left to me. If you
are reading this letter, you have rejected my request to
care for my little Sylvia.*

Request? More like a bludgeoning over the head with
a gravestone. Christopher fought the urge to ball the
paper in his fist and toss it into the surf rolling around
the rotting timber breakwater.

She has been a daughter to me all these years.

Then why hide her away?

Her mother was my first and only love. She chose another, but my feelings remained constant. Now, all I can do for my beloved Marguerite is take care of her little girl, Sylvia. My poor Marguerite, so tender in her emotions, dragged down into the pit of hell by viciousness and vice.

These were words a Gothic novelist like Mrs Radcliffe would have been proud to write. Gritting his teeth, he forced himself to read on.

Understand, my dear Christopher, her father deserted his child and continues to deny her. I have spent my life and most of my money trying to prove her claim.

You must succeed where I have failed. The duke must pay for his crime.

Please, do not let me down. You are Sylvia's only hope.

John Christopher Evernden.

The word *hope* had been underlined several times.

He was supposed to guess the name of this duke? He turned the paper over to see if it contained the answer on the back. Nothing. Was he supposed to walk up to each of them in turn and accuse them of siring a French bastard?

Damn. His uncle must think him some sort of knight on a white charger, riding around the countryside rescuing damsels in distress. Questionable damsels at that.

It was the sort of thing Garth would have jumped at when they were boys. And Christopher would have followed behind, cleaning up the mess. A fool's errand. The old man had to be addled in his pate. Sylvia Boisette had been brutally clear about her mother's occupation.

But not the daughter? For some obscure reason, he wanted to believe Uncle John's assertion she was his ward and nothing more. In the face of a statement made by a man facing death, Christopher ought to believe in her innocence as a matter of family honour, despite her wanton behaviour earlier today.

A sudden image of her siren smile, the languorous removal of her gloves, fired his blood. Hell, did he have no self-control where this woman was concerned? Was desire mingled with disgust colouring his judgement?

Whatever the case, the almost nonexistent funds for her support left the workhouse as the only solution unless he succumbed to her blackmail.

He stared blindly at the tumbling surf and grating pebbles.

She needn't know how much would be left after the sale of the house. He could add to the balance, just be rid of her. He certainly had enough blunt left from the tidy profit he'd made on the last cargo of silks from the Orient. Even after purchasing a half-share in a ship bound for America, there was more than enough left to see Mademoiselle Boisette comfortably settled.

It would solve the problem. *If* he could be sure she would leave his family in peace.

He stuck the note in his pocket alongside the agreement drawn up by Tripp, pushed to his feet and headed towards town and the comfort of his inn. He'd think about it some more over dinner.

Taking hasty decisions on an empty stomach only resulted in trouble.

Chapter Three

At the crunch of wheels on gravel, Sylvia turned her gaze from her beloved cliffs to the Evernden carriage rolling through the gate.

Thirsty for one last memory, she wheeled in a slow circle, the coarse fabric of her plain, grey wool travelling cloak twisting about her legs. Above her, white against grey, crying seagulls hovered on a breeze alive with the boom of crashing surf and a smattering of rain. Weighed down by the lessons she'd learned as a child, she drank in her last view of the rambling mansion's warm red brick framed by windswept larches. One could never go back.

The matching chestnuts slowed to a halt at the front door. All loose-limbed athletic grace and conservative in a black coat, Mr Evernden leaped down. The wind ruffled the crisp waves of his light brown hair. His handsome face brightened when he caught sight of her.

Warmth trickled into her stomach. Her mind screamed danger.

He waited as she strolled across the drive to his side, then glanced at her green brassbound trunk beside her valise on the steps. 'Is this everything?'

She had packed only the most practical of her clothing. She nodded. 'All I need.'

The coachman tied her luggage on the rack at the back and Mr Evernden swept open the carriage door. 'Are you ready, Mademoiselle Boisette?'

He held out his hand to assist her in. A small, polite smile curved his firm mouth and green sparks danced in his eyes.

Awareness of his size and strength skittered across her skin. She stilled, frozen by the odd sensation. Last night, his note had indicated his agreement to take her to Tunbridge Wells. After performing the harlot yesterday, dare she trust him? Prickles of foreboding crawled down her back.

She ignored his proffered aid. 'Quite ready, Mr Evernden.' Maintaining a cool expression, she stepped into the well-appointed carriage and settled on the comfortable black-tufted seats.

He followed her in, his musky sandalwood cologne heady in the confined space. Lean long legs filled the gap between the seats as he lounged into the squabs in the opposite corner. He gave her a sharp glance, then rapped on the roof and the carriage moved off with a gentle sway.

The window afforded glimpses of white sails skimming the spume-capped grey waves of the English Channel, an impenetrable moat around the castle of her past.

'Another wet day,' he said.

She kept her gaze fixed outside. 'Indeed.'

'Having caused us to freeze all winter I understand there are predictions that the Tomboro volcano will also ruin our spring.'

The masculine timbre of his voice resonated a chord deep inside her. For no apparent reason, her breath shortened as if his size and strength and even his cologne pressed against her chest. She clenched the strings of her reticule in her lap. 'So I have heard.'

An awkward silence hung in the air.

He cleared his throat. 'We will stop at Ashford for lunch and arrive in Tunbridge Wells before the supper hour.'

'Thank you.'

Tunbridge Wells and Mary Jensen and her future. Her heart swelled with optimism and she touched the locket at her throat. Everything would be all right.

An impatient sigh gusted from his corner. He shifted, stretching out his long legs until his shining black boots landed inches from the edge of her skirts.

For all his outward appearance of ease, tension crackled across the space between them. Determined to ignore it and him, she focused her gaze out of the window.

He eased his shoulders deeper into the corner. She glanced at him from beneath her bonnet's brim and cast a professional eye over his attire. After all, a successful modiste kept *au courant* with the latest styles, male and female, and she had met few members of the *ton* hidden away in Dover.

His buff unmentionables clung to his well-muscled legs, a smooth second skin over lean, strong thighs. Her pulse quickened.

Unable to resist the tempting sight, she let her gaze drift upwards past narrow hips to his broad chest, the close cut of his black coat, unmistakably Weston. Above an intricate, snowy cravat, she followed the column of his strong neck to his patrician profile, then to his hair arranged *à la Brutus*. A stray lock fell in a wave on his broad forehead. No dandy, just the quiet elegance of a man comfortable with himself.

As if he sensed her perusal, he turned his head and glanced at her from beneath half-lowered lids.

Cheeks burning, she flicked her gaze to the view.

Not another glance would she spare for her escort. Mary and her shop must be the focus of all her attention. *Their shop.* She hugged the thought to herself, a glimmer of warmth in a chilly world. Although small, according to Mary it was situated one street from the centre of the spa. No longer as popular as Bath, the Wells continued to attract older members of the *ton* because of its proximity to London. But Mary's last letter had arrived six months ago. Her business must be thriving if she could not find the time to write.

'*Mademoiselle?*'

Her stomach lurched.

Merde. She had all but forgotten him. Taking a deep breath, she willed her heart to stop its wild fluttering and forced frost into her tone. 'Miss Boisette, Mr Evernden, since I plan to make my home here in England.'

He raised a brow. 'Boisette is hardly an English name?'

He was right. It was the name her English mother had used in her new life in Paris, a life where she preferred not to shame her family name. Sylvia had simply adopted it. 'It is how I wish to be addressed.'

A furrow formed above his patrician nose, but he inclined his head. 'As you wish.'

'I prefer to be addressed as Miss. Both of my parents were English. Also, there is no need for polite conversation, since after today we will never meet again.'

His firm mouth tightened and his nostrils flared as if he held back angry words. 'As you wish, *Miss* Boisette.'

The carriage turned north away from the coast and he gazed out the rain-spattered window at the passing hilly countryside.

She let go of her breath. She infinitely preferred the heat of his anger to the other warmth she'd sensed deep in his eyes. Yesterday, he had been furious as she removed her gloves. Furious and fascinated.

Therein lay the danger. While he might have convinced the softhearted Monsieur Jean as to his honourable nature, she knew better than to trust any man.

Painful pinpricks ran over her shoulders. At any moment he might press her to make good her offer from the previous day. The dangerous game she played might yet be lost. She squeezed tighter into her corner of the carriage.

They reached Ashford around mid-day and lunched at the King's Head. There, in clipped sentences he explained the document setting out the terms under which he agreed to provide her with the promised funds. Sylvia signed it and he produced a velvet purse containing twenty-five guineas, the rest to be forwarded from his bank within two weeks. With new horses put to, the carriage jolted its way across country to their final destination and at long last, the coach bowled into Tunbridge Wells. Sylvia leaned forward for a better view of the High Street and the famous spa at the bottom of the hill. The town was smaller than she expected. It didn't matter. The infusion of funds from her uncle and the two of them sharing the work—and she would work night and day—it could not help but be a success.

The coach eased into a narrow lane and pulled up outside a timbered, bow-fronted shop with swathes of cloth draped in the window. Mr Evernden reached for the door handle.

Her heart beat a rapid tattoo. She did not want him to realise the unexpected nature of her arrival. She placed a hand on his sleeve.

The hiss of his indrawn breath shivered to the pit of her stomach.

She drew back, startled. Shaken by her response to that faint breath, she tried to keep her voice steady. 'If you would request your coachman to put my luggage on the road, I will not put you to any further inconvenience, Mr Evernden.'

He turned the door handle. 'It is no trouble at all, Miss Boisette.'

Stubborn man. She raised a brow. 'I prefer not to arrive here blatantly accompanied by a young gentleman of the *ton*.'

His expression turned grim and he dropped his hand. 'It is impolite to leave you in the street, but it shall be as you desire.' He sat back. 'I wish you all the best in your new life, Miss Boisette, and bid you good day.'

His stern remoteness appealed to her far more than effusive politeness. He'd acted the perfect gentleman in all their dealings, while she had treated him to an outrageous display of hot and cold. No doubt he thought the worst of her. A pang of regret held her rigid for the space of a heartbeat. She must not care about his opinion. She reached for the door. 'Thank you.'

She stepped out on to the slick cobbles.

At Mr Evernden's order, the coachman heaved her belongings down beside her and climbed back on to his perch.

Shocked to discover her hand shaking in trepidation, she knocked on the door, all the while aware of Mr Evernden's intense gaze on her back. She turned, raised her hand in farewell, and the carriage moved off, affording one last glance of Mr Evernden's stern profile in the window.

The door opened to reveal a freckle-faced girl of about

ten. Behind her, a passage led into the depths of the first floor and a narrow set of stairs wound upwards. Mary had never mentioned a child. She must be the maid.

'Can I help you, miss?' the girl asked.

Sylvia took a deep breath and smiled. 'Is Miss Jensen home?'

'There ain't no Miss Jensen at this address.'

Sylvia frowned. 'Are you sure?'

'Of course I am. I live here, don't I?'

'Who is it, Maisie?' a voice called from upstairs.

'A lady looking for a Miss Jensen, Ma,' Maisie yelled back.

A plump, dark-haired matron in a chintz gown, a chubby baby on her hip and a question on her face, clattered down the stairs.

Foreboding quaked in Sylvia's chest. She took a shaky breath. 'My name is Sylvia Boisette. I'm here to see Mary Jensen.'

The woman shook her head. 'She's gone, miss. The landlady said she fell ill and her brother fetched her back to London more than five months ago.'

The entrance to the Sussex Hotel at the back of the promenade hummed with activity. Coaches rumbled in and out, grooms struggled with frisky teams, ostlers ran to and fro and passengers, rich and poor, milled around in controlled confusion in a yard rich with the smell of horse manure and stale ale.

Sylvia tried to make sense of the bustling chaos. She dug into her meagre store of small coins and gave a ha'penny to the boy who had carried her trunk from Frog Lane.

He touched his cap and dashed off, whistling a merry tune.

Oh, to be so youthful and carefree. Sylvia couldn't remember a time in her life when she hadn't been anxious about something. She clutched her reticule to her, where the slip of paper with Mary's new address, which the plump matron had given her, resided. And right now she was about to embark on an exceedingly risky course. Respectable females rarely travelled by common stage. But then she had never been considered respectable.

She had no option. She would not waste her small store of guineas on expensive modes of travel. Nor could she afford to lose them to footpads or pickpockets. Since no one in the yard appeared to notice her, she unlocked the trunk and hid the purse of guineas in its battered depths. Rising, she caught the eye of a passing lackey in brown livery.

'Can I help you, miss?'

'Please take my trunk inside.'

He moved aside to allow a gentleman and his lady to pass through the entrance into the lobby. 'Have you a room bespoke, miss?'

'I just need one small chamber.'

'I dunno. You best check with the master. Your luggage will be safe enough with the porter while you go and see what Mr Garge has to say.'

He hefted her trunk on his shoulder and staggered to the stable entrance with Sylvia marching behind. He dropped it beside an elderly porter seated on a wooden box outside the mail-coach ticket office and storeroom. Another carriage rattled into the yard and the lackey raced off to meet it.

Sylvia smiled at the porter. 'I plan to catch the first coach to London tomorrow morning. If you would be so good as to see my trunk is placed on it, I would be most grateful.'

A pair of twinkling brown eyes looked at her from beneath straggly grey brows and the weathered face creased into a smile. 'I'll be more than pleased to oblige, miss,' he said. 'You gets your ticket in there.' He jerked his head towards the office.

'Thank you.' She gave him a penny and went inside to pay for her ticket. By the time she had completed her purchase and come outside, the porter had dispensed with her trunk. The door to the storeroom seemed sturdy and there were bars at the window. Hopefully, her money and her small cache of jewellery would be safe enough. Valise and hatbox in hand, she entered the inn.

One side of the wide entrance hall housed a counter. Across the way, a confusing array of doorways and passages led off in various directions. A bell sat next to the guest book on the counter. She rang it.

Moments later, a short, fat, florid-faced landlord in a black coat and striped waistcoat bustled out of the dining room door. 'Good evening, miss. Can I be of assistance?'

'Good evening. I will be catching the six o'clock stage tomorrow morning and require a single room for the night.'

'The name, miss?' he asked, running a stubby finger down the list in his book.

'I do not have a reservation.'

He looked behind her as if he expected someone else. 'How many in your party, miss? We are very busy today. I am not sure I can accommodate you.'

'There's no one else in my party.'

He frowned. 'Didn't you just arrive with this gentleman?'

Sylvia glanced over her shoulder. A young sprig of fashion in a many-caped driving coat and stiff shirt points swept through door.

'I am travelling alone. I... My maid took ill at the last moment.'

The landlord lowered his beetle brows. 'This inn's for Quality and their womenfolk don't travel alone. You'd best take yourself off to the Two Aitches.'

She blinked. She must have misheard. 'Where?'

'The Hare and Hounds, on the London Road. It has rooms for the likes of you. Now be off.'

The likes of her? Was her past somehow written on her forehead or branded on her cheek? Heat scorched through her veins. He had no right to treat her like some low-class female because she travelled alone and the last thing she wanted to do was wander the town looking for a room. 'My good man—'

She drew herself up to her full height and pierced him with a cool stare. 'You must have something. A small chamber will suffice.'

The landlord tapped a sausage of a finger on his reservation book. 'Well, I might have something,' he allowed. 'Not a very big room and no private parlour. I'll have to check with the missus.'

The gentleman behind her coughed and the harried landlord looked past her. 'If you'll just stand aside, miss, I'll look after this here gentleman and then I'll see what can be done.'

A hot admonition jumped to her tongue, instantly quelled. Forced to be patient or lose her only chance of a room, she drew back into the corner and watched as the innkeeper folded his stout body in half. 'Lord Albert, how good to see you again. What will it be today, a private parlour? We've got a nice bit of roast beef on the spit that might take your fancy for dinner.'

The fashionably attired young dandy with an elaborately tied cravat and rouged cheeks caught Sylvia's scornful glance over the landlord's bowed head. He winked.

Her stomach dropped. Foolhardy indeed, if she attracted the attention of this young fop. She schooled her face into chilly disdain and stared at the opposite wall.

Undeterred, the dandy gestured in her direction. 'Why, Garge, I believe this young, er…lady was here before me.' He spoke with a pronounced lisp.

Garge's face darkened. 'I'm looking after her, sir. She has to wait until I have some time.'

From the corner of her eye, she watched Lord Albert's gaze rake her from head to toe. Damn him for his impudence. Tapping her foot, she favoured him with her iciest stare.

His smile broadened. 'Perhaps I can be of some assistance, miss? I'd be delighted to be of service.' He giggled.

He actually giggled. Sylvia opened her mouth to give him a set-down, but the landlord's scowl did not bode well and she pressed her lips together.

The landlord's colour heightened. 'I'll have none of them goings-on under my roof, Lord Albert. I run a respectable house, I do.'

'I was only offering to share my room, Garge.' The dandy smirked.

Mortified, she stiffened her spine and raised her chin. 'I have a room.'

The landlord glowered. 'Not here you don't.'

Oh, no. He couldn't have changed his mind, not now. 'You said—'

'I made a mistake. We're full up.'

'As I said,' Lord Albert interjected, with a flourish of his silver-headed cane and a sly smile on his thin lips, 'I would be more than willing to accommodate you.'

Couldn't the mincing puppy see the trouble he was

causing? Sylvia wanted to shake him. 'Sir, I would be obliged if you would mind your own business.'

The landlord turned his broad back on her as if she no longer existed.

For goodness' sake. She wasn't asking for the moon. All she wanted was a room for the night. She picked up her valise and sidled around him, preparing to argue.

A hand touched her sleeve. 'If you wish,' a faintly lyrical voice murmured in her ear, 'I could guide you to the Hare and Hounds Tavern. It's not such a bad place. I am sure they have a decent room.'

She swung around and found herself hemmed in by a man of medium height and a wiry frame, who must have entered the entrance hall from one of the passages. His dark green coat had seen better days and the brim of his black hat shadowed all but his lean jaw and a flash of crooked teeth.

She shook his hand off her arm. Another gallant gentleman with less than honourable intentions, no doubt. 'No, thank you, sir.'

He touched her shoulder. 'You won't get any change out of Garge, here. You will no doubt fare better at the Hare.'

In a flurry of capes, Lord Albert strode over and pointed his cane at the newcomer's chest. 'Stand aside, sir,' he lisped. 'Garge, this young lady is under my protection. I insist you provide us with a room immediately. Isn't that right, my dear?'

He caught her fingers and pressed them to his moist lips. Sylvia pulled away, but for all his fragile posturing, his grip held firm. He drew her closer.

Nausea rose in her throat and her skin crawled at the touch of his hot, damp fingers. A violent urge to flee, a fear she hadn't known in years, quickened her pulse. But she needed this room.

'Unhand me, sir.' With a jerk, she freed herself. Disguising her panic with a chilly glare, she took a deep breath.

'The young lady is with me.' A quiet, but firm voice came from behind her.

Sylvia whirled around. One hand resting on the door-frame, his shoulders filling the entrance to the dining room, Christopher Evernden glowered at Lord Albert.

A warm glow rose up her neck and warmed her cheeks. The shabby man uttered a muffled oath and seemed to fade into the shadows as quickly as he had appeared.

The landlord thrust his jaw and pendulous chins in Mr Evernden's direction. 'Now don't you start, sir. This young person ain't spending the night at this inn with any of you randy gentlemen.'

Heat raced from the tips of her ears to her toes. An irresistible urge to slap the landlord's fat face clenched her fist.

Mr Evernden shot out a large hand, grasped her wrist and dragged her out of Lord Albert's reach.

She gasped and pried at his fingers. She wasn't a bone to be fought over by men acting like curs. 'Let me go.'

'I say, old chap,' the dandy drawled. 'I saw her first. Find your own ladybird Or get to the back of the queue.'

His high-pitched giggle scraped her nerves raw. She prayed for the floor to open up and swallow her whole. Or, better yet, for lightning to strike the simpering popinjay.

Merde. How had things come to this pass?

'The lady is with me.' Suppressed violence filled Mr Evernden's tone. All semblance of reserve gone, he radiated anger. Eyes the colour of evergreens in winter, he took a menacing step towards the mincing dandy.

Things were definitely growing worse. How typically, brutally male. She pressed back against the wall.

Cursing, Garge inserted his bulk between the two men eyeing each other like fighting cocks. He placed a heavy hand on each man's shoulder. 'I'll have no brawling in my house, gentlemen.'

Lord Albert recoiled, dusting off his coat as if Garge's touch had soiled it. 'I'm sure I don't care that much for the gel.' He snapped his fingers. 'You shouldn't leave her loitering about in public houses, if you don't want her accosted.'

'Exactly,' Mr Evernden replied with an exasperated glance at Sylvia.

Did he think to blame her because Lord Albert was a despicable rake? She returned stare for stare.

Lord Albert drummed his fingers on the counter's polished wood.

Mr Evernden glared at his back, then turned to the bristling innkeeper. 'Now, landlord, a room for Mademoiselle Boisette, if you please.'

Garge grunted. 'You ain't welcome here, sir, not you or your bit o' muslin, not nohow. I'll have your carriage brought around and your bags brought down.' He shook his head and muttered, *'Mademoiselle* indeed. Whatever next? This is a respectable house, this is, and Frenchies ain't welcome, nor their fancy men, neither.'

He turned to Lord Albert and bowed. 'I apologise for that, my lord. We don't usually get riff-raff in here. Now we've got that bit of unpleasantness out of the way, Lord Albert, I assume it's your usual room?'

A dull red suffused Mr Evernden's lean cheeks. He didn't speak. He grabbed the valise and hatbox from Sylvia's hand and strode outside.

Head held high, Sylvia trotted after him. No matter

what he thought, she had done nothing wrong. If he dared say one word of criticism, she would provide her opinion of the whole male population.

'Wait here,' he said.

Long strides carried him across the cobbled yard. Neatly dodging a liveried lackey running at full tilt with a tray of tankards to a waiting tilbury, he disappeared into the stables.

Nonplussed by yet another startling change in her circumstances, Sylvia waited as instructed. Gradually, her thoughts took some order. It seemed she would have to try this Hare and Hounds after all.

Nearby, a gentleman assisted a woman in a red-plumed bonnet into a shiny black barouche. A terrier, chased by two scruffy urchins, barked at the wheels of a departing coach. As it rattled beneath the archway into the street, she thought she glimpsed a figure flat against the wall. She peered into the gloom, but saw nothing but shadows.

More to the point, she needed a plan. She darted a swift glance around the courtyard, seeking inspiration. With nowhere to stay and Mr Evernden once more in command, she seemed to have come full circle.

'Miss Boisette.'

She stared in astonishment. The voice came from Christopher Evernden, but instead of his comfortable town coach, he perched high on a maroon-bodied curricle pulled by two ebony horses. An ostler dashed up to hold the nervous team and Mr Evernden leaped down.

She backed away. 'Where's your carriage?'

'I sent it back to London with my servant.'

Gallivanting around the countryside in an open carriage with a strange man reeked of danger. 'I'm not riding in that.'

He stalked to her side. 'Either you get in or I'll pick you up and put you in. Your choice, but make it quick.'

The set of his jaw and the angry glitter in his eyes said he would have no compunction about throwing her into the horrible thing. And yet, for all that he towered over her, she felt not the slightest bit afraid.

'Very well. I will ride with you as far as the Hare and Hounds.' At least the rain had ceased.

He handed her up. The fragile equipage rocked precariously on its long springs. While she settled herself with care on the seat, she admired the high-priced cattle in the traces. Mr Evernden obviously knew horses.

The team tossed their heads and stamped their feet. The rackety thing lurched. She grabbed for the side. It was worse than any ship.

The moment Mr Evernden climbed into his seat and took up the reins, the groom released the bridles. Solely in charge of the spirited pair, Mr Evernden glanced around him. With a dexterous twist of his strong wrist, he flicked his whip and set his horses in motion.

She'd heard a great many tales about young blades who drove like the wind in their sporting carriages. More often than not, they broke their necks. She curbed the desire to hang on to his solid-looking forearm.

In moments, the carriage eased its way through the archway. No sign of the man she thought she'd seen loitering in the shadows and yet the hairs on her neck prickled as if someone was watching. Oh, for goodness' sake. Now she was imagining monsters on every corner. The events of the afternoon must have rattled her nerves. Her biggest problem sat at her side.

They turned out on to the road.

'I assume you know where to find this Hare and

Hounds?' she asked, pulling her cloak tight against the chilly air.

'I didn't say I was going to the Hare and Hounds.'

She stared at the hard line of his profile. He kept his gaze fixed on the road ahead, but the flickering muscle in his strong jaw boded ill.

'Then where are we going?'

'You'll see.'

Once more, something uncomfortable writhed in her stomach. Alone with this man, she had nothing but her wits to defend her and half the time they seemed to go begging where he was concerned. 'I expect I shall see, but I would prefer to know.'

He gave a short humourless laugh. 'What difference does it make? You're going, whether you wish it or not.'

Chapter Four

'If you are wise, you won't cause any more trouble,' he said and pulled out to pass a slowly moving town coach.

Sylvia gripped the side of the curricle and shot him a glare designed to freeze 'Without your interference, there would have been no trouble.'

'I suppose you didn't almost cause a mill back there, cosying up to some namby-pamby, titled puppy with more hair than wit.' He fired her a hard glance. 'And just what were you doing there, anyway?'

The mill, as he called the altercation, was entirely his own doing. 'My affairs are not your concern.'

A muscle jerked in his jaw and his anger sparked across the space between them. 'Really? We'll see about that.'

Prickles raced down her back. Until his resentment subsided, she risked more than sharp words from the bristling male at her side. And if he overturned this ridiculous vehicle, it would be the perfect ending to a perfectly awful day. She sat back, determined not to say another word.

The carriage bowled along at a smart clip, his strong hands grasping the ribbons with practised assurance. The spirited team ate up the road, passing everything in its path.

The traffic thinned. Signs of habitation dwindled to the occasional farm along the road. The clouds rolled away and the horizon disappeared into hazy dusk, while sunset gilded the tops of distant trees. She nibbled her bottom lip. Just how far did he intend to travel? If they went too far, she would not get back to Tunbridge Wells in time to catch the morning coach.

Her trunk. How could she have been so stupid? She clutched at Mr Evernden's sleeve.

A stony expression met her gaze. 'What?'

'I left my luggage behind.'

'You can collect it in the morning.'

The savage edge to his tone and the vicious flick of his whip above his horses' heads gave her but a moment's pause. 'We must go back. What if it is stolen?'

'Miss Boisette, if you think I would set foot in that place again… I have never in my life been ejected from anywhere, let alone a common inn.' Anger vibrated from him in waves.

She quelled a sudden urge to laugh at his injured expression. 'Then you have me to thank for a novel experience.'

He scowled.

She'd gone too far. She edged away a fraction.

'It's an experience I could have done without,' he said. 'And I'd liefer not go through it again. If it is not too much trouble, I would appreciate your behaving with suitable decorum at this next inn.' Despite his repressive tone, he no longer sounded furious.

A sideways glance revealed his lips in a slight curve. 'Gad,' he muttered, staring straight ahead. 'A novel experience.'

Her lips twitched. She pressed them together, but not before she knew he'd caught the beginning of her smile.

'Don't worry about your trunk,' he said after a brief silence. 'It will be safe at the Sussex Hotel. The landlord appears to run a tight ship.'

'As we found to our cost.'

He smiled. 'Indeed.'

Her breath caught somewhere between her throat and her heart. The grin made him younger, almost boyish. His eyes crinkled at the corners and danced with green pinpricks of light. Unable to resist, she smiled back.

The travelling must have sent her wits to sleep. Signs of friendliness posed risks she dare not entertain. Men were dangerous enough without encouragement. She straightened in her seat and braced herself for what might lie ahead.

At a crossroads, he slowed the horses and turned them off the London Road. Sylvia tried to read the signpost, but the faded letters flashed by too fast. High hedges and overhanging trees cast deep shadows in the rutted, twisting lane. A flutter of disquiet attacked her stomach. 'Where *are* we going?'

'Somewhere we will be welcome, of that I can assure you. It is not far now.'

Did he have to be so mysterious? This stiff young man at her side thought her a wanton. So he should. She'd behaved like a strumpet, gambling everything on his desire to be rid of her. What if he changed his mind? Alone with a young and virile man, who-knew-where, tasted of risk.

Better him, than one of those other men at the Sussex Hotel. Better? A sudden tremble shook her limbs. She clenched her fingers around her locket, a familiar anchor to her past in the storm-tossed ocean of an uncertain future. If it came to a confrontation, somehow she had to make him understand she was not like her mother.

The Bird in Hand's mullioned windows flickered with warm light, a lighthouse in the deepening dusk. Wood smoke scented the cool air and the front door stood open in welcome.

Christopher hadn't been here since his grandmother had died, but it looked the same as always. The blackened Tudor timbers breathed permanence, despite the green of new thatch and a recent extension to the adjoining stables. A plaque over the weathered oak door boasted of hosting Good Queen Bess in the year fifteen hundred and fifty-six—along with half of England's other inns. He brought the horses to a stand.

A balding groom ran out from the stables and grasped the team's bridles.

A wonderful aroma of roasted meat filled Christopher's nostrils and set his mouth watering. If he could count on one thing, it was Mrs Dorkin's cooking.

'How pretty,' Miss Boisette said.

'Yes.' Christopher rolled his stiff shoulders. 'And I can guarantee we won't be turned away.'

'I am pleased to hear it.' Strain edged her voice.

The paleness of her countenance startled him. *Now* she felt nervous? She should have been a little more concerned back at the Sussex, a great deal more worried, based on his judgement of Lord Albert's intentions. The prancing ninny had his hands all over her. His gut churned.

But she had stood up to him, held her ground. He couldn't but help admire her courage, when it would have been so easy to flee, or to give in to the lordling's blandishments. And beneath the courage, he'd sensed a very real fear.

Thrusting the recollection aside, Christopher climbed down and reached up to help her alight. He caught her by the waist. Slender and lithe beneath his fingers, the heavy wool of her drab gown and grey cloak did little to disguise her womanly curves. The urge to bring her close and let her slide down his body shortened his breath.

Hell. He was no better than the popinjay at the inn.

Arms rigid, he placed her on the ground away from him, once more surprised by her small stature. For some reason, he imagined her taller. Something about her innate dignity and solemn demeanour added to her height. She had more pride than a duchess when she wasn't playing the wanton.

'Mr Christopher.' Gladness rang in the voice calling out through the door and Christopher turned to greet the generously proportioned matron who burst into the courtyard. She wiped her hands on her snowy apron and held them out in welcome.

He winced. Heaven knew what she'd say about him turning up with an unchaperoned female. He smiled. 'Mrs Dorkin. How are you?'

'Why on earth didn't you write and tell us you were coming?' she said in mock-scolding tones and her forefinger wagging. 'I would have aired the sheets special, just like your mother always ordered at the big house.'

Bloody hell. As if he needed more tender care than he'd suffered already. 'Mrs Dorkin, this is a friend of the family, Miss Sylvia Boisette.' He turned to Sylvia. 'Mrs Dorkin cooked for my grandparents at their estate near here.'

'I'm pleased to meet you,' Sylvia murmured with a smile.

Relief washed through Christopher. At least she wasn't giving dear old Mrs Dorkin her frosty face. In the old days, the cook had been his only ally against the army of doctors who insisted he eat nothing but gruel. Fortunately, she believed a lad needed his nourishment.

'We were supposed to lodge at the Sussex Hotel tonight,' he said, opening his arms in a gesture of regret. 'But somehow they let our rooms go. I do hope you can accommodate us?'

Mrs Dorkin placed her hands on her ample hips. 'The Sussex Hotel, is it? And you no more than a stone's throw from the Bird? I'm surprised at you, Mr Christopher. Come in, do. It's late and you must be tired.'

She waved a hand in the direction of the front door. 'I've a nice bit of roast pork on the spit and there's some cottage pie and I think a capon or two—cold, mind—left over from Sunday. Now then, Mr Christopher, I know that finicky appetite of yours, I'll expect you to let me know if none of it takes your fancy.' She shook her head. 'Mercy me, I am sure to find some cheese somewhere and I baked bread this afternoon.'

The warm chatter eased his tension, the way it had calmed him as a boy racked by fever. He gestured for Miss Boisette to step inside. Shadows like bruises lay beneath her huge cornflower eyes. She looked exhausted and scared.

Damn it. The wench had been bold enough an hour ago in the face of the innkeeper's rudeness and Lord Albert's obviously dishonourable intentions.

Christopher clenched his jaw. He couldn't entirely blame the young rakehell. He'd acted like any other hot-blooded male faced with an irresistible opportunity. And Miss Boisette certainly was all of that. Why the hell had she not stayed with her friend? Suspicion reared an ugly head. Perhaps she had followed him, thinking him an easy mark after his generosity.

Mrs Dorkin pitched her voice into the back of the house. 'Pansy! Dratted girl, never around when you need her.'

A scrawny wench came at a run, her cheeks as red as if she'd been roasting her face instead of the pork.

'Show the young lady up to the second-floor bedroom.' Mrs Dorkin smiled at Sylvia. 'You'll find that's the best room, miss. Quiet.'

'Thank you,' she murmured.

Christopher grinned at the plump matron, much as he had when he had lived at his grandmother's house. 'Mrs Dorkin, we are starving. Anything you could do to hurry dinner along will be much appreciated.'

'Dinner in half an hour, don't be late.' Mrs Dorkin's voice faded away as she travelled into the depths of the old inn. 'Maybe I have some of the nice fruitcake I baked for the vicar last Sunday. You always liked fruitcake…'

Shoulders slumped, Sylvia started after the maid.

Christopher put a hand on her arm. 'I should have warned you. She's a dear, but she loves to talk.'

'She seems very kind. I hadn't realised just how famished I am. All that talk of food…'

The faintness of her voice, weary posture and attempted smile caused him a pang of guilt. Curse it. No wonder she looked ready to wilt, she'd eaten almost nothing at lunch.

Unwelcome sympathy stirred in his chest. This was the first time today he'd seen her control slip. His questions would wait until after dinner.

He caught a glimpse of a well-turned ankle as she followed the maid up the stairs. Even worn to the bone, she radiated female sensuality. No wonder men rushed to her aid, lust burning in their eyes.

The low-beamed room with overstuffed chairs and easy country atmosphere comforted Christopher like hot punch on a cold night. Half-empty serving dishes cluttered the sideboard against the wall.

Pleasantly full, he set down his knife and fork and stared at the woman across from him. The warmth of the fire and her few sips of red wine had dispelled her earlier pallor. The faint glow in her cheeks and the sparkle in her eyes rendered her utterly lovely.

Mrs Dorkin hadn't asked him any pointed questions about Miss Boisette's presence under his protection. No doubt she'd seen and heard enough about the Evernden men and their dissolute ways not to be surprised at Christopher's arrival with one of the world's most beautiful women on his arm.

Despite her assertions, Miss Boisette needed proper male protection. The scene at the Sussex proved it.

He ran an appraising glance over her and frowned. Her severe brown gown couldn't be drearier. Come to think of it, the nondescript grey cloak and black poke bonnet she wore to travel in were also exceedingly dowdy. To all intents and purposes, she dressed like a governess or lady's maid.

Christopher wanted to see her in something more elegant, lighter, perhaps the colour of sapphires to match her brilliant eyes. Something lacy and filmy that left little to the imagination. Something like Lady Delia, Garth's last fling, had worn when Christopher had dropped in on their love nest one afternoon.

The image of Sylvia Boisette's curvaceous form clothed in a wisp of silk stirred his blood.

Her small white teeth, with their adorable tiny space in the centre, bit into a petit-four. What would that moist, soft mouth feel like against his lips or on his…?

Bloody hell. He didn't need this. He pushed his plate away.

Her wanton behaviour yesterday and in Tunbridge Wells had his thoughts in the gutter. If she had stayed where he had left her, they wouldn't be in this fix. If she had dressed like a lady, the young lordling might not have been so ready with his insults and the landlord might have given her a room without question.

'Don't you have something smarter to wear?' he asked.

Blue heat flashed in her eyes. Quickly repressed, it hinted at higher passions beneath her cool distant beauty. His groin tightened. Mentally, he cursed.

'Why would I?' she asked. 'I plan to become a shop-keeper, not a courtesan.'

Her flat tone delivered a dash of cold water to his lust. He watched an expression of satisfaction dawn on her face. She intended to disgust him. What game was she playing?

He'd been billed enough for expensive clothes by the last woman in his life to know quality when he saw it. 'The mourning gown you wore to my uncle's funeral was well cut and in the height of fashion. Made from the finest silk, if I'm not mistaken.' He waved his glass in her general direction. 'I'm sure my uncle preferred you in something more attractive.'

Pain shadowed her eyes before she shuttered her gaze. 'That part of my life is over.'

He took a deep swallow of wine. 'Really? Then what were you doing at the Sussex Hotel?'

'Seeking a room for the night.'

'With Lord Albert, no doubt.'

Outwardly unruffled, she did not shrink from his gaze, but her hand clutched the locket at her throat. 'No.'

A low blow, he silently acknowledged, remembering the panic in her eyes when Lord Albert slobbered over her hand. Damn it, every time he thought about it, he wanted to throttle the snivelling fribble.

What the hell was the matter with him? He never let

a woman distract him. Miss Boisette had caused him nothing but anxious moments. 'While we are on the subject, perhaps you would like to explain why you tipped me the double?'

'Tipped you the double?' She wrinkled her nose.

The urge to kiss away the furrow on her brow swept through him. He wanted to do more than that. Even with a frown, her incredible beauty numbed his mind and shortened his breath. His blood thickened. Never had a woman tempted him like this one.

He drew in a deep breath, crushing his desire. Dalliance with his uncle's ward or mistress—which he no longer believed—remained out of the question if he wanted to preserve a grain of family honour.

Hell. He needed to get rid of her and continue on his way to the Darbys'. He set his glass down, the chink loud in the quiet room. 'Come clean, Miss Boisette. Why did you not stay with your friend? You took money to go into business and within an hour of my leaving you, I find you at a common inn hanging on the arm of some young coxcomb.'

Arctic chill frosted her gaze. 'Are you implying that I took the money under false pretences?'

'I demand an explanation.'

'You have no right to demand anything. You brought me here against my will and if you try to touch me, I will scream bloody murder.'

It seemed he now had her full attention. This beautiful young woman, who behaved like a trollop one moment and an ice queen the next, needed a good shaking. 'Do you really think the Dorkins will pay any attention?'

Stark terror leaped into her eyes, bleakness invading their clear, cold depths like a plea for help. Fear hung in the air as thick and choking as smoke.

What did a woman like her have to fear from him? She had tossed more lures at him than a falconer to an ill-trained hawk. And he'd almost come to her fist, jessied and hooded.

Enough. He would do his duty and see her settled and he would see it done his way. Calmly, logically. The methods he used in his business dealings.

He poured a glass of wine from the decanter at his elbow and schooled his face into pleasant cheerfulness. 'I must apologise. My anger is directed at Lord Albert and that damn innkeeper.' Hell, the recollection caused his blood to simmer all over again. 'However, we did have an agreement, one you proposed and appear to have broken.'

She didn't speak, but stared at her empty plate as if trying to weave some new web of lies.

He pushed a plate of comfits in her direction. 'Here.'

A pathetic peace offering, yet it eased the palpable tension.

Sylvia gazed from the heaped pink-and-white sugared almonds on the blue dish to his face. Emerald fires burned deep in his hazel eyes, not the usual blaze of a lusty male, but a deep slow burn that fanned the embers in the pit of her own stomach to flame.

A tremor she could only identify as fear quivered in the region of her heart. Without him she was stranded. All her money, apart from the few coins in her reticule, had been left behind in Tunbridge Wells.

Trapped. A shiver shot up her spine. And he was right. She did owe him an explanation. She took a deep breath. 'My friend, Mary Jensen, moved her business to London.' She hoped he did not hear the hitch in her voice at her lie.

He frowned at his glass, then stared her straight in the eye. 'I thought she expected you?'

She sighed. Obviously, he had paid attention. 'There was some error in our communication. She left a forwarding address with the new tenant. The woman forgot to mail on my letters, therefore Mary did not know about your uncle's unexpected demise.'

His intense scrutiny made her shift in her seat. She had the strong sense he did not believe her.

'And?' he said.

She shrugged. 'I must now go to London.'

'You have her address?'

'I do.'

'What is it?'

'I don't see why—'

His mouth turned down and his eyes narrowed. 'I'm sure you don't. But you are mistaken if you think I am going to drop you off at a coaching house in the morning without knowing your proposed destination.'

'You agreed to drive me to Tunbridge Wells. Your obligation ends there.'

'I offered to drive you to the bosom of your friend and that is where my duty ends.'

The quiet emphasis in his voice made it clear he would not listen to further argument. She hesitated. It would do no harm to give him Mary's directions. Once she reached London, she would never see him again.

'Very well.' She dived into her reticule and handed him the dog-eared paper with Mary's new address.

He gazed at it silently for a moment. 'Dear God. The Seven Dials. Do you have any idea what sort of place that is?'

Her stomach plummeted. 'Not good, I assume.'

'I wouldn't worry if it were just not good, as you put it. It couldn't be worse. It houses London's worst slums and most dangerous criminals.'

'Mary Jensen is of a perfect respectability,' she flashed back. *Incroyable.* She'd lost her grip on her English.

'Not living in that neighborhood, she isn't.' He tossed the paper on the table next to a hunk of fruitcake.

His innuendoes wearied her; the whole day had tried her patience, and the strange, nerve-stretching aware-ness between them exhausted her most of all. She was an idiot for leaving Tunbridge Wells in his carriage. She would have been much better off at the damned Hare and Hounds.

'What does it matter? I am not of a respectableness enough for you or your most esteemed family. The sooner we make our own directions, the better, *n'est ce pas*?'

'Do not raise your voice to me, *mademoiselle.*'

'And do not dictate to me.'

She stood.

He followed suit with easy grace, looming over her, green pinpricks of anger dancing in his eyes. 'I would not have to dictate to you, if you had been more forthright in your dealings with me. It is my duty to see you safely es-tablished somewhere and I will not brook an argument.'

Golden in the firelight, he stood like a knight of old surrounded by the armour of righteousness. Trust him, her heart murmured with a little skip. Let him enfold you with his strength, urged her body with a delicious shiver. An urgent warning clamoured in her mind. *You are no better than your mother.*

'I do not accept your right to give me orders.'

He bowed. 'I suggest you go to bed. We will discuss what is to be done in the morning, when your nerves are less overset.'

She almost laughed in his face. Monsieur Jean must have lost his mind putting her in the hands of this dutiful and stuffy Evernden nephew.

'Nerves, Mr Evernden, are for pampered darlings with fathers and husbands to protect them while they lie about on *chaises* with vinaigrettes and hartshorn complaining of headaches. I don't have the luxury of nerves.' She headed for the door. 'We will certainly discuss this further *en route* to catch the mail in the morning.'

She turned in the doorway. 'We will need to be up at five. I hope that is not too early for you?'

His open mouth gave her satisfaction enough as she swept out of the room and up the stairs.

Chapter Five

Christopher paused on the front step of the inn and lit his cigar. The night air cooled his cheeks after the Bird in Hand's blazing fire and his argument with Miss Boisette. Abstracted, he ran a hand over the thick wooden door, the raised studs and black iron bands rough beneath his fingertips. Hard to imagine that the man who had built this door had died more than two centuries ago and the tree from which he carved it had probably grown for two centuries before that. Those were times of knights and lords and deeds of daring. What would those men think of this world now?

The faint haze of his smoky breath drifted in front of his face. He drew on his cigar and savoured the acrid burn on his tongue and the mellow aroma in his nostrils. He needed a walk to restore some sort of order to his body and his mind before he retired for the night.

He left the warm light of the inn and strode down the tree-arched lane, stretching muscles cramped from the journey. Amidst the sparse spring leaves of the canopy above his head, stars winked their steel-bright messages in a stygian sky.

A wooden stile broke a gap in the dense hedgerow and he leaned against its rail. The full moon hovered yellow, fat and lazy above the horizon. Scattered lights twinkled along the dark slash of river valley meandering through rolling meadows.

He'd wandered this countryside as a boy while quarantined from disease-ridden London and his family. They had visited him here at his grandparents' estate from time to time, but his father had insisted on residing in London.

He stared into the gloom, trying to identify boyhood haunts. He and Garth had ridden this country hard during school holidays. He grimaced. More often than not, Garth had been flogged for some of their more daring exploits, always taking the punishment for leading Christopher astray. He hadn't needed much leading. But deemed too sickly to receive his share of the blame, Garth had taken it for both of them. Garth never seemed to care, but he had ceased to spend much time at Hedly Hall once he went away to school and Christopher hadn't visited it in years. Too busy keeping on top of his business interests.

An owl hooted. Distant hooves beat the familiar rhythm of a gallop on the hard-packed earth. The drumming stopped, heralding a late-night visitor to the inn.

His mind flew back to Sylvia, the gorgeous vision of sensual womanhood he had seen in Dover, the frightened, but determined, girl at the Sussex Hotel. He smothered a curse. Stubborn woman. She had him out here pacing in the night air while she no doubt was tucked up in bed, dreaming of London, with a gown of the sheerest muslin covering every lithe inch of her. He grimaced. He didn't care what kind of gown she wore; he wanted to see it on her. He wanted to slide it from her alabaster skin the way she'd stripped off her gloves. He wanted what lay beneath.

His arousal, a low controlled thrumming during dinner, spiked with urgent need. What the hell was the matter with him? He never had any trouble controlling his base urges when confronted with members of the opposite sex. Not even the most famous of London's courtesans had heated his blood to the point he could think of nothing but slaking his lust inside her delicious body.

No matter how dull the attire covering her enticing curves, the longer he spent in her company, the more he wanted to explore her swells and hollows.

He groaned. He'd have more success knocking out Gentleman Jackson than battering his loins' demands into submission. Damn John Evernden for foisting the wench on him.

No one need know if she became his mistress. The idea lit in his mind like a beacon. In London the news would make the rounds in a heartbeat, but tucked away at his country house in Kent, their liaison would be discreet enough. No one would know he'd taken his uncle's ward under his protection.

He would know. And Garth would accuse him of hypocrisy the moment he guessed. He closed his eyes in silent contempt. Was he as bad as the rest of the Evernden men when it came to loose women?

Damn. There had been enough scandal in the Evernden family and he had sworn not to add to it.

He dropped the remains of his cigar, a smouldering red spark in the night, and ground it beneath his heel as if quenching the fire in his veins. If only it were that easy. He turned and strode for the inn.

What the hell should he do with her, then? The thought of a bordello chilled his blood. A lady's maid? A seamstress? Apparently, she had some talent in that direction.

Idiot. She was French. A married friend had complained bitterly about the cost of his French governess. If, as Christopher suspected, this friend in London proved to be a hum, why not palm her off on some country squire seeking to elevate the prospects of his hopeful brood?

Because he wanted her.

Hell fire. A wry smile twisted his lips at the way his mind bent towards the urgings of his body.

He rounded the bend. A lantern lit the sign of the Bird, a clenched fist with only the head of a bright-eyed robin visible. The door lay open, but the parlour window was dark and blank.

What would Mrs Dorkin say if he requested a tub of cold water to be sent to his chamber? She'd likely think he'd run mad and predict his death from pneumonia.

Tension locked his spine and he rubbed the back of his neck. A good strong brandy before bed would relax him and take the edge off the want clawing at the heart of his resolve.

Maybe two.

A brown gelding lifted its head from the trough on the stable wall. A nice beast, perhaps a little long in the leg, it had been ridden hard judging from the steam rising from its flanks.

Christopher ducked his head beneath the lintel and made his way through a narrow passage to the back of the house and the dimly lit taproom. Behind the long bar, Jack Dorkin, jolly and fat on his wife's cooking, greeted him with a nod.

Dorkin put down a pewter tankard and his drying cloth. 'Something for you, Mr Evernden?'

'A brandy, please. Make it a double.'

Dorkin lifted a bottle and shook it. 'I'll have to go to the cellar,' he muttered. 'Won't be but a moment, sir.' He swung up a trapdoor in the floor and clattered down the steps.

Christopher leaned one arm on the battered oak bar. A couple of country labourers in traditional smocks, clay pipes clamped in whiskered jaws, clacked domino tiles in swift sure movements. An occasional chuckle or mutter indicated the state of play. A shepherd, his dog at his feet, nursed a tankard on the settle beside the red brick medieval hearth. Out of the corner of his eye, he caught a movement in the shadows at the far end of the bar. In a pool of light cast by an oil lamp, a square strong hand, the wrist covered by the cuff of dark green coat, lifted a mug. The horseman.

Christopher nodded. 'Good evening.'

The hand raised in greeting. 'The top of the evening to you too, sir.'

Irish by his brogue.

'That's a fine piece horseflesh you have there,' Christopher said.

'Aye, an' it is and all,' the man replied. He threw a coin on the counter. 'I'll be wishing you a good night, then.' He stood and, with a slight bow, placed his hat on his head and sauntered out of the bar. The flickering lamp by the door illuminated his rangy frame and lean jaw, then he was gone.

Where had he seen the man before? Christopher rarely forgot a face, but right at the moment he could not place this one.

'Here's your brandy, Mr Evernden,' Dorkin said, his cheeks puffing in and out. 'Sorry it took so long. I keeps me best stuff locked up. Can't trust the help these days, you know.'

'Who was that?' Christopher asked, his gaze fixed on the doorway.

'Dunno, sir. Just popped in on the off chance, like. I've never seen him afore.'

Christopher picked up the goblet. 'Cheers, Dorkin, and thank you.'

He wandered to the bench opposite the shepherd and stretched out his legs to the fire's warmth. He savoured the smooth amber liquid on his tongue.

Oh, yes, this was the best stuff all right. Definitely French and certainly an improvement over a cold bath, if not as effective.

A scuffling noise invaded Sylvia's consciousness. It couldn't possibly be time to rise. Her eyelids refused the order to open and she submerged into the opaque veil of sleep.

A sound like fingernails on glass tormented her ears. The maid must be scratching at the door to wake her. She had to get up. She must not miss the coach to London. She groaned. Just a few minutes more, then she would open her eyes. She wriggled further beneath the warmth of the blankets.

Stupid. The inability to sleep after leaving Christopher Evernden in the dining room did not give her an excuse to lie in bed. He reminded her of a disapproving older brother, except nothing brotherly lingered in the depth of evergreen eyes flecked with brown. His steel-hard resolve to do his duty and his ingrained sense of honour pulled at her like the full moon on the ocean. Not to mention his handsome face.

An ache squeezed her heart and her breath hitched at the pain. Burrowing into the pillow, she shook her head in denial. No handsome face would lead her down the path to ruin and misery. No. She would not let another Evernden man break down her carefully constructed defences.

A sliding noise and a bang jolted her fully awake. She stared into the gloom. It wasn't morning. A pale square of light glimmered on the wall opposite the window; the rest of the room lay in deep shadow.

She turned over.

Oh, God! Outlined by moonlight, a head and shoulders filled the window frame.

Fingers of ice held her body immobile and squeezed her throat. She opened her mouth to scream. A faint croak emerged.

The dark shape dropped to the floor with a muffled thud. This had to be a dream. She swallowed what felt like gravel.

The shadow lunged at her. Shivers of dread clawed down her spine, breaking the frigid clasp of fear. She kicked the bedclothes aside. A heavy weight landed on her, driving the breath from her lungs, pinning her down. A warm calloused hand covered her mouth and nose. She fought for air. The smell of tobacco filled her nostrils and she tasted salty sweat. She flailed her arms, kicked out at him. Her heart pounded in her ears.

Not again. This couldn't happen to her again.

Her lungs begged for air. Her head swam; darkness crept to the edges of her vision. She flailed her arms. He grunted as her fist made contact in the region of his head. His weight shifted, his grip eased. She closed her teeth hard on the soft flesh of his thumb. Sweat and tobacco soured her tongue.

He cursed.

Triumph surged in her veins. She gulped at the sudden sweet rush of air and squirmed from beneath him.

'Don't touch me,' she cried. 'Get out.'

'I'm going,' he said, shaking his injured hand. 'An' like it or not, pet, you're coming with me.'

'No.'

She dived off the bed towards the door. Her elbow struck the bedpost and sent agonising tingles shooting to the tip of her little finger. Bent double, she clutched her arm to her chest.

'Help,' she screamed. '*À moi.*' Would no one come to her aid?

He raised his hand, his fist clenched around something black. She ducked.

The blow snapped her head back. A sharp pain, a flash of light, then sinking blackness rose up and swallowed her.

Christopher opened his eyes, his heart racing. What the hell? It had sounded like a woman's scream.

He groaned. It must have been a bad dream, either that or some lusty knave was hard at it with a red-faced maid. The sour thought only made his own fantasies of Sylvia more frustrating.

The mist of sleep and the fog of brandy slowly cleared. Good God. He'd lain down fully clothed. He'd clearly spent far too long with Dorkin and his finest French brandy before coming to bed.

A thud overhead sent him bolt upright.

Devil a bit. Miss Boisette must be pacing the floor.

More bumps. The hair on the back of his neck stirred, his skin prickled. It didn't sound like pacing. It sounded more like a battle. What the deuce was going on up there? He leaped off the bed, flung open the door and peered into the hallway.

A whispered curse from above directed his attention up the stairs. Caught in the dim glow from the lantern on the landing, a man stood rigid, ready to step down. In his arms, he carried something large and white like a bundle of sheets. A servant?

'Identify yourself,' Christopher ordered.

The man let his burden slide to the floor. A pair of slender legs and trailing blonde hair gleamed before they disappeared into the shadows.

Sylvia?

Christopher dashed up the stairs. The man swung a bag at his head. Sylvia's valise. Christopher ducked. He charged the man's gut with his shoulder.

His opponent grunted, stumbling backward. Christopher bunched his fists. Disadvantaged by the man's position above him, Christopher couldn't get a clear swing. The man flung himself forward. A sharp elbow jabbed Christopher in the ribs. Air rushed from his lungs. He doubled in pain. The man shoved him hard against the balustrade and hurtled down two flights of stairs. He crashed out through the front door, still clutching the bag.

Gasping, Christopher started after him.

Damn. He couldn't leave Sylvia. He turned and took the stairs two at a time to her side.

As still as death, she lay sprawled on the planked landing, her face pale and her lips bloodless in the lantern's flickering light.

Bile rose in his throat. Dead? He knelt and lifted her wrist. Her pulse beat strong and steady. He ran his hands over her limbs and her torso. Thank God, no blood.

He chafed her cold hands. 'Sylvia.'

She didn't move.

He pulled her nightgown down to cover her shapely calves and picked her up. Her head fell back, revealing her slender throat and a bruise behind her ear. Rage like molten metal surged through him. Damn the blackguard for striking a woman. If he ever got his hands on him, he'd kill the bastard.

He hesitated. He couldn't leave her here or take her

to her own room in case the damned rogue came back. Instead, he carried her down to his chamber and laid her on the bed.

'Mr Evernden.' Dorkin's voice sounded shocked. 'What are you doing with that there young lady?'

'Damn it, Dorkin. Don't just stand there gawking. Miss Boisette is hurt. Fetch a doctor.'

'I'll get the missus,' Dorkin said. 'She'll know what's best. Mr Christopher, I never would have thought it of you.' Dorkin hurried off.

Christopher stared at his departing back. What the devil did he mean? He glanced down at the practically naked girl on his bed. Dorkin must think that he… Hell. Now he'd have some explaining to do.

He eased the counterpane from beneath her and pulled it up. He smoothed her hair back from her face. Unbound it had the texture of silk. He investigated the lump on her tender skin behind her ear.

The cur had struck her a vicious blow. A sick feeling washed over him. What kind of man would do that to a woman? Why had this man attacked her? Not just attacked, he'd tried to abduct her. He shook his head. Beautiful she might be, but people didn't go around stealing females because they were beyond-reason lovely. Not in this day and age, for God's sake. Unless some rogue thought Christopher would pay to get her back?

He enclosed her cold fingers in his hands, trying to warm them, his gaze on her pale face. Damn, she was exquisite. And he'd been right about the nightgown. He'd seen far too much of her beneath it. Her limbs were every bit as lovely as he had imagined and twice as tempting.

Need ripped through him like a torturer's knife pressed against his ballocks.

He cursed under his breath. He had to put a stop to

this, and soon. In the meantime, he kept his gaze fixed on her face. Where the hell was Mrs Dorkin, anyway? Sylvia might die before she got here.

He felt her pulse again and sighed with relief to discover its steady rhythm. A rhythm that in no way matched the tumult of his own erratic heartbeat.

Hell's teeth, his racing heart had nothing to do with the scantily clad Sylvia and everything to do with his burning need to catch this criminal. He should be chasing the villain, not sitting here holding her hand.

Limp and white, her long slender fingers lay like a bird's broken wing in his large palm. The hand of a lady. Except that this lady was a courtesan's daughter.

'Now then, Mr Christopher Evernden, what's all this I hear?'

Thank God. Mrs Dorkin would know how to care for Sylvia. He moved aside to let her get to the bed.

Her face full of anxiety, Mrs Dorkin leaned over and peered down at the unconscious girl.

'Miss?' she said. 'Can you hear me?'

Sylvia drifted through thick grey fog.

A moan increased the pain in her head. She opened her eyes. A fuzzy moon-face hung over her. She shuddered. What did he want with her?

She put up her hands to ward him off. 'Don't touch me, you whoremaster,' she yelled. 'Get away from me, you pig.' She struck out with her fists.

'Lawks,' moon-face said.

'In English, Miss Boisette.'

Mr Evernden's voice.

What was he doing in her room? Why had he climbed through her window?

'You unholy bastard.' She tried to sit up. The room spun around her, nausea rose in her throat.

'Miss Boisette, speak English and for God's sake mind your language. You sound like a Paris trollop.'

French. They were speaking in French. She tried to get her mind working. Someone had filled it with treacle. Her temples throbbed.

A firm hand pressed her back against the pillows.

'Now don't you take on so, miss.'

It was Mrs Dorkin whose face hung over her in a shifting blur. Sylvia blinked the mist from her sight.

'You've had a nasty bump on the head, dear,' Mrs Dorkin murmured, smoothing her hair back. 'Pansy will be along in a minute with a compress. You lie nice and quiet and you'll be all right in no time.'

Sylvia gazed around the room. This was not her room. She stared past Mrs Dorkin at Christopher standing at the end of the bed. Another man hovered in the doorway behind him.

Christopher wore a shirt open at the throat and looked decidedly tousled. His expression held concern. What had he done to her? The last she remembered, they had been arguing at dinner.

'Why am I here?'

Christopher frowned. 'Someone tried to abduct you.'

'Someone? Who? Why?'

'I don't know. Did you not see who it was?'

A rough lilting voice came back to her, a growl close to her ear and full of menace. *And you're coming with me, pet.*

'He came in through the window. He spoke French with a strange accent,' she said.

Christopher leaned forward, his expression intent. 'What sort of accent?'

Sylvia shook her head. 'Hard to tell. He whispered.'

'Exactly what did he say?'

'He said I had to go with him.' Her limbs trembled as the fear rushed back.

Christopher's expression hardened. 'He got you halfway down the stairs. Luckily, I heard you cry out.'

She remembered the feel of his hand on her mouth, the taste of his skin on her tongue. She shuddered. 'He smokes cigars,' she said.

'How on earth could you possibly know that?' Suspicion darkened his eyes.

'He covered my mouth with his hand. I couldn't breathe, so I bit him. I tasted cigars.'

Admiration flickered in his eyes, replaced by worry. 'Good God, he might have killed you.'

Yes, she believed he might have. The man who had whispered in the dark was capable of anything, even murder. A shiver shook her at the recollection of his hands on her body. She had to leave here. He might return.

She pushed herself up on her elbow. An ache throbbed in her skull. She touched the back of her head and winced as her fingers encountered a tender lump. She closed her eyes, seeking relief.

'Now, now, miss, what did I say?' Mrs Dorkin said. 'You lie down. You've had a nasty shock. Mr Christopher, your questions must wait until later.'

'I must get up.' Her voice quavered, but she refused to acknowledge her weakness. 'I have to catch the stage to London.'

'Not today, you won't,' Mrs Dorkin pronounced. 'Ah, Pansy, there you are. Bring that bowl over here.'

The maid sidled around Christopher and set a bowl and towels on the bed next to Mrs Dorkin.

'Go on now, Mr Christopher,' Mrs Dorkin said. 'And you too, Dorkin. This young lady has had a nasty scare and a bad knock. I'll see to her head, and after some willow bark tea, she's going to sleep. Out you go. At once.'

Sylvia sent Christopher a look of appeal. 'I have to leave today. What about my trunk?'

A frown creasing his forehead, Christopher shook his head. 'Listen to Mrs Dorkin, Miss Boisette. Don't worry about your things, I'll look after them.'

He didn't wait for her to argue and Mrs Dorkin didn't listen to her protests.

Fatigue washed over Sylvia. As limp as the week-old lettuce she'd prized as a starving child running the streets of Paris, she sank back against the pillows and welcomed the cold compress Mrs Dorkin applied to her aching head.

Christopher took Dorkin outside and they scoured the perimeter of the inn, looking for signs of the intruder. Above the old kitchen at the back, the thatched roof sloped within three feet of the ground and Dorkin pointed out a pile of stones against the wall. 'He must have used them to climb up.'

Cold moonlight revealed broken thatch where the intruder must have stood to force open the second-floor window. Dorkin peered at Christopher. 'Very strange goin's on, sir. Why would anyone want to abduct the young lady?'

Since Christopher had asked himself the same question without an answer, he shook his head. 'I'm not sure.'

Most importantly, he didn't want a whole bunch of gossip about this. Travelling with a woman of less than savoury repute was bad enough; talk of tonight would just increase speculation. Christopher would come off just as badly as Miss Boisette and neither of them deserved it.

'I suspect it was a mistake,' Christopher said. 'Or someone thought to ransom her because she is travelling under my protection. I think it is best if we do not say anything to anyone else about this until I can speak further to Miss Boisette.'

Whatever Dorkin thought about the affair, he simply nodded his agreement, his close connections to the influential Everndens ensuring his loyal silence. With no particular expectation of finding anything, Christopher walked out to the lane. A black shape lay amidst the rough grass on the verge. He picked it up and turned the hat over in his hands.

There was nothing remarkable about the fairly common black felt hat worn by the lower orders. The man in the bar tonight had worn just such a hat. Christopher frowned. Had the man dropped it when he rode away or was he Sylvia's midnight visitor? If so, there remained the question of why? He tucked it under his arm and followed Dorkin into the inn.

Chapter Six

Christopher gazed into the window of the most well-known dressmaker in Tunbridge Wells, taking in the lengths of brightly coloured muslins and satins and the assortment of gloves and hats and other more personal articles of ladies' apparel laid out before him. He tugged at his cravat.

He did not want to do this.

He had no choice. The damn rogue who attacked Sylvia had stolen every article of her clothing along with her bag and when Christopher had presented himself to the porter at the Sussex Hotel, the fool proudly announced he personally saw to putting the young lady's chest on the six o'clock coach. When Christopher upbraided him about the folly of sending the baggage without the owner, the man had shrugged and said the lady was very positive in her request. She could pick it up at the London office as soon as she arrived there. Meanwhile, Sylvia had nothing to wear but her nightgown.

Two ladies stepped around him and entered the establishment. The younger one slid him a curious glance.

Inwardly, Christopher cursed. He definitely didn't want to do this. Garth might take pleasure in overseeing his mistresses' adornment, but Christopher preferred to give them the money and send them shopping.

Hell and damnation. He'd spent the past two days doing nothing but things against his better judgement. Well, he'd damned well had enough of dancing to other people's tunes. Sylvia would travel to London under his escort and no argument. Last night was all the evidence he needed of the danger she faced travelling alone.

First, he'd buy her some clothes and then he would drop her off with this friend of hers. After that, he would wash his hands of the whole business and head back to Sussex as originally planned.

Perhaps a closed carriage would be a better mode of travel given the dreadful weather this year. He could leave his curricle at the Bird and take a post-chaise. He shook his head. Then he'd be left in London with no means of transportation. Bloody hell. She would just have to put up with it.

He squared his shoulders and strode into the cluttered shop. Manikins draped with swathes of cloth posed in front of shelves filled with fabrics of every hue. The two women ahead of him dithered over a tray of ribbons. Christopher flicked through a book of fashion plates on a side table and waited. One page pictured a blue gown with a modest, but attractive, neckline. He liked blue and it matched the colour of her eyes. Perfect.

He fixed the middle-aged dressmaker with a stern look. Rows of purple ruffles on her billowing lilac gown made her ample bosom all the more impressive.

She bade her other customers farewell and bustled to his side. 'How can I be of service, sir?'

'I want to buy a gown for my sister.'

On her way out of the door, the younger woman sniggered. Christopher ignored her.

'Yes, sir,' the smiling seamstress said.

The woman's knowing expression told him she did not believe a word. He narrowed his eyes and spoke firmly. 'My sister is having a birthday and I wish to buy her a gown, in blue, today.'

The woman frowned. 'It will have to be ready-made, sir.'

'Of course.'

The woman pulled a sheet of paper out from under the counter and stood with quill poised, looking at him. 'If you would provide her sizes, I will look and see what I have in stock.'

Sizes. God. He knew nothing about sizes. He took a stab at it. 'She's slender and petite.'

'Height?'

He held his hand at shoulder height. 'Her head comes to about here.'

'Waist?'

Christopher stared at her. 'Er…' He'd held her by the waist yesterday. He recalled the feel of her slender body under his fingers. He held his hands in a circle, not quite touching each other. 'Like this.'

'Eighteen inches, I should think,' the woman said, scratching on her paper.

'Chest?'

Christopher held himself steady, refusing to be put off, despite an overwhelming inclination to flee the store and forget the whole thing. How would a brother know that kind of thing? He wouldn't. He shook his head.

The woman tutted. She looked down at her own well-endowed figure. 'Like me?'

Perish the thought. 'Smaller. Quite a lot smaller.'

The woman crossed to a manikin and held her hands cupped in front of it. Christopher could tell that she had done this before. 'Like this?' she asked.

The shape of the woman's hands were nothing like the small upthrusting breasts beneath the nightgown he'd glimpsed in the small hours of this morning. He swallowed. 'Not so round.'

'Ah,' the woman said, her lips pursed. 'Lisette, dear. Do come out here a moment.'

A young woman in a stiff black gown cut high to the neck emerged from behind a yellow curtain beyond the counter. The shopkeeper swung her around by the shoulders to outline her figure's profile. She pulled the gown tight at the sides, revealing a pert and shapely figure.

'How about like this?'

He pushed the disturbing image of Sylvia's breasts, coupled with visions of her legs, her golden hair hanging to her waist, to one side. The girl was close enough to Sylvia to make no difference. 'Yes. About like her, perhaps a little more slender.'

The woman bobbed a curtsy. 'I'm sure we have something to your liking, sir. I'll be but a moment.'

Christopher approached a display cabinet and leaned against it, looking in. The case contained gloves and little lacy things. Soft and delicate things he imagined Sylvia wearing at night or beneath her gown. Filmy, clinging garments designed to hug soft feminine curves. Curves which felt so right in his arms. Curves he'd had no business touching and which were likely to disturb his mind and his body for a very long time.

Disgusted with the turn of his mind, he flung himself into a gilt chair jammed between stacks of cloth, his gaze fixed on the brightly coloured bales, refusing to think about Sylvia at all.

He didn't have long to wait for the woman to return.
He stared at the froth of garments draped over her arms.

'I brought you a morning gown in blue-and-white
muslin. Something for daywear, I think you said? I also
took the liberty of bringing an evening gown, right for
almost any function. This shade of rose is all the rage
and truly lovely. No lady would be disappointed.'

He hesitated. Decisions never bothered him, but he
had no idea what Sylvia liked. 'I'll take them both.'

The woman smiled. 'She is a lucky lady to have a
generous…brother like you.'

He gritted his teeth at her impertinence, but leashed
his temper. It didn't matter what she thought. 'I also
need things to go under those, and a hat, gloves, you
know the sort of thing.'

The woman's face lit up as if she'd been given a gift.
'Yes, sir,' she said. 'Might I suggest—'

'Just put it all together. Everything a lady will need
for two days. I will come and collect them in half an
hour, if it's not too much trouble.'

'No trouble at all, Mr Evernden,' the dressmaker said,
rubbing her hands together.

He mentally cursed his stupidity. He'd lived not five
miles from here during his youth—was it any wonder she
knew him? She would also know he did not have a sister.

In the dark passage outside the parlour, Sylvia
prepared herself to face Mr Evernden over luncheon.
She smoothed her hair and swallowed a gasp when her
fingers encountered the tender spot in her hairline
behind her ear.

A shudder ripped through her. Who would want to
abduct her in the middle of the night and steal all her
clothes? The thought left her feeling shaky, unlike herself.

It seemed so peculiar. And now she found herself further indebted to Mr Evernden. She glanced down at the gown he had purchased for her. A fashionable high-waisted blue muslin with a generous amount of lace in the neckline and pretty puffed sleeves, it must have cost a fortune, it and the rest of the items he'd brought back from Tunbridge.

Spine straight, she pushed open the heavy oak door and stepped into the front parlour Mrs Dorkin reserved for her most favored guests.

Newspaper in hand, Mr Evernden rose to his feet and bowed. 'Good afternoon, Miss Boisette. I hope you are feeling more the thing?'

The deep timbre of his voice and his concerned expression drove all thoughts from her mind, except how handsome and large he looked framed in the bow window. This man had saved her life last night. A fluttering warmth danced in her veins. 'Thank you. I feel much better.'

Afraid her eyes would give her away, she dropped her gaze to the table. 'My goodness.' A basket of bread, a cold ham and platters of fruits, cheeses and other delicacies lay spread out on the table in front of him.

His warm chuckle reverberated from his chest. 'I hope you are ravenous.' He gestured to the banquet. 'I certainly can't eat all this myself and Mrs Dorkin will be most put out if we do not do it justice.'

He went around the table and pulled out the chair for her. 'Please, sit down.'

The calm easy manner soothed her jangled nerves and, as she settled into the chair, the scent of his sandalwood cologne filled her senses. She risked a smile.

His eyes widened a fraction and a heat flickered in their green depths.

A fire ignited beneath her skin. Her pulse tripped and quickened. She felt warm and shivery all at once. She stared down at her hands folded in her lap and noticed their tremble. The blow to her head had affected her more than she thought.

He returned to his seat.

She wove her fingers together, stilling them. 'Thank you for purchasing this gown, Mr Evernden. I am sorry to put you to so much expense.'

His gaze travelled over her, appreciation in their depths. 'It certainly fits well enough and the colour matches your eyes.'

The urge to smile back, to simper like a schoolgirl, tugged at her lips. She caught it and held it at bay. 'I would have preferred something a little less fashionable, but I do thank you.'

His mouth twisted in a wry smile and he raised a brow. 'There was little else to choose.'

She hadn't meant to hurt his feelings. 'It's a lovely colour.'

He grinned, cheerful and boyish. Her foolish heart skipped a beat.

'I hope the other items were to your satisfaction?' he asked.

A laugh rose in her throat at his smug expression. Never had a man charmed her like this. Razor-sharp claws of fear tore at her stomach. Fear of her own weakness. She kept her expression and smile cool. 'Yes, thank you.'

He cocked his head to one side as if puzzled, then shrugged. 'Allow me to help you to a slice of ham.'

She unclenched her stiff fingers and passed him her plate. 'Thank you.'

On it, he placed a roll, some wafer-thin ham and three asparagus spears, bright green against the white china.

'That is enough,' she murmured.

'You must keep up your strength after last night, Miss Boisette.' He added a slice of chicken.

He returned her plate and filled his own.

They ate in a comfortable silence.

'May I pour you some coffee?' she asked.

'Please.' He pushed his cup and saucer towards her and she filled it. The earthy aroma wafted up. It was as if they were a married couple. A painful yearning ached in her chest. She would never have a husband.

'You are very attached to your locket, Miss Boisette.' A small jerk of his chin brought her to realise she clutched the heart-shaped gold at her throat.

'It is the only thing I have left of my mother. The only thing I brought to England from Paris.'

A muscle flicked in his lean jaw at the mention of her origins and pain stabbed her heart. No gentleman would want to be reminded of her background.

After a mouthful of coffee, he placed his cup on the saucer and gave her a long steady stare. 'I'm afraid we must discuss last night. Do you have any idea why this man might want to abduct you?'

Nausea rolled in her stomach. The reason that had occurred to her was not something she wished to discuss with any man, particularly one as straitlaced as this one. 'I have no idea at all.'

'Did you recognise his voice? Can you describe anything about him?'

A hoarse low whisper echoed in her ears and a bitter taste touched her tongue. 'As I said before, he spoke French, but the accent was odd.' She shook her head and winced at the ache. 'He seemed familiar. Someone I've met.'

He stared at her, eyes narrowed, intent. 'Where?'

'I'm sorry, I can't remember.' The recollection of enveloping darkness rolled over her. She touched a hand to the lump behind her ear.

'Dorkin is of the opinion we should call in the local magistrate. I'm not so sure.'

The thought of the authorities made her shiver. Her blood froze the way it had when she had been a child on the streets in Paris at the sight of the National Guard. She strove to keep the panic from her voice. 'I prefer to leave for London immediately. There must be a later stage I can catch.'

He frowned. 'Quite honestly, I also would prefer not to become entangled in a lengthy enquiry. The circumstances of our travelling together are rather unfortunate. However, I cannot allow you to continue your journey by public transportation. After last night, surely you must see the danger?'

Unwelcome warmth glowed in her heart at the genuine concern in his eyes. She made one last-ditch attempt to stave him off. 'People travel quite safely that way every day, Mr Evernden. Last night's events were perpetrated by some rogue trying to rob the inn. I was the unfortunate victim.'

He gave her a long searching look. 'I wish I felt sure it was a random act. I think I saw the fellow in the bar last night. He struck me as a man with a purpose.' Determination shone in his eyes and hardened the set of his jaw. 'Whatever the case, I will see you safely to London.'

Christopher eased his team around the tight turn on to White Lyon Street. He narrowly avoided a marauding band of sailors propositioning a group of tawdry trulls flashing their wares like exotic birds in the moulting season. Ragged men and women huddled in doorways. The dreary rookeries of London's East End crowded in on them.

He glanced at Miss Boisette's wooden expression. 'Your friend must have her business in a different part of town.'

'Yes, I expect so.' She sounded far from sure.

The weather had remained unusually fair and the drive had passed amicably. As they whiled away the time on the drive, he saw in her laughing replies hints of the sensuous woman who had teased him close to madness in Dover.

Strangely, his uncle seemed to have educated her more like a male friend than a female. She was well versed in the classics, Plato and Aristotle, and fond of the French philosopher Descartes. She had decided opinions on all of them.

Her fine mind would be wasted in a dress shop. She'd make a perfect companion with whom to spend the evening hours after mutually satisfying physical intimacy. The thought sliced through his idle musings. Had he lost his mind?

Awareness of her delightful feminine form scorched his hip. He shifted away and glanced around. Late afternoon lengthened the shadows between the buildings at an alarming rate. The district's evils were well known to him from his occasional business dealings here. He pulled up in front of a three-storey tenement house with peeling paint and an air of disreputable decay. A broken shutter hung from an upper storey. Filthy rags replaced glass here and there across the face of the building.

A frown creased her forehead. 'This is it?'

He nodded and signalled to a skinny youth with a shorn head and enormous ears slouched against the wall. 'Hold the bridle.'

The boy leaped forward.

Christopher climbed down. He gave the lad a stern glance. 'No funny business and I'll give you a penny.'

Red-rimmed assessing eyes stared back. The lad wiped his nose on a tattered sleeve. 'Right you are, sir.'

Christopher helped Sylvia down from the carriage and across the stinking kennel running with the day's effluence. She stared at the narrow door bearing the number they sought, took a deep breath and knocked. The sound echoed off the dank walls along the street.

Nerves of steel would avail her little in a place like this. Anger burned in his gullet. How could she possibly think of living here? It seemed too rank, too desperate for such a bright jewel. With half an eye on his carriage and the unsavoury youth at the team's heads, he drummed his fingers on his thigh.

The door opened a crack and a dirty face and two dark eyes peered out at them. Christopher didn't blame the occupant for caution in this neighborhood.

Sylvia took a small step back. She looked at the paper in her hand. 'Does Mary Jensen live here?'

'Aye.' The door widened to reveal a man in the rough garb of a labourer, his coal-dust-blackened face pierced by a pair of wary bloodshot eyes. The man's gaze ran over her, then took in Christopher and the carriage beyond. 'Who wants her?'

'My name is Sylvia Boisette. She used to be my governess.'

The man seemed slow to absorb the words, but finally he nodded. 'I'm her brother. Mary is sick in her bed.'

'I wonder if I might see her?'

The girl was persistent if nothing else. Christopher felt admiration well in his chest.

'Aye, ye best come in, then.' He glanced down at

himself. 'You'll have to excuse my dirt, I just got in from work at the coal yard.'

An honest trade, at least. Christopher removed his hat and followed Sylvia into a dingy hall.

'This way,' Jensen said.

'Who is it, Bill?' a shrill voice called.

'No one,' he shouted back. 'Visitors for Mary.'

A woman, brown wisps poking out from beneath her cap, bobbed her head around a door along the passage. Her eyes widened at the sight of Sylvia and practically popped out of her head when she focused on Christopher. She joined them in the narrow corridor.

'This is my wife,' Jensen said.

'Lord have mercy,' Mrs Jensen said. 'You be that French girl she's always talking about. The one that was going to help her at the shop.'

'Yes, Sylvia Boisette,' Sylvia said.

Christopher heard relief in Sylvia's voice, but a chill of premonition told him that the worst was yet to come. No respectable woman would willingly live in this part of London. He couldn't leave Sylvia here. The thought hit him like a dunk in a horse trough on a cold day.

He placed a hand on her shoulder. 'I don't think this is such a good idea.'

She ducked out of reach.

'Who's that, then?' Mrs Jensen asked, with a nudge of her elbow. 'Your fancy man?'

'He drove me here.'

Christopher wanted to throttle Sylvia. She had dismissed him as if he was some sort of lackey, a coachman no less. Well she was about to find out that he considered himself a whole lot more.

'Mary's in the back room,' Jensen said.

He led the way into a cell of a room with flaking

plaster walls, a truckle bed and a table beside it. On a narrow cot, a woman lay beneath the sheets, her skin like rice paper over blue veins. She opened her dark-circled eyes and slowly focused on the invaders of her cloister.

'She's on opium for the pain,' Jensen announced.

Sylvia sank to her knees beside the bed. 'Mary,' she said, her voice husky.

Christopher felt like a voyeur in this room of suffering. The familiar smell of illness, sickly sweet and vile, hung in the air and turned his mouth sour. 'I will wait for you outside, Miss Boisette. Don't be long.'

Questioning, Sylvia glanced up at him, tears hanging like bright diamonds on her lower lashes, her eyes deep pools of sorrow.

'I mean it, Miss Boisette. Ten minutes.' He headed for the front door and the fresh air of the street. Fresh. What a joke. Thick with smoke and the stink of rotting refuse, it was a slight improvement on a room full of death waiting to claim its own.

Damn it all. This time, Sylvia Boisette would do as he instructed. He didn't want to have to go back in there and haul her out.

Sylvia took Mary's frail hand in hers. 'What happened?' she asked gently. 'You never replied to my letters. When I went to Tunbridge Wells you had left.'

Mary's soft brown eyes closed for a moment. 'I'm sorry,' she whispered. 'I thought it was the ague at first. Before I knew it, I could scarcely crawl out of my bed.'

Sylvia pressed her palm to Mary's forehead. Hot and clammy to the touch, it told the story of her friend's suffering. Sadness filled her heart. 'Tell me what I must do to help you.'

Mary shook her head.

'It's a canker in her lungs,' her brother said from behind. 'Ain't nothing can be done, what we ain't already done.'

For all their poverty, the room seemed clean, the sheets smelling of soap, the floor swept. She glanced at Mary's sister-in-law. 'There must be something?'

'Mary's got a bit of money put by and we've been using that for the doctor and the medicines.' Mrs Jensen bit her lip. 'When that's gone, I'm not sure what we'll do.' With a glance at the woman on the bed, she lowered her voice. 'It may not be much longer, though.'

It seemed so unfair that someone as vital as Mary Jensen should be brought to such an end. Sorrow filled Sylvia's heart and tears choked her throat. She picked up the skeletal white hand and stroked it. 'You must get well,' she said, her voice thick. 'I'm relying on your skill with a needle. I have many new designs sketched out.'

'John Evernden is dead, then?' Mary whispered.

Sylvia nodded. 'A few days ago.'

'He left you well settled?'

If there was anything surer, Mary Jensen didn't need to hear about Sylvia's troubles. She smiled and indicated the door. 'His nephew.'

Mary frowned. 'Lord Stanford? I've heard bad things about that young man.'

A rush of tenderness filled her for a person who cared enough to worry about her at such a time. There had been few enough of those in her life. 'The younger brother. He's a good man.' He was, she realised. For all her annoyance at his interference, he had been kind and honourable.

A cough racked her friend's fragile form and Sylvia picked up a glass of water from the small night table. She lifted Mary's head and helped her to drink.

Mary gave her a wan smile of thanks. 'I'm glad you're settled, then,' she said so softly Sylvia had to bend her head close. 'You don't belong here, Sylvia. There's too much sickness and squalor. Don't worry about me. Bill is a good man and takes care of me.'

'As good as I can,' Bill spoke gently.

Sylvia's heart gladdened at the thought that Mary had relatives to care for her. A family's love made all the difference at a time like this. But she and Mary had been such close friends; she did so hate to lose her.

Mary's eyes slid closed.

'Best leave her, miss,' Bill said. 'She tires easy. She'll talk about this visit for days, she will. In between the opium, like.'

The steady rise and fall of the thin chest beneath the covers seemed peaceful. Sylvia stood up and smiled at Mr Jensen. 'If you ever need anything, please let me know.' How? How could he let her know? She took a deep breath. 'Mr Evernden will know my whereabouts should you need to reach me.'

As soon as she settled her own affairs, she would see what she could do for Mary. She wiped her eyes on the heel of her hand.

'This way, miss,' Bill Jensen said.

Out in the ugly street, she stared back at the gaunt building. Poor Mary. And just when life had seemed so full of promise. How unkind the fates could be. In laying Mary low, they had twisted Sylvia's path until she could no longer see her way.

Up and down the grimy street full of shadows and dirt, her gaze sought answers. With nowhere to go, no plan, no future, confusion washed over her. She knew nothing of London. She would have to find somewhere to live, some means of earning a living.

She wiped her eyes on her handkerchief and straightened her shoulders. She did not believe in fate. One made one's own destiny. And who knew, perhaps she would be able to come back and help her loyal friend.

Like a candle flame on a dark winter's night, Christopher guided her towards his carriage with gentle sympathy.

'Where now?' she asked, too tired to care.

'Now we go to Evernden Place on Mount Street,' he said and lifted her into the curricle.

Chapter Seven

The wall sconces remained unlit in his mother's upstairs withdrawing room. Christopher was not surprised to see his mother stretched out on a *chaise* asleep. She liked to nap before dinner and dance until dawn.

In repose, she looked younger than her forty and some summers. The gathering gloom gave her skin a fine and delicate appearance and her pale green gown showed off her still youthful figure.

'Mother,' he murmured.

Her eyes flew open and she sat up with a start, reaching to straighten her cap, a mere wisp of lace perched on silver-stranded blonde curls. 'Christopher, darling. What on earth are you doing back in town so soon?'

He strode to her side and carried her proffered hand to his lips. 'What?' he asked. 'Are you not pleased to see me?'

She waved her handkerchief at him. 'Naughty boy. Of course I am. I am merely surprised. You intended to visit friends, did you not? I did not look to see you for at least a fortnight.'

'Unfortunately, things did not turn out quite as

expected,' he replied, unable to fully obliterate the wryness in his tone.

An expression of dismay crossed her face. 'Were things so very bad at Cliff House? It just seemed so disrespectful for no one from the family to attend.'

Christopher sat down on the chair next to the *chaise*. 'Aunt Imogene and Uncle George put in an appearance.'

She pursed her lips. 'Oh, you poor dear. Now I'm sorry I asked you to go. It must have been simply dreadful.'

Dreadful didn't quite describe the past two days. Interesting, challenging, but as the face of Miss Sylvia Boisette intruded on his thoughts, he knew he would not have missed it for the world.

'It wasn't so bad. Aunt Imogene finally got the ormolu clock, so we've heard the last of it.'

'But why did you return home?'

His face heated under her intense scrutiny. She always knew when he was keeping something from her. He had better get this over with. 'Something happened.'

Her eyes lit with interest. 'You met someone?'

Christopher stemmed a groan. For the past few months, his mother had been trying to match him up with one suitable female after another. He'd been running the gauntlet of gently bred débutantes dressed in white at every function he attended. Hence his planned flight to the country. Unfortunately Miss Boisette and her problems had put it all out of mind.

'It is a little difficult to explain. You see, Uncle John left me with the care of his ward, Mademoiselle—'

'His ward?' his mother shrieked.

She never raised her voice except at Garth, and never in a shriek. Damn. 'Mother, you must listen. Uncle John left Miss Boisette in my care and I offered to drive her to a friend of hers in Tunbridge Wells.'

With a small sigh of relief, she raised a languorous hand to her temple. 'My word, child, you had me thinking you had brought that dreadful woman here.'

'Er...actually, I did.'

She sat bolt upright. 'You did what?'

He could not see a way to cushion the blow and readied himself for the peal she would ring over his head. 'I brought her to London with me.'

Twin spots of colour glowed on her cheeks. 'You brought his paramour to London?'

'Miss Boisette is downstairs in the drawing room.'

'Downstairs in my drawing room?'

Better she sound like a parrot than a banshee. 'Yes, Mother, that is what I have been trying to tell you. Her friend had left the Wells. I brought Miss Boisette here because she had nowhere else to go.'

His mother reached for his hand. 'Is it not enough for your brother to have no morals—now you, too? Tulwyn thought better of you, Christopher. You will oblige me by taking her back where she came from, at once.'

'I can't, Mother. The house is sold.'

'Surely there are places for women like her?' The corners of her mouth turned down as if she'd sucked on a lemon. 'Your father found them easily enough in his day. Take her to one of those.'

Christopher had never seen her so haughty or so heartless. 'She was Uncle John's ward.'

'Is that what she told you?'

The venom in her tone set his teeth on edge. He got up and strode to the window, staring into the street. It had been a mistake to bring Miss Boisette here. What with his father's behaviour in his last years and Garth's dissipated ways, how could he expect his mother to accept her? But he would not drop Sylvia off at some inn like so much rubbish.

He paced back to his seat and took his mother's hand in his. 'Mother, we cannot turn her out on to the street, no matter how much you dislike it. Uncle John left her in my care. If I take her to a hotel in London, surely word of it will be all over town in a day or so. You would not like that, would you?'

She shook her head doubtfully. 'Christopher, everyone knows about her. He brought her back from France and hid her away in that house of his. It doesn't matter what he called her, she was his mistress. Your father said so.'

The echo of his earlier misgivings hit a nerve. Sylvia had behaved disgracefully at Cliff House. Since then, her demeanour had been exemplary, but what if she treated his mother to a taste of her wantonness? He grimaced. 'She is less than half his age.'

His mother moaned and reached for her smelling salts on the table beside her. 'And that's what makes it so disgusting. Oh, Christopher, please. I can't bear to have another scandal in the family. How could you?'

Dash it all, he was making a pig's ear of turning his mother up sweet. 'I don't want a scandal either. That's why we have to find her a position as a governess as far away from London as possible.'

She pressed her handkerchief to her eyes as ever-ready tears welled up. 'A governess? You have run mad. I shall appeal to Garth. Lord only knows what he will say.'

Hell. He never fought with his mother. He'd seen her cry enough over his father and be driven to distraction by Garth. Gentle persuasion worked far better with her than harsh commands. Too bad his father hadn't discovered the secret.

Absently, he leaned forward and shifted the tea tray to sit dead centre on the rosewood table. 'I'm sorry, Mother, but you haven't met Miss Boisette and you are judging her without giving her a chance.' Much as he had himself, for God's sake. He glanced up at her. 'I'm not asking you to introduce her to the *ton*; I just want you to help her find a position. It doesn't have to be with one of your friends, just a decent family in need of a French governess.'

Lady Stanford gazed at him through watery blue eyes. 'I don't know anyone of that sort. What respectable family would allow a disreputable woman to educate their children?'

Mother had learned never to say no, she just found more difficulties. 'No one has to know anything about her past. As soon as she finds a position, she will leave. That is what you want, is it not?'

She pouted. 'I still don't see why we are responsible for this female.'

'I explained all that.'

Tears spilled over and coursed down her pale cheeks. 'Oh, Christopher, how could you?'

Reaching for every ounce of patience at his command, he rubbed his palms over his knees and prepared for battle. For one brief moment, his father had his sympathy.

Above the marble mantel, a portrait of a knight in a full-bottomed wig and shining ceremonial armour returned Sylvia's gaze with a half-smile. This Evernden ancestor must be from the last century. The way his green-flecked hazel eyes crinkled at the corners reminded her of Christopher.

Too tense to sit on one of the green-and-cream

brocade sofas artfully arranged against the wainscoting, Sylvia circled the room inspecting the assorted bric-à-brac on elegant Sheraton tables. On the far wall hung the painting of a woman also from the last century. Powdered and rolled over her ears, her hair rose to startling proportions, topped off with white ostrich plumes. Sylvia vaguely remembered her mother dressing her hair that way.

'Extraordinary hairdo, ain't it?'

Sylvia jumped. She swung around to the man who spoke in such a contemptuous tone.

The word *satanic* leaped to her mind as she took in midnight-winging brows, a full mouth curled in a sneer and waving black hair. Inches taller, but of slighter build than Christopher, she guessed he must be Lord Stanford. The widening of his brown eyes told her she'd surprised him also.

'Stanford, at your service, madam,' he said with a gallant bow. He gestured to the portrait behind her. 'My mother, the dowager Lady Stanford.'

They had not been introduced, but she couldn't very well ignore him in his own home. 'Sylvia Boisette,' she replied.

Recognition flickered in his dark eyes. He raised an eyebrow.

'I'm waiting for Mr Evernden,' she explained.

An appraising glance ran from her head to her toes and seemed to see right through her clothes.

Hating the surge of heat in her face, she stiffened.

A rakish smile quirked one corner of his mouth. 'Well, good for Kit. Welcome to my abode, Miss Boisette.'

His home. She mistrusted the tenor of his scrutiny and the gleam in his dark, wicked eyes. She held herself aloof. 'Thank you.'

'And where is my younger brother? Hardly courteous of him to leave you kicking your heels here by yourself. Would you like some tea, or could I offer you something a little stronger after your journey? Wine, perhaps?'

Heavens, his deep lazy drawl sounded pleasing to the ear. 'No, thank you. Mr Evernden went to speak to Lady Stanford.'

The eyebrow shot up again. 'Bearding the lioness in her den, hmm. Christopher has more bottom than I.'

His lips twisted at her blank stare. 'Please, won't you be seated and make yourself comfortable?'

He placed her hand on his arm and led her to the sofa by the fireplace. She perched on its edge.

He lounged next to her, one long arm resting along the sofa's back, his hand inches from her shoulder.

She had tried to persuade Christopher not to bring her here, but he had refused to set her down at an inn. He had insisted she would be welcomed at Evernden Place and his mother would find a way to help her. The wolfish expression on the sinfully handsome face so close to her own reinforced her misgivings.

The silenced crackled with tension.

'It is a very pleasant house you have, Lord Stanford,' she managed.

'Thank you. What brings you to London, Miss Boisette?'

The steel beneath the lazy tone demanded an answer. Damn Christopher for leaving her alone. 'I intended to live in Tunbridge Wells, but unforeseen circumstances forced a change in my plans.'

'How very…unfortunate,' he murmured, staring at her mouth.

She winced at the sarcasm and the heated stare. His assumption rankled, but she had known how it would be the moment she had agreed to travel with Mr Evernden. 'I can assure you my presence here is wholly your brother's idea. I asked him to leave me at a coaching inn. I am quite capable of looking after my own affairs.'

Amusement glimmered in obsidian depths. 'How refreshing.'

She had the distinct impression this was some sort of game and she played the mouse to his cat. She touched the locket at her neck, seeking its comfort.

With the grace and menace of a panther, he rose to loom over her. 'I think I should go and see what is keeping my brother. I shall return in a moment.'

She nodded and watched him leave with an overpowering sense of relief.

Whistling softly, Garth mounted the stairs, knowing exactly where to find Christopher and his mother at this hour of the day. He paused in the doorway, a bitter taste in his mouth as he watched the affected fluttering of his mother's handkerchief and her pouting mouth, as she listened to the low voice of her adored younger son.

For once it seemed that Christopher had earned her wrath. It would do him good to receive the edge of her tongue until she found some reason to blame Garth for his brother's fall from grace. After all, Christopher was the beloved son, the one who looked like an Evernden and not a cuckoo in the nest.

To hell with the lot of them. He held the title whether his foolish fashion-plate of a mother liked it or not.

He sauntered into the room, stretching out his hand. 'Kit, I see you couldn't stay away. Who is the ravishing creature in the drawing room?'

Christopher's eyebrows snapped together and he gave Garth an intent look as they shook hands.

'Ravishing?' Lady Stanford cried. 'Christopher, you never said anything about ravishing. How can I help find a governess position for someone with her reputation who is ravishing to boot?'

'A governess, eh? What a waste,' Garth mused. 'She didn't strike me as that sort.'

Christopher glared at him. 'You don't know anything about her.'

Garth shrugged.

'Is she really beautiful?' Lady Stanford asked.

'Stunning,' Garth replied.

Christopher glowered.

'That settles it,' Lady Stanford said, swinging her feet onto the floor with a rustle of skirts. 'I will have nothing to do with her. I don't care what you say, Christopher, I can do nothing to help the girl. Send her away at once.'

The idiot must really be smitten if he thought to foist his ladybird off on Mother. Fascinating. 'If Christopher wants to invite Miss Boisette to stay here in *my* house, I am sure I have no objection. And if he feels obligated to find her a position as a governess, then I believe we should do everything we can to assist.'

Lady Stanford wrung her hands, but Christopher's expression lightened and he clapped Garth on the shoulder. 'Thank you. You won't regret it. Despite her unfortunate…er…background, she is truly unexceptionable. You will have no reason to find fault with her manners, I promise you.'

He swung around to clasp his mother's hands. 'Mother, I'm sure you will be able to help her if you would just put your mind to it.'

'Since Garth insists,' his mother said with a sniff, 'there is no more to be said. As he says, it is his house now.'

Garth ignored the slightly baleful stare that accompanied the words. His mother's borderline insults no longer troubled him. While she never quite came out and spoke her mind, her dislike always simmered below the surface. As a child, he'd been mystified by her cold disapproval. As an adult, he'd seen right through her hypocrisy. Christopher, on the other hand, seemed oblivious to underlying tension filling the Evernden household. Garth could only imagine his brother's resentment if he ever discovered the truth.

A chill ran down his spine. He shrugged it off. He didn't give a tinker's damn.

For now, Miss Boisette would provide an entertaining diversion. A cat among the pigeons. Or was she a pigeon for the cat? He almost licked his lips. She would relieve his boredom, annoy the hell out of his mother and he might even get a rise out of even-tempered Christopher.

'Miss Boisette is very welcome to stay here as long as she wishes,' Garth said.

Christopher strode towards the door. He halted in the doorway and glanced at his mother. 'I will bring her to meet you at once.'

Lady Stanford patted her hair. 'I'm sure I look a perfect fright. I really must tidy myself.'

'You needn't bother,' Christopher said with a grin. 'You always look beautiful.'

Garth swallowed a cutting remark as his mother simpered. She wasn't worth the effort.

'Thank you, dearest,' Lady Stanford said. 'However, I am sure she would like to freshen up after her journey. Have Merreck take her to a chamber on the fourth floor. I will see her in the drawing room in one hour.'

Christopher frowned. 'The fourth floor?'

His mother raised a haughty brow. 'A governess, Christopher, not family.'

Garth silenced a chuckle at Christopher's obvious displeasure. What had the lad expected? That his uncle's paramour would be treated like a long-lost cousin? Even Christopher couldn't be that naïve. 'Best trust Mother in issues of protocol, old chap.'

Christopher grimaced and strode out.

Garth strolled to his mother's side and kissed her hand, barely grazing her white skin. He glanced into her clouded blue eyes with a laconic smile. As usual, she fretted about her darling younger son. Had she ever looked that anxious about himself? He kept his expression bland. 'So, our Kit is finally breaking the rules. And what a sublime creature she is, to be sure.'

'Oh, never say so, Garth. You can't be serious. Tell me the truth now—is she really lovely?'

'Devastating.' He sank into the chair beside her.

'As head of the family, you must do something, Garth. You must put a stop to it, not encourage him in this madness. He says John left her in his care. But to bring her here... Think of the scandal if people should learn of it.'

Always the scandal, always afraid what others would say. And it had rubbed off on to Christopher, poor idiot. Anyone would think Mother had walked with the angels all her life. He allowed himself an ironic smile. 'As to that, my dearest mama, my advice is to let things run their course.'

Lady Stanford pouted her pretty lips. 'I never thought Christopher would turn out like you.'

He curled his lip and inclined his head a small degree. 'Thank you, my dear.'

Her cautious glance gave him a modicum of satisfaction. Since he now held the purse strings, she occasionally realised just how obliged to him she was.

'Christopher,' he said, 'is too sensible to embroil himself with someone so far beneath him in any serious way. Don't worry, he will come to his senses.' He smiled wickedly. 'I intend to give him a little help. I find myself quite charmed by her.'

'Not you, too,' she cried.

Did she have to be so obtuse? 'The worst thing you can do is try to set Christopher against her. The more you oppose it, the more likely he will be to dig in his heels. You know how stubborn he is.'

'Just like his father.' She sighed. 'Well, if you truly think so.'

Just like his father. She said it so innocently, so sweetly, and buried the knife a little deeper. As usual he shrugged it off. 'I do. Someone of her ilk is bound to give him a disgust of her in short order. You know how particular he is in his notions of propriety. And perhaps I can provide some assistance.' He looked forward to it.

Thoughtfully, she gazed at him. 'I suppose so. I am relying on your help, Garth.'

If it suited Mother to believe he was helping her, he saw no reason to object. He had his own game to play and the thought of toying with this particular morsel pleased him exceedingly.

He took her hand and patted it. 'Always your willing servant, *dearest* Mama.'

Sylvia unpacked her few belongings in the sort of room one would give to a poor relation or an upstairs servant. In addition to the bed, it provided a wardrobe, a washstand and mirror and a writing desk. Dull cream-painted walls and a small window looking out on a noisy London street made it a far cry from her apartments at Cliff House. She pushed the past firmly back where it belonged.

Sighing, she dropped her bonnet on the bed. She poured cold water in the white china bowl on the washstand and washed her face and hands. A glance in the mirror showed her that the day had taken a toll on her hair. She repinned it in a severe bun, an appropriate hairstyle for a governess. Her new life.

Tomorrow, she would seek her lost trunk at the coaching office at the George in Southwark where the Tunbridge Wells coaches arrived in London. On the short journey from the Jensens', Christopher had suggested she consider applying for a governess position. Taken aback at first, the more she thought about it, the more viable it seemed. Certainly, opening a dressmaking business with only the few guineas from the sale of Cliff House and without the help of a skilled seamstress was out of the question. Working in an attic or basement as an unskilled needlewoman held little allure. Unless there was no other option.

A governess. Her eyes stared curiously back at her from the glass. She knew too few children to know if she had the patience or the skill, but surely it could not be too difficult? It was certainly a respectable occupation. Take it, embrace it, no matter the cost to her pride, her mind encouraged. If she could find a suitable position with a wealthy family, she would save all her earnings and open a dress shop some time in the future.

She strolled to the window and looked down into the busy street. There were numbers of people going about their business in the early evening: carters, fruit sellers, flower girls, and rich folks beneath umbrellas. A well-dressed boy skipped through puddles on the pavement, trailed by a woman in sombre grey. His governess? It did not look so bad.

Other people, shabby and aimless, wandered down the street. A man in a long black coat and a black hat pulled down low leaned against the lamppost on the distant corner. He looked oddly familiar, but every street corner in London seemed to attract loitering males and beggars like the bedraggled old woman hunched against the railings opposite. Sylvia shivered. She would not become that woman.

A knock on the door broke her thoughts and she hurried to open it.

'Are you ready?' Christopher asked, flashing her the charming smile that sent her heart beating a little too fast.

She nodded and forced a smile. Everything depended on her interview with Lady Stanford. Sylvia had been the object of enough disapproving glances during her life with Monsieur Jean to know not to take anything for granted. A recollection of the instant assumptions in Lord Stanford's dark eyes reminded her to be cautious.

Once more, she wished Christopher had not bought quite such a fashionable gown. Her own clothes would have presented a much better appearance for someone seeking work.

She rested her hand on Christopher's arm and he led her downstairs.

The dowager Lady Stanford, with her oldest son standing behind her, sat in state on a sofa in the same drawing room where Sylvia had waited earlier. She instantly recognised Lady Stanford as the woman in the portrait, even without the elaborate wig. The blush of youth captured by the artist had long since faded, but she remained a handsome woman dressed in the first stare of fashion in a Pomona crepe morning gown over a white satin slip from beneath which matching green slippers peeped. The cashmere shawl covering her shoulders must have cost a fortune.

An intense desire to make a good impression swept over Sylvia in a wave, but the dowager's frigid expression chilled her hopes. She resisted the urge to turn tail and run. She needed this woman's assistance. She would endure anything if it provided her with the means of becoming independent. She kept her expression remote and curtsied deeply on Christopher's introduction.

'I am so sorry to hear of your misfortune, Miss Boisette.' Lady Stanford's cold tone disheartened Sylvia further.

By misfortune, did she mean John Evernden's death or the loss of her trunk? Sylvia looked to Christopher for some explanation, but Lady Stanford waved a wisp of lace and continued. 'I understand from Christopher that the friend you were relying on to help you is ill and you would like me to help you find a place with a suitable family.'

No doubt the ill luck referred to Sylvia's presence. She maintained her calm expression. 'Yes, my lady, if it pleases you. I am skilled in watercolours and drawing. I speak fluent French.'

A wry expression twisted Lady Stanford's face. 'I am glad my husband's brother provided you with such a good education.'

Despite her quaking limbs, Sylvia forced herself to speak calmly. 'Mr Evernden was exceedingly generous.'

The words sounded dreadful and Lady Stanford's face froze into a mask of indifference.

Sylvia winced at the upward slant of Lord Stanford's mouth.

His lazy drawl broke the stiff silence. 'Miss Boisette, allow me to seat you.' He sauntered to her side, took her hand in gallant style and led her to the sofa opposite his mother.

He lounged next to her, his long legs brushing her skirts. Christopher frowned at his brother.

Lord Stanford glanced across at Lady Stanford. 'Mother, it is good of you to offer Miss Boisette your assistance. It is certainly not something where I could be of any value.'

Lady Stanford's expression became horrified and she twisted her handkerchief around her fingers. 'Good heavens. I should think not indeed. Just imagine the reaction of any of our acquaintances if you were to recommend Miss Boisette to them.'

Christopher's face darkened and he glared at his brother. 'No one suggested he would.'

Lady Stanford gave a long-suffering sigh and forced a stiff little smile. 'Since Christopher is so insistent, I will do what I can. To be frank, I know very few matrons with young children, Miss Boisette.'

Sylvia glanced at Christopher. Her heart squeezed painfully at the discomfort in his eyes. When he said nothing, her stomach dropped to the floor. She should never have let him persuade her to come here.

His earlier kindness had lulled her into thinking he no longer held her in contempt. She began to reconstruct the wall of ice around her heart, her defence against a world that despised her. 'I do not wish to put you to any trouble, my lady. I believe I might easily find a position through advertisements in the newspapers.'

'It's no trouble at all, is it, Mother?' Christopher said.

Lady Stanford sighed again. 'Of course not.'

Sylvia didn't believe a word of it and nor did Lord Stanford from his sardonic smile. He seemed entertained by the discord permeating the room.

'Thank you, Mother,' Christopher said, sitting beside Lady Stanford. 'I know Miss Boisette is grateful for any help you can provide.'

Sylvia gritted her teeth. She would be grateful if the promised position materialised; until then all she could do was hide her resentment at Lady Stanford's disapproval. 'Indeed,' she said.

'Well, now that's settled,' Lady Stanford said. 'Christopher, I do hope you will accompany Garth and me to Covent Garden tonight. Mr Macready is quite the latest rage. I know you hadn't planned to go, but Garth never stays until the end and I would so appreciate your company on the drive home.' She smiled expectantly.

Christopher nodded, a trifle unwillingly, Sylvia thought. 'As you wish.'

Lady Stanford, it seemed, used a mixture of delicate nerves and guilt to get her way. By now, Christopher must thoroughly regret bringing Sylvia to meet his mother.

'Perhaps Miss Boisette could accompany us?' Christopher said, his expression brightening. 'I am sure you would enjoy the play.'

His open smile sent Sylvia's heart leaping into her throat. He wanted her to go with them. Against her will, a glow of joy melted a brick in the chilly wall around her heart.

Covent Garden. An unlooked for courtesy. For a moment, Sylvia imagined attending one of London's fashionable playhouses in the rose-silk gown Christopher had purchased until she caught the horrified expression on Lady Stanford's face.

She packed ice into the chink. 'No indeed, Mr Evernden. Your acquaintances would think it very odd for a woman seeking a place as a governess to attend the theatre as your guest.'

Not to mention her disreputable background. That thought raced across Lady Stanford's face.

Christopher's mouth thinned to a straight line. Disappointment that his mother was right? Lord Stanford engaged himself in removing a piece of lint from his sleeve. Embarrassment charged the air.

Her face blank, Sylvia dared them to utter what was on their minds.

A deep chuckle from Lord Stanford broke the uncomfortable silence. 'I don't know about the rest of you,' he drawled, 'but I am sorely in need of my supper.'

'And so unusual of you to join us, Stanford dear,' the dowager said, with a downward curve to her mouth.

'I would not miss it for the world,' he replied with a small bow. 'After all, it is not every day we have such a charming guest for dinner.' His hooded gaze left Sylvia with the impression she was the main course.

She acknowledged his supposed compliment with a stiff nod.

Lady Stanford's expression would have soured a bowl of cream.

Giving his brother a sharp stare, Christopher rose and strode to Sylvia's side. 'Good Lord, yes. You must be ravenous after all the travelling today, Miss Boisette.' He took her hand and brought her to her feet. 'Allow me to escort you into the dining room.'

'Mother,' Lord Stanford said, rising and holding out his arm.

Christopher gave Sylvia a little grimace as they followed Lord Stanford and his very proper mother.

Unsure of his meaning, she felt only relief at surviving the interview, if not in good order, at least with her dignity intact.

Chapter Eight

W hat better way could she spend an evening than hemming a handkerchief in the Everndens' drawing room? Sylvia stifled a yawn and set another small stitch in the fine white lawn.

The theatre would have been better. She forced the thought aside. She had no reason to envy the Everndens their evening and she needed this time to get her thoughts in order after the sinking of her well-laid plans by poor Mary's illness. Having found herself in uncharted waters, she needed to set a new course. The governess idea might well provide a welcome haven.

In the meantime, to counteract her feeling of obligation to the grudging Lady Stanford, she had offered to make herself useful during her stay. She had begun right away by fetching Lady Stanford's shawl from the drawing room when she complained of a draught.

Christopher had encouraged her with a nod, Lady Stanford had seemed a little less frigid and Lord Stanford had raised a cynical brow. So here she sat, usefully employed on one of Lady Stanford's indispensable scraps of lace.

A clock in the hall chimed the hour into a silent house. Ten o'clock. Preferring not to hear about the play, she folded the needlework and placed it in the basket beside her chair.

The door swung open. She started, her heart picking up speed.

In full evening dress, Lord Stanford loomed in the doorway. A quizzical smile leavened his chiselled features. 'Miss Boisette, did I startle you? I was not sure I would find you still downstairs.'

He probably thought she should scuttle off to bed like an upstairs maid. She wished she had, given that everything about this man smacked of danger. Unlike his younger brother, who wore his sense of honour on his fair and open countenance, Lord Stanford hid his thoughts behind a mask of cynicism. 'I did not expect you back so soon,' she said.

He chuckled. 'Oh, I left during the first intermission. The house was sadly lacking in interesting company. I thought I might find more amusement here.'

Dread clenched her stomach. 'You flatter me. I can assure you I am not in the habit of amusing gentlemen and I am just about to retire.' She rose to her feet.

As solid as any door, he leaned a shoulder against the doorjamb. 'Come now, Miss Boisette, I'm certain I detected a distinct unwillingness on my brother's part to leave such delightful company at home. You have been travelling together, have you not?'

Sylvia kept her expression aloof and her gaze steady on the wickedly handsome untrustworthy face. 'Lord Stanford, you are quite mistaken. Mr Evernden simply undertook to escort me to my destination.'

His gaze lingered on her mouth, before rising to her eyes. 'To a friend who seems as elusive as fog,

Miss Boisette. Or do I call you *mademoiselle*?' he murmured.

The dread clawed its way up into her throat. She stepped forward, meaning to pass him, but he didn't move. She stopped two steps away. 'My friend's illness was as much a surprise to me as it was to your brother. Now, if you will excuse me…'

He reached out and put one finger under her chin. His dark gaze raked her face. 'Unbelievable,' he muttered. 'You are exquisite. But you know that, don't you? You are quite wasted on my brother. He is far too strict in his notions to appreciate your undeniable charms.'

She held her ground, resisting the temptation to slap his smiling mouth. 'At least your brother is a gentleman, my lord.' An honourable gentleman. She bit back the words, fearing to push him too far.

He laughed. 'So, you've got claws too. I like spirited women.'

She swallowed a gasp, meeting his gaze with a silent stare.

His lips curled. 'Oh yes, Kit is definitely a gentleman.' He made it sound like an insult. 'You know, I could offer you a much better arrangement than ever my brother would. I have an exceedingly well-appointed house in Blackheath and you would find me most generous. You would lack for nothing now, or later when we go our separate ways.'

Warmth stole up her neck and into her face at his callous assumption that she was available to the highest bidder. She kept her hands relaxed at her sides. She needed Lady Stanford's help to find a position and it wasn't the first time she had been forced to swallow her pride.

Look to the future and survive the present. In a respectable position, a situation where no one knew her history, she would not be subject to this kind of humiliation.

She kept her smile cool. 'I thank you for your offer, my lord, but I am not in the market for a protector. I have other irons in the fire.'

He regarded her silently for a moment. When he spoke, his soft tone held a warning. 'You're a hard little piece, ain't you. You know, Miss Boisette, I would not want to see my brother embroiled in any sort of...difficulty.'

Sylvia blinked. If it wasn't so out of character, she might suspect him of trying to protect his sibling. Or had Christopher, suspecting her growing attraction, sent his brother to warn her off? An unexpected pang caught at her heart. 'I acknowledge my debt to your brother and I certainly would not dream of diverting him from his familial duty.'

A dark brow flicked up and he nodded. 'Even if you are not interested in him, Miss Boisette, I am sure you have noticed his interest in you. Whether by accident or by design, it is a problem I would rather avoid. I hope you will not repay his kindness by putting him under some further obligation.' He flashed a charming smile.

She bit back a heated retort and smiled sweetly. 'He has fulfilled all of his obligations, my lord.'

'I'm pleased to hear it.' He placed one languid white hand on the doorframe, blocking her passage. 'If you change your mind about my offer, you will let me know, won't you?'

She lifted her chin. 'Highly unlikely, my lord.'

Lord Stanford eased away from the door to let her pass. 'Too bad,' he drawled. 'But I'm glad we had this little chat and understand each other.'

She understood very well. She had just been told to keep her unworthy claws out of his precious brother. Her foolish heart ached for something she had known all along she did not deserve. Pride straightened her spine. 'I too prefer frankness, Lord Stanford.'

She cast him a careless smile on her way past and swept through the door. She barely avoided colliding with Christopher. He looked from her to Lord Stanford and frowned.

'Back already?' Lord Stanford asked.

His gaze fixed on Sylvia, Christopher nodded. 'I have some documents to sign. My man of business wanted them first thing in the morning.'

'Quite the businessman these days,' Stanford said, a cutting edge to his tone.

Christopher shrugged. 'I thought you were going to White's tonight?'

'Indeed I am. I came home to change and found Miss Boisette alone with her needlework. I became so entertained by our conversation I quite forgot the time.'

Christopher's expression darkened. 'I see.'

Sylvia stared at him. Just what did he did see? That his brother had spent the last fifteen minutes warning her off? Or that the dissipated rake had offered her a *carte blanche*? To her annoyance, fire burned her cheeks. She wasn't the one who should be blushing— it was his horrid brother.

Tears prickled the backs of her eyes. What on earth was wrong with her? It didn't matter a damn what either of them thought of her. She ducked her head. 'If you will excuse me, gentlemen. I am going to my room.'

Lord Stanford bowed elegantly. 'Goodnight, Miss Boisette.'

Christopher hesitated as if he wanted to say something. Whatever it was, Sylvia could not stay to hear it. One more insult and she might really cry. She brushed past him.

'Goodnight, *mademoiselle*,' Christopher said to her retreating back.

The ironic note in his voice almost caused her to turn back. Men. They were all the same. She held her back straight and marched up the stairs.

'I see you managed to pry yourself free of the clinging vine.' Garth's words echoed up the stairs.

'Damn you, Garth, but you're an insulting cur to our mother.'

'So I am, dear boy.' His sardonic laughter rang out as Sylvia reached the landing. She shivered. Bitterness seemed to hang over Lord Stanford like a shadow.

Over the past week, Sylvia had run errands for the fragile Lady Stanford to the best of her ability. Lady Stanford had generously said she wasn't sure what she would do without Sylvia's help when she left. But there was no doubt about it, Sylvia would be leaving.

Today, she had promised to return a novel to Hookham's on Bond Street. After receiving directions to the famous lending library from the haughty butler, she put on the grey merino and brown pelisse she'd taken to wearing since the return of her trunk. Since her only bonnet had been stolen, she wore the high-crowned, blue confection decorated with pink rosebuds purchased by Christopher in Tunbridge Wells.

Outside, a fine drizzle slicked the streets and coated everything with damp soot. A little nervous about her first expedition in London, she stepped out smartly.

Around her, horse-drawn equipages crowded the road. Coalmen and other tradesmen filed by in a variety of creaking and rumbling wagons. Barouches trundled sedately over the cobbles and young bloods perched in their sporting curricles turned their heads to stare at her over high shirt points. She avoided their gazes.

Shouts, horses' hooves on cobblestones, whistles and catcalls added up to an almost unbearable din. Unpleasant and unnameable smells invaded the smoky air, mitigated only by the scent of cinnamon wafting from a cheeky lass selling sticky buns and the floral perfumes worn by the well-dressed ladies she passed. The noise and the dirt reminded her too much of her childhood in Paris for comfort.

Cliff House and her hitherto secluded existence seemed hundreds of miles away. She prayed for a position with a family who resided in the country.

In Hookham's, she returned Lady Stanford's novel, collected the one on order, then spent a happy hour feasting on the vast selection of books on the floor-to-ceiling shelves. When she emerged into the street, the rain had ceased and Bond Street thronged with gentlemen and ladies sauntering along the pavement. They browsed the shop windows and chatted with acquaintances, their stylish attire and carefully coiffed hair proclaiming their wealth and status.

Sylvia studied the dressmakers' displays as she strolled along. The array of gowns and bonnets dazzled her with their variety of fabrics and styles. An unusually fashioned morning gown in green sarsenet trimmed with points of white satin caught her attention. How cleverly the fabric had been cut on the bias. With a regretful sigh, she stored the idea away and picked up her pace.

A black town carriage drew up at the curb's edge beside her. A footman jumped down and blocked her path.

Jolted out of her reverie, she stepped to one side.

'Your carriage, miss?' He nudged her towards the open door.

She shook her head. 'You are mistaken.'

He put out an arm. 'There's a gentleman friend of yours inside.'

Christopher?

She peered through the open door. A man with a hat pulled low and a muffler over his face sat in the shadows.

The footman took her arm. 'In you go, miss.'

Hot pinpricks flashed across her back. She jerked her arm out of his reach. 'This is not my carriage.' She turned to push past him.

His portly body blocked her. He thrust her back towards the lowered steps.

Her throat dried. 'Take your hands off me.'

Heart hammering, she glanced around for aid. No one appeared to notice. She clutched the string of her reticule, heavy with her borrowed book, and judged the distance to his head. If she hit him hard enough and ran, even in hampering skirts, she'd easily outdistance such a fat man. She stepped closer. Her heart picked up speed.

Garth waited for a hackney to drive by, then stepped off the curb, tossing a penny to the street sweeper who cleared him a path.

Damn, but Madame Eglantine had been in fine fettle last night. He grinned to himself at the recollection.

A couple of servants arguing on the footpath caught his idle glance. The woman looked ready to assail the fat fellow. He drew in a sharp breath. What the hell was Miss Boisette doing on Bond Street brawling with a footman? This young woman collected admirers, the way he collected snuffboxes. He strode towards them.

Miss Boisette's expression turned to relief, her colour rushing back in a flood. Perhaps he would make one of her collection after all. The already pleasant morning had just improved by leaps and bounds.

He composed his expression in a bored smile. 'Miss Boisette, is aught amiss?'

The lackey mumbled something and retreated. He clambered on to the box of the nearby carriage. Its occupant slammed the door shut and the coach forced its way into the traffic.

Garth stared after it. 'What the deuce is going on?'

'He offered me a ride.' Her voice shook. Clearly she remained upset, despite her outward calmness.

'Someone you know?'

Distress once more clouded her expression. 'A case of mistaken identity, I believe.' She sounded too uncertain for him to believe her, the cheating little haggage. She must think him a fool. No one would mistake that face of hers for another.

He toyed with the idea of chasing the carriage down and getting to the truth. Rot it. It would put a dumper on his plans. There was a team of bays he wanted going on the block today at Tattersalls. If he didn't beat the rush, he'd lose them.

She gazed up at him. Never had he seen such intensely blue eyes. He flicked a glance over her and imagined her naked. His blood stirred.

No wonder Christopher wanted to hang on to her. Garth chewed on the inside of his cheek. Christopher had better watch his step with this one or she'd have him leg-shackled before he blinked. Not a chance. His brother was far too sensible. In fact, no fun at all. Perhaps this young lady would enjoy a bit of sport. If so, Garth was more the man for the job.

He held out his arm. 'Come, I will see you home.'

Still trembling inside, Sylvia took Lord Stanford's

arm. While the speculative expression on his face caused an unpleasant flutter in her stomach, she felt safer with him than with the man in the carriage. Had it really been a mistake, as she first thought, or did it have something to do with the man at the inn? Surely not.

Slowly her heartbeat returned to normal and she felt calm enough to glance at her escort. Dressed in his evening clothes from the night before, the dissolute young lord had definitely not slept at home. In her youth, she'd seen too many men leaving at dawn in their evening clothes to question where he'd been.

Lord Stanford shot her a penetrating glance. 'What on earth *are* you doing out here alone, Miss Boisette?'

A fair question, considering. 'I returned a library book to Hookham's for your mother.'

'You should not go out alone.'

'I could hardly ask a maid to go with me.'

'Why not?'

She stared at him. Did he think she was not aware that her position in his home was under sufferance? The servants certainly knew it. 'I'm not exactly a guest.'

His frown deepened, but he did not take issue with her statement. He glanced down the street in the direction the coach had disappeared. 'Tell me who he was.'

She gave him a cold glance. 'The man was a stranger.'

'Then you should not have stopped to speak to him.'

This was beyond all. Now he was accusing her of wrongdoing. 'Lord Stanford, I had no intention of getting into that carriage, *je vous assure*; I was never more pleased to see anyone in my whole life as when you arrived just now.'

The expression in his dark eyes warmed. 'I beg your pardon, Miss Boisette, I believe I mistook the matter.

Come, a truce. Whoever the blackguard was, he is a coward. We will not give him another thought.'

If only it were that easy.

With only Sylvia for company at lunch, Lady Stanford toyed with the food on her plate. When she signalled to the footman to take it away, Sylvia noticed she had barely touched the roasted breast of pheasant or the aspic.

'Miss Boisette,' Lady Stanford said, while the footman poured coffee, 'I have some good news for you. I meant to tell Christopher, but he left so precipitously this morning, he didn't give me the opportunity.' She paused and frowned as if puzzled. 'Ah, well. A friend of mine knows of a family looking for a governess.'

At last. Now Sylvia could get on with her life. She put down her knife and fork. 'That is good news.'

'Yes. The family lives in Wiltshire and they are in London for a short stay. Apparently, they have sought a governess without success for quite some time. It seems as though I have hit on the perfect solution. Mrs Elston will come for tea at four this afternoon and interview you.' She beamed. 'Now, what do you think of that?'

'My lady, I cannot express enough my appreciation for your help. I will do my best to make a good impression on Mrs Elston.'

Lady Stanford pursed her lips. 'I sincerely hope you will.'

The murmur of men's voices, interrupted by shouts of triumph or groans of despair, rumbled around White's gaming room. Across the green baize table from Christopher, Garth scribbled on a scrap of paper and dropped it on top of the pile of guineas. 'I'll raise you a pony.'

The dim light from the lantern above their heads did nothing to deaden the reckless glitter in Garth's eyes. He seemed to be well on the way to half seas over.

A trifle warm himself, Christopher had drunk only half the quantity Garth had imbibed in the past two hours. Damn Garth for an idiot to bet another hundred on the single queen in his hand when she wasn't even trumps.

He raised his eyebrows at the crumpled vowel. 'Under the hatches again?'

Garth shrugged. 'Is my note not good enough for you?'

Christopher gritted his teeth at the sarcasm. 'Of course it is.'

His own hand wasn't very good, but it would take the trick. His facility with numbers never let him down, no matter how much he imbibed, and he never relied on blind luck. Something Garth ought to know by now.

'I need a drink.' Garth signalled to a passing waiter for another bottle. 'No mistake, though, she's a diamond of the first water,' he said, picking up their earlier conversation on the subject of Mademoiselle Boisette.

They'd been around this topic once. 'Leave well enough alone.'

'But a governess.' Mock pain edged Garth's tone. 'What a waste of delicious womanhood.'

'It's what she wants.'

'It's what she says she wants. Women never say what they mean.'

Christopher felt the hackles rise on the back of his neck. A hot rush of something unpleasant closed his throat. He forced his words past it. 'What the hell are you talking about?'

One side of Garth's mouth curled in a sneer. 'Women. They are all the same. You just have to find the key to unlock the gate. Usually jewels, or money.' He chuckled.

'I don't much like your sense of humour.'

Garth flashed him a grin. 'I thought we'd agreed never to argue over the fairer sex. They aren't worth it.'

They had. Years ago, when they had come to blows over the milkmaid at their grandmother's house. They'd agreed to let the woman choose and she'd decided on the older, far more experienced Garth. They'd never competed for a female again. Until now. The thought didn't sit well in Christopher's stomach. 'Then stay away from Miss Boisette.'

'Bloody hell, don't be such a dog in the manger. You don't want her, therefore she's fair game.'

Want was far too weak a word to describe the insistent throb low in his groin each time he saw or thought about her. 'She wants to be a governess.' Now he sounded like a sulky schoolboy denied a treat. He tossed off his brandy, then stared at his glass. Damn. At this rate he'd be under the table before the end of the evening.

'You're a damned fool.' Garth threw an impatient glance at the money on the table. 'Are you in or not?'

Christopher wanted to be inside Sylvia's slender body. Buried to the hilt in her hot, sweet flesh. He pushed one hundred guineas into the pile. 'I'm in.'

Garth scrawled on another slip of paper with a flourish. 'Two hundred.' He flicked the paper on to the growing pile.

Christopher stared at it. The raving idiot.

Garth leaned forward. 'If you think I'm going to let an Incomparable hie off to be a drudge in Wiltshire with a parcel of brats instead of warming my bed, you are more of a bloody fool than I thought.'

It was all Christopher could do to stop from reaching out and choking Garth with his bare hands. His brother would love that. 'She's not interested. She's as cold as a mountain stream.'

The waiter arrived with a bottle of brandy, filled both glasses and set the bottle at Garth's elbow.

With a deep sigh of contentment, Garth leaned back. 'Now that's where you are wrong.' He raised his glass in a toast, then took a deep swig. 'Take it from an expert. There's a hot spring beneath the frigid waters waiting for a man to dive in. Haven't you seen that smile?'

Rarely. A vivid image of her performance at Cliff House filled his mind, the teasing way she removed her gloves, her tempting smile with its fascinating tiny fault. The same smile she had bestowed on Garth a week ago, after the theater.

The thought of Sylvia with Garth sent sparks of anger chasing through his veins. He snapped his cards face down on the table. 'You bastard. If you go anywhere near her, I'll murder you.'

Garth's inscrutable gaze rose from contemplating the dregs of brandy in the bottom of his glass. His sneer deepened. 'Do you really think you can?'

Probably not. Garth was a crack shot and an expert duellist, but Christopher, with his greater bulk, might have a chance at his own sport, boxing. He glared across at his brother. Tension crackled across the table, palpable in the thick air.

Two men playing chess across the aisle from them perked up in their deep armchairs. An argument always attracted a crowd.

Christopher lowered his voice. 'Don't think I won't. Stay away from her.'

'Don't let that angelic face fool you. If you want her, take her. Otherwise, get off the pot,' Garth said crudely. He gestured at Christopher's cards. 'Your play.'

Garth deserved to lose. Christopher closed the fanned cards. 'Your trick.'

A frown on his face, Garth reached for the discarded hand.

Lurching to his feet, Christopher nudged the table. Cards and guineas and promises to pay tumbled to the floor.

Garth glared at him. 'Don't play me for an ass, brother.'

Christopher bowed. 'I wouldn't dare now, would I? I'll see you later.'

Garth slanted him a wry look. 'Not if I see you first.' He reached for the brandy bottle. 'I'll give you one day and then it's open season.'

The desire to plant his knuckles in Garth's leering face made Christopher clench his fists. He took a deep breath to steady himself, nodded and sauntered off to find his hat and coat. He needed to talk to Miss Boisette about her smile.

Tonight.

Chapter Nine

'Come in,' Sylvia called out at the rap on her chamber door. At last, the scullery maid with her supper. The only sure way to prevent another encounter with Lord Stanford. She hastened to clear the clutter from the writing desk.

'Good evening, Miss Boisette.'

She jerked around, hand at her throat.

Christopher. Why now, after avoiding her all week? 'Mr Evernden. I'm sorry, I thought you were Lucy with the tea tray.'

His shoulders spanned the doorway of her small chamber. 'I am sorry to disappoint.' The corners of his eyes crinkled as a charming smile curved his lips, the reserve of the past few days replaced by an expression of warm appreciation.

Awareness of his maleness, his aura of controlled strength, unfurled in a strangely pleasant flitter in her stomach. Warmth rushed up her body to heat her face. She retreated. 'It is no disappointment. Indeed, I had wanted to seek your advice.'

'Good. I wanted to talk to you.' He strolled to the bed

and with a sigh slouched back against the headboard. His weight dipped into the cream cotton bedspread as he hitched up one long leg.

Her breath caught in her throat. He looked so comfortable, so right, on her bed. The last place she ever expected to see him. The flitter turned into the wild beating of a bird trying to escape.

He grinned. 'Won't you sit down?' He seemed unusually relaxed.

The straight-backed wooden chair at the writing desk offered safety and distance. After turning it to face him, she perched on its edge.

'I expected to find you in the drawing room,' he said. 'I hope we haven't made you feel so unwelcome you feel obliged to hide up here in the evening.'

Unable to voice her real reason, she avoided his frank gaze and gestured to the bedside table. 'I borrowed a book from Hookham's and hoped to finish it before I leave.'

'You are leaving, then?' His voice held regret.

She clenched her hands in her lap. 'I have been offered a position.'

He nodded. 'So I understand.'

The quiet murmur and calm expression gave her courage to go on. 'The family lives in Wiltshire. There are four children, all rather young. I'm not sure it is exactly what I had hoped for and yet Lady Stanford is convinced it is the best offer I am likely to receive, given my lack of experience.'

The candle beside the bed bronzed the plains and valleys of his angled face and flickered in his eyes as he shot her a quizzical look. 'You are asking my opinion?'

A tremor shook her hands and she fingered her locket. 'It sounds foolish to hesitate, I know.' She attempted a bright smile. 'My only other option is to visit a friend in Paris.' She'd written to Denise, but she hated the thought of returning to France. 'I'm sure your mother is right. It is the best solution.'

His voice lowered, thickened. 'There is another option.'

She'd half-expected this, half-dreaded the thought of refusing him. Her hands trembled. Unable to bear the tension of waiting for the words she despaired to hear, she rose and went to the window. Lamps twinkled along the street like diamonds on a necklace. 'What option?'

The bed squeaked, then a wall of heat shimmered at her back. His hands, large, warm, dropped to her shoulders. His face, reflected ghostly in the glass, bent close to her cheek. 'Stay with me.' His breath tickled her ear.

At least he had the courage to ask for what he wanted. She could say nothing. Since the moment they had met, she'd denied and resisted his pull. She turned in his arms. Brandy scented his breath and mingled with sandalwood and musky male, a heady combination.

For long moments, she savoured the feel of him close, the correct words refusing to form in her mind, let alone on her tongue. 'I must not,' she forced out.

His gaze lowered to her mouth and his head angled down. 'You must not or you do not want to?'

She stared at his full, sensual lips, glimpsed the dappled forest green of his eyes. Oh, she wanted, but not what he had to offer. He'd splintered the wall of ice around her heart, exposing it, vulnerable and raw, to his power to wound.

The heartbreak in her mother's eyes grazed her memory. 'I think it is best if you leave.' The words tore her in two.

'Don't think,' he murmured and captured her mouth with his.

The warm, moist touch of his lips branded her mouth.

Shock waves of shivering heat tore through her chest and settled deep in the pit of her stomach.

Drowning in her blood's molten heat, she clung to his solid form, melted against his hard body, her arms inching around his neck without permission. A hard thigh pressed between her legs and she angled her hips into it. Urgent need pulsed deep in her core.

His heart hammered against her chest. She yearned to open to him, to trust him. Insidious need had softened her heart and weakened her will. He had slipped past her guard.

Her lips parted and his tongue teased at the corners, plundered her mouth, drove her to a need so great, she arched her back. His hands ran over her shoulders and down her spine, lighting fires of longing. Her body cried yes in sly encouragement.

A small sound escaped her throat.

He cupped her buttocks and pulled her hard against the ridge of his arousal with a soft groan.

By all the saints, he wanted her, Christopher acknowledged. She haunted his dreams. Warm and soft in his arms, she felt right, perfect in fact.

Damn Garth and his hints. Had she yielded to him? The thought crashed over him like cold surf. He broke the kiss and closed his eyes against the demands of his body. If he didn't stop now, he'd take her right here, under his mother's roof, and be damned.

Breath rasping in his throat, he grasped her shoulders and stepped back. Her beautiful blue eyes, hazy with passion, stared up at him; her lips rosy and moist from his kiss called him back. He would not share her. 'I have a small house in Kent, less than a day's drive from town. We can live there. I can stay at Grillon's when I have business in London.'

Sorrow shadowed her face and her gaze dropped to the floor.

'What?' he asked.

A brittle laugh broke the silence 'I thank you for your flattering offer, but I find I must decline.'

She made it sound as though he'd handed her a bouquet of poisonous weeds. Clearly, he'd missed something along the way. Damn the brandy he'd drunk. He recalled Garth's mocking words. She must want more. 'You will find me generous and, when we part, I promise you will never have to worry about money again.'

'No. Thank you.'

The flat-out rejection hurt more than he wanted to acknowledge. 'It can't be worse than playing nursemaid to a pack of unruly brats.'

She raised a brow. 'I disagree.'

An impression of tears in her crystalline eye panicked him. He never panicked. Damn drinking too much and damn her. One moment she played the Jezebel, the next her repertoire consisted of untouchable ice maiden. He didn't like either role.

'Oh, come on. We both know you are no gently bred female straight from the schoolroom.'

She averted her gaze. 'I am not interested.'

Suspicion roiled through his gut. Garth had been just a little too smug. The demon leaped out of the abyss in his mind and into his mouth. 'If you are seeking a man with a title, I can assure you my brother's no green 'un to be taken in by that lovely face of yours.'

Her head jerked around. Shock, dismay and something far worse mirrored in her gaze. Guilt.

Hemmed in by the small chamber, he paced around

the foot of the bed, logic slipping beyond the grip of his hazy mind.

She shrank back as he swung around to face her.

'Don't give me that innocent look,' he said. 'I saw your true colours in Dover. And I saw the way you smiled at my brother, while all I see are cold stares.'

Her face became wooden, her eyes remote. He'd hit a nerve.

With shock, Sylvia heard the slur in his words and saw the way he rocked on his feet. He was drunk. She'd been so pleased to see him, she hadn't noticed. She swallowed. Men in their cups were hard to manage. Strong and heavy and mean.

He rubbed a hand over his chin. 'Sylvia. Don't hold out for Garth.' His tone held a warning. 'He knows I have first option.'

She gasped. They'd bargained for her between them. She eased around him and pulled open the door. 'I want neither of you and you, sir, are sotted. You will oblige me by leaving immediately.'

He stared at her, stark disbelief in his face, then his lip curled in a sneer. 'Oh, so now you play the prim and proper lady again.' He laughed, low and bitter. 'Well, let me tell you, *mademoiselle*, don't hold out for marriage. Even Garth knows better than that.'

Lord Stanford's proposal sprang into her mind and heat scalded her cheeks. Men only wanted beautiful women for one thing, and when they were satisfied they cast them aside.

How had she ever thought she could trust Christopher? Her throat burned with unshed tears; tremors shook her body. 'Get out. I have no more interest in you than I have in your brother.'

His eyes narrowed. 'I don't know what game you are

playing, but the sooner you find yourself a place away from this family, the better for all of us. I knew what you were the moment I set eyes on you.'

Her heart bled from his unjust words, but she would not let him see how he had wounded her. Shattered pride would not allow it. 'Oh, and what is that?'

'A trollop.'

Bloodless, her heart shrank into a cold hard lump. The need to fight back, to wound him in return, straightened her spine. 'And Lord Stanford is exceptionally generous, I'm told, and very charming.'

A shadow darkened his eyes from green to brown. 'Then I wish you good luck.' He walked past her and closed the door with a violent softness.

It was the worst day of her life. First the incident with the carriage, then the awful Elston woman had offered her hard work for little pay and now Christopher had shown exactly what he thought of her. He hadn't wanted to kiss her; he had done it to prove she was the same as her mother. And she was. Just as weak and wanting.

Damn him to hell. Sylvia buried her face in her pillow and sobbed. And damn Mrs Elston and damn Lord Stanford. To the devil with them all. She dashed away the hot tears running down her face.

Merde. She would not turn herself into a drudge for a woman she could only describe as a harridan for the sake of respectability.

In her dreams, she had seen a different life, a comfortable home, laughing children, a man who would smile at her over his newspaper each morning with love and respect in his eyes. That dream would never be hers. She'd always known it. No decent man would marry her knowing her background and the sordid truth of her life in Paris.

Christopher Evernden and respectability were out of her reach.

...the sooner you find yourself a place away from this family, the better for all of us. Wasn't this what she wanted in the first place? To disgust him, so he would let her go? Then why this hollow sensation of loss? She rolled over on her back and stared at the sloping ceiling. Surely she had not expected him to be different? A pang twisted her heart. How foolish. How weak. She had actually started to trust him. Now she must get as far from him as possible.

She'd take up Denise's offer and join her in Paris. First thing in the morning she'd leave for the coast.

Christopher pressed his shaking fingers against his thumping temple and cursed the brandy he had drunk after leaving Sylvia last night. Self-disgust gnawed at his entrails.

He strode across the library to the fireplace and pulled the bell again. Where the bloody hell was Sylvia? It didn't take this long to find someone in this damned town house. At well past noon, she should be up and downstairs. It was bad enough that he had to face her to apologise without hanging around thinking about it.

'Kit, old chap,' Garth said, breezing in and picking up a newspaper. He glanced at the headlines as he spoke. 'If you want to make Darbys' place by nightfall, shouldn't you be on your way?'

In his black riding coat, skintight buff riding breeches and wearing his usual cynical expression, Garth epitomised the noble English rake about town.

Christopher nodded, then flinched at the pain the movement caused inside his skull.

Garth slouched into an armchair by the fireplace and turned to the racing page. 'Well?'

He didn't need Garth's sharp eyes focussed on him. He'd never hear the last of it if Garth learned what ten kinds of idiot he'd been last night. He glared at Garth. 'Well what?'

'Why are you still hanging about here?'

All he wanted to do was apologise to Sylvia and get out of London. The hurt in her eyes had floated before his face from the moment he'd opened his eyes, like an accusing Banquo's ghost. Shakespeare certainly knew how to portray a guilty conscience.

And why the hell was Garth so interested in his movements? For months, Garth hadn't spent any time in Mount Street, until this week. It all came back to the same thing. Miss Boisette. He glowered. 'I need to speak to Miss Boisette before I leave.'

Garth looked up from his paper. 'Actually, I rather wanted to talk to you about that young lady. Something rather untoward happened yesterday.'

Untoward? Bloody hell. She'd told Garth about his behaviour last night. Christopher strode to the window and looked out. Bright daylight burned red-hot needles into the backs of his eyes. His brother's flailing tongue could hardly make him feel any worse than he did, but he deserved it.

'Yes,' Garth continued, 'she really shouldn't be out on the streets on her own. She's far too lovely for her own safety.'

Christopher swung around and grabbed at the curtain as a wave of giddiness made the room pitch worse than a galleon in a hurricane. He took a deep breath to steady himself. 'What are you talking about?'

Frowning, Garth eyed him up and down. 'Are you all right, Kit?'

Oh God, not more brotherly concern. 'Yes. It's just a headache.'

A slow smile spread over Garth's face. 'You young idiot, you're jug-bitten.'

'What about Miss Boisette?'

Garth tossed the newspaper on the table beside him and stretched out his long legs. 'It was the oddest thing. A footman was pressing her to get into a carriage when I came along.'

'Whose carriage?'

'I didn't see the man inside, though she said there was one.'

The hairs on the back of his neck rose. Surely this couldn't have anything to do with the earlier attempt to abduct her? Could it? 'A case of mistaken identity?'

Garth looked unconvinced. 'She said so, but the lackey was pressing her pretty hard, I thought, and she looked terrified.'

'Why didn't you mention this last night?'

'I forgot.'

'Bloody hell. It can't be a coincidence.'

Garth shot a piercing glance from under his brows. ''Fess up.'

'It's not the first time there has been an attempt to abduct her. Someone tried to kidnap her from the Bird in Hand the night we stayed there.'

Garth's eyebrows almost disappeared into his hairline. 'Something you failed to mention.'

'I thought it was a random attack. Some Mohawk looking for a ransom.'

'Who knew you were there?'

'That's just it, no one as far as I know.' Christopher strode to the chair opposite Garth and dropped into it. 'Unless we were followed from Tunbridge Wells. There was some god-awful dandy at the Sussex Hotel. I just didn't think anything of it.' Mentally, Christopher reviewed the scene in Tunbridge Wells. He'd been so embarrassed; he'd put it out of his mind. He groaned.

'What?'

'There was another man in the lobby that day, a dingy fellow in the shadows behind her. A man very like the stranger at the bar in the Bird in Hand later that evening. He could have followed us. I didn't recall seeing him at the Sussex until right now.'

'No real reason to, I suppose.' Garth frowned. 'Who would want to kidnap a poverty-stricken female like Sylvia Boisette?'

Christopher raised his gaze to meet Garth's puzzled expression. 'Uncle John said she is the daughter of an English duke by a Parisian prostitute. He'd been trying to prove her claim.'

Garth whistled through his teeth. 'Which duke? Not one of the Prince's brothers, I hope?'

'He didn't provide the name. But it doesn't make any sense that he would want to harm Sylvia. Half the nobility have by-blows scattered around England. What difference would one from Paris make?'

Garth stilled. After a moment's hesitation, he shook his head. 'There's been some public mutterings about the morals of the nobility since the French Revolution, especially Prinny. It's not had much of an effect. The only duke I know who might have anything to lose is Huntingdon. He's supporting the introduction of a bill against prostitution.'

'How would you know? I didn't think you cared for politics.'

Garth brushed the question away with an impatient gesture. 'Huntingdon has all the passion of a crusader.

I heard him speak in the House a few weeks ago. The man positively frothed at the mouth.'

The radicals would certainly have a field day if Sylvia proved to be the daughter of such a moralistic Tory, but she had been explicit in her uninterest about her father.

Christopher frowned. Where the hell was she?

'Mr Evernden.' The butler hovered in the doorway, offering a silver tray with his nose so elevated he might have been holding a week-old chamber pot. 'The young person is not in the house, sir. One of the footmen recalls seeing her depart early this morning. I found these on the hall table.'

'Depart?' Christopher asked. A nasty sinking sensation invaded his sensitive gut.

'How early?' Garth asked.

'About five, my lord.' Merreck placed the tray on a green marble-topped table.

Suppressing an oath, Christopher retrieved the note addressed to him in fine neat script and left the one to his mother on the tray. 'Thank you, that will be all.' He waited until the man left before opening the sealed, plain white paper.

He read the few terse words and recalled the pain in her expression when she'd showed him the door last night. A strange sense of loss squeezed his chest. How sweetly her body had melded to his until he'd allowed jealousy of Garth to cloud his reason. He'd driven her away.

If she wanted to go to Paris that was her prerogative, provided she was safe. Every instinct told him she wasn't.

Garth stared at the paper. 'For Satan's sake, Kit. What does it say?'

'She's left for France.'

Christopher passed the note to Garth, who grimaced

when he finished reading. 'I can't say I blame her for not wanting to work for the Elston woman. She's a cheese-paring hag of a female by all accounts. But why France? There are plenty of others in need of a governess.'

Now the truth of what he had done had to come out. His stomach roiling, he rested his chin on his fist. 'I as good as called her a whore.' And that probably wasn't the worst of it, but it was all he was prepared to admit.

'Oh.' Garth sat silent for a moment. 'That would do it.'

He didn't need Garth's sarcasm to tell him he'd fumbled things. She was gone and that was all there was to it. She hadn't deserved what he'd said to her. She'd tried her best to behave like a respectable female, but she attracted trouble like jam lured wasps. She'd almost been abducted, not once, apparently, but twice.

'You are really smitten, aren't you?' Garth's question interrupted his train of thought.

He must be as transparent as glass. He tucked the note into his breast pocket. He thought about how much he liked her and swallowed. 'Aye.' His voice was strangely thick and gruff. His throat burned.

Garth grinned. 'Then you had better fetch her back. Get her out of your system.'

He forced himself to recognise the truth. 'It's you she wants.'

Garth raised a brow. 'Then she wouldn't have run away. Don't you know anything about women?'

'Obviously not. I stormed into her room last night and practically took her right then and there without a kiss-your-hand or by-your-leave. Then I told her she was dirt beneath *my* feet.'

Sympathy flashed in Garth's normally cynical eyes.

He didn't need sympathy. He wanted to hit something, someone, anyone, before the anger at himself exploded.

'Look, Kit,' Garth said and Christopher forced himself to listen, 'the only way to get her off your mind and out of your overactive conscience is to follow her and get her to listen to reason.'

For once Garth made sense. At least he'd be able to apologise. He would convince her to let him escort her to her destination. Or perhaps bring her back to London—and Garth. Anything to ensure her settled securely. After all, that was Uncle John's wish. 'Perhaps you are right.'

'I know I am. You can offer her far more than she'd ever get as a governess.'

Christopher's gut twisted. 'Or you could.'

After a sharp stare, Garth nodded. 'Before you leave, I'll get my man to mix you up a tonic for that head of yours. He has this amazing recipe. It really works. I should know, I drink the vile stuff every day.'

Everything suddenly seemed clear. If he left right away, he might stop her at Dover before she caught a packet to Calais and Mother would not know of her departure. When she returned, she could still take the Elston position or he'd make some other arrangement. He pocketed the note to his mother. 'I'll do it.'

'Right, come upstairs and I'll have him prepare it.'

'What?'

'The tonic.'

'To hell with that. I've got to get my horses put to.'

Chapter Ten

The sound of each shaky breath filled Sylvia's ears. Her heart knocked against her ribs. The pistol in the gloved hand of the hatchet-faced man on the carriage seat opposite remained unwavering, pointed at her chest. She licked her dry lips. 'Where are you taking me?'

He had introduced himself as Seamus Rafter when he swooped down and threw her in his coach outside the Lion d'Or. After that, he'd refused to say another word. He'd snatched her up on the way to catch the early *diligence* to Paris. She had instantly recalled him from the Sussex Hotel. Worse, she'd remembered his voice. He was the man who'd crept into her bedroom.

'You'll see soon enough, colleen.'

She jumped at the sound of his harsh voice in the confined space. Irish, then, not French. That was the reason for his strange lilting accent. 'What do you want with me? I demand you return me to Calais.'

His slate-grey eyes gazed unblinking back at her face. It was all she could do not to shudder. A lump welled up in her throat and prickles burned the backs of her eyes.

Years of iron control threatened to desert her. She swallowed her tears. She would not let him see her fear.

As the carriage turned off the main road on to a lane, it rocked and bounced worse than the Channel packet crossing from Dover. Her heart picked up speed until breathing became a chore. She clung to the handstrap for what felt like hours. When the carriage slowed and then halted, she wasn't sure she wanted the journey to end. Rafter gripped her wrist and hauled her down the carriage steps. He pulled her tight to his bony body. He smelled of stale cigars and sweat.

She tore at the hand around her upper arm. 'Let me go.'

Impervious to her struggles, Rafter propelled her along a weed-infested path towards a dilapidated grey stone mansion covered in ivy.

Sharpened by the harsh sunlight, his angular profile revealed nothing of his thoughts. Grey eyes as cold as polished steel stared straight ahead. When she dragged her feet, he simply tightened his grip around her shoulders and lifted her from the ground.

'Put me down,' she gasped, his hard squeeze crushing her ribs.

The house loomed closer. Paint peeled from the brown front door beneath the crumbling portico. She did not want to go in there. Her heart beat so hard it drowned out the sound of his steps on the flagstones.

The door swung open at his push. He hustled her inside, down a dark, narrow hallway and into a gloomy room.

'Why are we here?' she asked again, more to hear the sound of her voice than in expectation of an answer.

He released her arm and closed the door behind them.

Adjusting to the dim light, she stared around the room. Red velvet curtains fully covered the windows, gilt sofas with red upholstery stood against dark green walls illuminated by candles in three mirrored wall sconces. A sickening surge of familiarity washed through her. The gaudy furnishings were shabby and worn, the edges of the curtains frayed. Her stomach lurched. It seemed horribly familiar. 'What is this place?' She hauled in a shuddering breath. 'I demand an answer.'

Light eyes observed her with cold uninterest and his thin lips curled up in a sneer. He sauntered to the bell beside the fireplace and gave it a swift tug. It clanged in the nether regions of the old house like a call to the dead.

Sylvia eyed the door. If she could reach it before he did, she could be gone before anyone arrived.

'Don't try it, colleen.'

She glared at him. 'What do you want with me?'

'Nothing.'

She shuddered at the menace in his harsh indifference.

A frowsy, full-bosomed woman with red hair waddled in.

Sylvia clutched at her throat, all thoughts driven from her mind.

Madame Gilbert beamed, her full rouged lips parting in a simpering smile, her fat cheeks all but obliterating her beady, brown eyes. 'Why, *mon petit chou*. You do remember me. I am flattered.'

Sylvia swung around to Rafter. 'Why here?'

He leaned against the mantel, his lean face dispassionate. 'It's where you belong.'

'No.' She forced the croak from her dry throat.

Monsieur Jean had rescued her more than ten years ago, but she had never forgotten the groping, pawing hands, the pain, the bitter shame. Nor had she forgotten how Madame Gilbert paraded her before an old gentleman one evening. Young as she was, she had known what he wanted. Dread ate at her soul.

'Now, now, little one,' Madame Gilbert murmured, reaching out to touch her shoulder.

Sylvia's skin crawled. She pushed the pudgy hand away, her eyes on the door. She had to get out of here.

'You owe me, girl,' Madame Gilbert rasped. 'All those years I kept your mother when she was sick—she barely earned enough to pay for her own food, let alone yours. You will pay your debt, pretty one.'

The cloying scent of attar of roses over the smell of unwashed flesh and stale breath strummed at chords of remembrance. As the obese *madame* closed in on her, all the old terrors returned, the helplessness, the suffocating fear of being caught in a passageway or in her mother's room. Sylvia stumbled back until the backs of her legs came in contact with the edge of a sofa.

Trapped.

Madame Gilbert's beringed, damp fingers tipped Sylvia's face to the light.

She shuddered at the clammy touch on her skin. Bile filled her throat and threatened to choke her. Her worst nightmare had become reality.

Damn them. How dare they do this to her? A rush of hot anger released her numb mind. She jerked her head away. 'Don't touch me, *cochon*.'

Madame Gilbert's smile broadened. 'Magnificent. You are everything you promised to be all those years ago.' She turned her head and spoke to Rafter. 'You tell Milor', she'll be better than her mother. His secret will be safe.'

Rafter grunted. 'Watch your tongue, *madame*. You say too much.'

Milor'? Secret? Sylvia gazed from one to the other.

'Your father wants you back where you belong. Your

mother was a whore. It is your destiny,' Madame Gilbert said.

The room rocked. In all these years, she had never heard from her father. She sank on to the sofa. 'My father wants this?'

'You've said enough, old woman. If you say another word, the bargain will be broken and you will be dead.' The Irishman did not raise his voice, but the threat hung heavy in the dingy room.

Madame Gilbert cackled. 'It's all right, *mon ami*. All will be well now I have *mon petit chou* again.'

'*Salope.*' Sylvia spat the word at the vile woman who had somehow reached out from her past to claim her.

Madame Gilbert grinned. 'I see your command of French is as good as ever it was.'

She had reverted to the language of her childhood, curses and all. In those days she had fought for her right to survive. 'I am not staying.' She stood up and pushed past the *madame*'s solid wall of flesh.

'Temper, temper,' Madame Gilbert said. 'My gentlemen like a bit of fire in my girls.' She winked. 'But I demand obedience.'

She ran her hand down Sylvia's cheek. 'So soft and fine. I wonder who will pay the highest price to be first with you?'

Heat flamed in her face and she looked away.

Madame Gilbert's eyes narrowed. 'Your mother did protect you, did she not?'

Sylvia faced her interrogator. 'I know well enough what trade you ply.'

Madame Gilbert grimaced and shrugged, her voluptuous breasts jiggling in her low neckline. 'Then you know what is expected.'

Sylvia tamped down her rising panic. She must not

show weakness. 'I will not do this. I'll scream. I'll tell them you kidnapped me. You cannot force me.'

Rafter moved towards the door, a speculative expression on his face. 'You have your hands full, *madame*.'

The vast body shook as she chuckled. She stroked Sylvia's cheek. 'Fight all you want, little one. They will love it.'

A shudder racked her from head to toe. 'Don't touch me.'

'Ah, but not the first time,' Madame Gilbert crooned. 'The first time you will be gloriously accommodating, for you must learn.'

'I'll leave you to your business,' the Irishman said. 'I will come tomorrow for the paper in accordance with our agreement.' His expression hardened. 'Do not forget. It must be here when I return or it will go poorly with you. My patience is exhausted.'

Panic shortened Sylvia's breath. '*Monsieur*, do not leave me here. I have no intention of embarrassing my father. I will disappear. I will never speak his name.' She stretched out her hands to him.

The man paused, his hand on the door handle. He did not turn around. 'You know his name then, colleen?' He pulled open the door.

The terrible finality in his tone plunged her stomach to the floor. If only Monsieur Jean had not told her of his suspicions at the last, begged her to seek him out despite her objections, then she would not have made such a mistake. Frantic, she shook her head. 'No. I do not.'

Too late. The click of the latch behind him was the slam of a prison door.

She swung around and glared at Madame Gilbert. 'I have friends. They will look for me.'

The *madame* pulled the bell. 'The young Englishman you ran away from perhaps, *chérie*? You left him. He will not want you back after you have been here.' Her piggy eyes narrowed. 'Was it he who took what was mine to sell? If he comes near you, he is a dead man. There is no love for the English in this part of France.'

How did Madame Gilbert know so much about her? Rafter must have told her. He'd been following her, watching her.

She shuddered. And Madame Gilbert was right. She would get no help from the Everndens. No doubt Christopher was celebrating her departure. 'I have other friends.'

'Don't lie to me. Your so-called guardian is dead and the woman you hoped to live with is dying. There is no one.'

There was Denise. 'You are wrong.'

Madame Gilbert pulled an envelope from her pocket. 'Perhaps you are thinking of this?' Madame Gilbert waved her letter to Denise. Her last hope.

Sylvia failed to contain her gasp of disappointment as all hope of rescue fled. 'You have no right interfering with my mail.'

Madame Gilbert shook her head. 'Ah, *mon petit chou*, now there is only me.'

Her teeth wanted to chatter in tune with her trembling body. She clenched her jaw. She might be alone. But she was not helpless against an old and weak woman.

She edged towards the door. 'You cannot keep me here against my will.'

The *madame* raised a brow, her leering smile unwavering. She lowered her bulk onto the nearest sofa with a wheezy sigh. 'You think not, *chérie*?'

With a swift pull, Sylvia jerked open the door and stepped into the hallway. Broad and squat, his nose flattened and a jagged white scar across one swarthy cheek, a man with a straggling beard blocked her path. A leering toad. She stopped short.

'Alphonse,' Madame Gilbert said, 'meet Sylvie, our newest acquisition. She is not to go anywhere without my permission.'

Alphonse grunted and barred her path with one thick arm.

Sylvia glared down at him. 'Let me pass, oaf.'

He grinned.

She pushed at his arm and he shoved her backwards into the room. She stumbled, but managed to prevent herself from falling.

'Sit down, Sylvie,' Madame commanded.

'No.'

Alphonse lumbered forward and thrust her into a chair, then returned to his post in the hallway.

A smug smile slithered across the *madame*'s face. 'That's better. You will soon learn.'

Sylvia swung her head around at a noise at the door. Her heart lurched. Alphonse returning?

Instead, a hunched and wrinkled woman in a black maid's uniform pushed her way in. 'Gi' over, ye great lummox.'

'Jeannie?' Sylvia gasped.

The maid cocked her head sideways and peered up at Sylvia from beneath bushy grey brows. 'Aye. I heard you were back.'

Hope sprang in Sylvia's heart. The dour Scotswoman had stayed with Sylvia's mother through thick and thin, despite her Calvinistic disapproval of her mistress's lifestyle. 'You are still here?'

'Aye, Miss Sylvie. I always knew you'd return. Bad blood always proves true.'

Jeannie meant she had her father's blood. An old and well-remembered refrain.

Beyond Alphonse, two other women lurked in the shadowed corridor, their eyes curious, their faces painted. Not girls she recognised from the old days. No help there.

Madame Gilbert waved towards the door. 'Jeannie will show you to your room. The other girls will be along shortly to help you prepare.'

The words and smile threatened. Sylvia shook her head.

'I will ask Alphonse to carry you up, if you insist,' Madame Gilbert said.

The gloating glance from the dwarf-like Alphonse crushed the thought of resistance. Jeannie beckoned with a sly little smile. In despair, Sylvia followed her out of the door and up the stairs, aware of Alphonse's gaze at every step she took.

Jeannie led her to a chamber. Light struggling through a grimy window festooned with red velvet curtains revealed a straight-backed chair in one corner and a wardrobe in another, the whole dominated by a bed covered by white silky sheets.

The old woman pointed to the bed. 'Sit there and wait for *madame*. It's na more than ye deserve, let me tell ye.'

Tears blurred Sylvia's vision at the triumph in the old woman's tone. 'Why are you being so cruel? You used to be my friend. You loved my mother.'

Jeannie shuffled to the bed and turned back the sheet. 'That I did. More than my own life. I stayed with her in this heathen country until the day she died. Never a word of complaint from the poor wee lassie. Aye, nor of blame.' Her mouth turned down. ''Twas your fault, ye and the no-good man who stole her from her family, then got her with child and abandoned her.'

Jeannie twisted her head sideways on her hunched shoulders to look up at Sylvia. 'I hate ye both. And so shall ye both be punished.'

Sylvia recoiled from her venomous expression. 'You hate my father, yet you help him.'

'I've never helped him. I told Madame Gilbert he'd pay. And he did. He bled freely, just like my sainted mistress coughing up her lungs and bleeding and bleeding, till I couldna' wipe the blood from her lips fast enough.'

Jeannie's wrinkled face twisted into a mask of hate. 'Then the war got so bad, even Rafter could no' get in or out of Paris. Niver mind that the Irish sided with France. After that, there was no money for food or medicine.'

Sylvia sank on to the bed, sickened as she imagined her mother unable to work at all and with no money to pay the doctor.

'Oh, aye,' Jeannie said, her watery eyes gazing into the distance at the scenes playing out in her head. 'I stole and I even tried whoring, but with my face and form I never got naught but pennies from drunks and sailors.'

Regret, dark and painful, crushed Sylvia's soul. She should have stayed. 'But why do you hate me, Jeannie? What did I ever do to hurt you or my mother?'

'If she'd have never bore you, he'd never have left her. I know it.'

'That is hardly my fault.'

Jeannie's gnarled hands shook. She twisted them in her apron and glared at Sylvia. 'You selfish little bitch. You left her to die with niver a thought for her who bore ye and fed ye and kept ye by the toils of her body. You left her when she needed you most. Dying she was. Your beautiful little body could have kept her alive.'

The bitterness in the old woman's tone struck Sylvia like a blow. Jeannie had expected her, a child of eleven, to provide for her mother. And, Sylvia realised with shock, she would have if her mother hadn't sent her away.

She sank down on the bed. The sheet clenched in her fingers felt slippery and cold, like the tears on her cheeks when she learned what her mother and Monsieur Jean had done that long-ago day. She gazed at Jeannie, desperate to be believed. 'I didn't want to go. I didn't want to leave her. I missed her so much.'

A sob broke free. She swallowed the lump in her throat. 'Monsieur Jean was kind and generous, but I would have given up my life to stay with *maman* to the end.' Husky and raw with emotion, her voice broke. 'She was all I had. I loved her.'

Puzzlement in her tired eyes, Jeannie stared, then sank to perch next to her. 'D'ye mean John Evernden forced you to leave with him?'

Sylvia cast her mind back. 'He never said we were leaving. She sent us for pastries. The carriage just kept going and going, further and further. Then he put me under a blanket in the coach. It was a game, he said, hide and seek from the bad soldiers. I must have fallen asleep. When I awoke we were in England. They tricked me. He told me I would never see *maman* again.'

Tears glazed Jeannie's eyes and she swiped at them. 'Aye. She was that set on saving you. But she pined away after. I couldna' forgive ye. My poor sweet lady that was so beautiful, so sweet and loving, and they all left her to die.'

Scalding tears trickled down Sylvia's cheeks. She envisaged her mother's last days, saw again the face that had become vague and misty over the years, only a faint likeness in her locket to remind her. The memories sharpened to vivid pictures of blonde hair, sallow skin and unhealthy flushed cheeks. Dark circles outlined luminous blue eyes full of pain and soul-deep hurt. Jeannie was right. Sylvia should have stayed.

She placed an arm around Jeannie's bony shoulders. 'I'm so sorry. Thank you for taking care of her. I know she loved you just as much as you loved her.'

Jeannie pulled a handkerchief from her apron pocket and blew her nose. 'Aye. She did. I didna' tell her where the extra money came from to feed the two of you. 'Twas between me, the *madame* and the Irishman. She never would have let me take money from that bastard. She loved him, y'see, and she wouldna' listen to reason.'

Jeannie dabbed at her eyes. 'They were so happy when they first came to France. I thought he loved her too. Then the troubles started. All the nobles left Paris. A message came from the old duke for him to come home, but he wouldna' accept your mither. They couldna' make up their minds.'

The old maid wrung her hands. 'Then it was almost too late. The embassy closed and British soldiers were sent to take us all to a boat, her and the duke. We got separated from him in the confusion. He got to the boat, we didna'. Rafter was a soldier then. He brought us to Madame Gilbert's to hide.'

Rafter? Suspicion uncoiled like a loathsome snake in Sylvia's stomach. 'Rafter brought you to Madame Gilbert's?'

Lost in the past, Jeannie stared into the distance. 'We waited and we waited, but he niver came back. But we had to eat. Your mither was two months gone with you and, in the end, Madame Gilbert gave her no choice but to work. All the old friends were gone from Paris, or had lost their heads, ye ken. After you were born, you had to be fed. Rafter came back to see his old friend Madame Gilbert a few months after your birth with the news the Duke wasna' interested in your mither. I decided your father would pay. I found the paper that Marguerite said proved who you were tucked away with her trinkets. I gave it to Madame Gilbert.' Her face lit with a smile of triumph. 'For a while things were easier, he sent money to keep us in France. He'd do anything to keep the both of ye a secret, Rafter said.'

Sylvia froze. She placed a hand on Jeannie's arm, jerking the old woman back into the present. 'Wait a minute. Are you saying there really is proof I'm his daughter?'

'Aye. But Marguerite wouldna' use it. If he didna' want her, then she said she didna' care, not for herself. So I took it to pay him back. I niver dared tell her what I'd done, even when she discovered it gone that day when Evernden took ye.'

Sylvia got up and went to the window. Outside the day was bright, the sky blue, while inside this dreadful house everything seemed dark and twisted. 'What did the paper say?'

The old woman slumped and shook her grizzled head. 'I canna read. But they came home one day giggling like naughty children with the paper. They must have known then that she was with child.' Jeannie's claw-like hands clenched. 'Everything was a game to them in those days. A game against his father.'

Sylvia's mind whirled. All those years Monsieur Jean had sought proof, and it was here all the time. 'Why did my father deny us all these years?'

Sorrow crumpled Jeannie's wizened face. 'I don't know, lassie. I just dinna' ken. I suppose he didna' love her as she did him.' Her old eyes filled with tears again. 'You look just like her. Ah, I'm right sorry, lass. I should never have told them about John Evernden whisking ye off. It fair makes my heart weep to see such loveliness wasted. It's inner beauty what counts. She had it and now I see it in you too.'

With a heart aching so much she thought it would break, Sylvia hugged Jeannie's bony body close. 'My father should not have abandoned her and nor should I.'

'Dear God,' the old woman moaned. 'What have I done?'

Footsteps and female voices sounded on the stairs. They jumped apart.

'That's Madame Gilbert,' Jeannie said, wiping her eyes. 'And the other girls, coming to settle you in.'

The sounds drew close and Jeannie stood. 'I must go. I'll help ye if I can, Sylvie, with my last breath, so I will.'

The door opened. Madame Gilbert waddled in with what looked like a bottle of medicine. Three girls in tawdry, revealing gowns, their eyes bright and hard and distant, followed her in.

'That will be all, Jeannie,' the Madame said, her smile treacle-sweet. 'You can leave Sylvie to us.'

Christopher felt an utter idiot lurking in a hedge like some peeping Tom. The rented hack flicked its tail at the flies on its sweating, dun-brown flanks. He'd pushed the nag hard to catch up to the travelling carriage containing Sylvia and her escort after he caught sight of the blue bonnet he'd bought in Tunbridge Wells. It had passed him on his way in to a Calais inn in search of her.

Cradling the horse's nose to keep it silent and still, he peered through the hedge. The dusty black coach turned around in the narrow lane outside the unremarkable house. Large and square, it had tangled bushes encroaching on the path to the front door. Weeds infested what must once have been a rose garden, while ancient ivy clung to the grey stonework, draping the upper windows. It appeared to be the kind of country house a gentleman might own, if it weren't so neglected. Yet for all its apparent state of disrepair, the ruts in the lane indicated frequent visitors.

Into this house Sylvia had waltzed, encircled within the protective embrace of the Irishman from the Bird. A friend or a lover? A pang pierced his chest. He didn't want to believe it.

Damnation. Was he about to make a fool of himself over a strumpet, a beauty who tempted him against all his principles? He'd only wanted her because he couldn't have her. Lust. Nothing more.

Yet he wanted her still.

He cursed. Perhaps she'd plotted with this man to blackmail the Evernden family. In that case, why had she left without the rest of the money Christopher had promised her?

While he stood here wondering like a besotted fool, matters of business awaited him in London, important matters she'd driven from his mind. He'd wasted enough time over a woman who had so quickly found another protector. He mounted and brought the horse's head around.

A door slammed.

He glanced over his shoulder.

The Irishman sauntered down the steps and out of the front gate. Alone. A smile curved his thin lips. He set what looked like a brand-new hat on his head at a jaunty angle. With a brief word to the coachman, he climbed inside.

The hairs on the back of Christopher's neck prickled. Despite all his logic, something about this felt wrong. He had to know if Sylvia and this man meant trouble for him and his family. He had to know Sylvia was all right.

He edged the horse deeper into the hedge's shadow

and watched the coach rumble and sway down the lane. Nothing about the house revealed Sylvia's purpose in coming here. If it was an assignation, why had the man left so soon?

He recalled the farm labourer hoeing a field a mile or so down the lane. He would know who owned the house. Careful to keep out of view of the windows for the first few yards, Christopher retraced his tracks to where the lone man toiled, his hoe swinging in rhythmic arcs. The peasant looked up when Christopher drew close. He leaned on his implement and touched a hand to his forelock. The lines in his weathered face deepened as he squinted up.

'Who owns these lands?' Christopher asked, with a sweep of his arm.

'Today, milor'?'

Christopher frowned. 'What do you mean?'

A grin revealed rotting teeth and further creased the labourer's crumpled face. 'They used to belong to le Duc de Verendelle, then they belonged to the peasants, then to Bonaparte. Now?' He spread his arms wide. 'I don't know. I just do what I have always done, milor'.'

Christopher understood the man's confusion. Since Bonaparte's departure for St Helena, the government of France under Louis XVIII had yet to organise itself. Lands were still being parcelled out to their former owners. 'Then the land does not belong to those who occupy *la grande maison*?' He nodded back in the direction of the house.

The grin widened, black eyes twinkled. 'No, milor'. Though it is true that many a furrow is ploughed there. They do not work the land.'

'Speak plainly, man.'

'Why, milor', 'tis a bordello. Only *les filles de joie*

live there now.' He grimaced. 'Though I have only heard tell of it. It is not for the likes of me. Only men like the mayor and rich merchants can pay their prices. And men like you, milor'.' The leathery face leered up at him.

Prostitutes? Christopher's mind reeled. He couldn't imagine it. A vision of the day he met her flashed into his mind. If that was the true Sylvia, then he could picture it very well. A cold hand seemed to fist in his chest. He was a stupid fool to follow her like some callow youth.

He flicked a *sou* to the peasant and, not wishing to arouse suspicion, he continued in the same direction as before. As he rode, he cast his mind over her entrance into the house. The Irishman had held her tight against him. She appeared willing enough.

Damn her to hell. He needed to know, to hear that this was what she wanted from her own lips.

He doubled back and once more observed the house from the shelter of the hedge on the other side of the lane.

Blank-eyed, the shade-covered windows stared back at him. He tied the horse to a hazel tree and circled the house. At the back, he discovered a stable from which the sounds of at least one horse emanated. Smoke drifted from a chimney on the low wing jutting at right angles from the main house. Probably the kitchen.

None of the back windows were open. Fresh air seemed unpopular in this establishment. Apart from breaking a window, he did not see any way in.

Hell fire. If the old peasant told the truth and it was a brothel, who more likely to seek its services than a hot-blooded gentleman? He jogged back to his mount. Pulling the horse behind him, he marched boldly up to the front door and rang the bell.

The man who answered his summons barely reached his chest, but the aggression in his stance and the brutality in his pugnacious face marked him for a bruiser. 'Yes?'

Christopher raised a haughty eyebrow in true Garth style.

The glowering gnome raked Christopher with an appraising look, then pushed the door wide. 'Welcome, *monsieur*. Tie your horse to the post and come in. May I take your coat and hat?'

'I'll keep them, thank you.' He retained a firm grip on his cane. The sword hidden within might be needed. The swaggering ox ushered him into a murky parlour. 'I will tell *madame* you are here.'

Christopher strolled to a shabby couch and made himself comfortable. He grimaced at the filthy furnishings. They had certainly seen better days.

The *madame*, a red-haired, gargantuan woman of indeterminate age, bustled in.

He maintained his nonchalant expression as her avaricious eyes took in his dress, his jewellery and his physique. He resisted the temptation to tug at his cravat.

He obviously passed muster, because she smiled coquettishly. 'I am Madame Gilbert. How can we be of service to you, *monsieur*?'

He waved a languid hand. 'I was told you have some of the best women this side of Paris. I find myself in need of some female company.'

'You were informed correctly, *monsieur*. Most of my girls used to work in Paris before the troubles and well know the taste of aristos. Do you have any preferences? They are all excellent, clean and experienced in all the arts. The *vice Anglais*, if you desire?'

Christopher kept his expression bland at the mention of an aberration favoured by Englishmen who had developed a taste for the birch switch at public school. He had never gone away to school.

'I prefer blondes,' he said. 'Slim and young.'

The *madame* nodded and waddled out.

Christopher leaned back against the sofa and forced himself to appear nonchalant as he imagined Sylvia's surprise, or anger. Hell, perhaps this wasn't such a good idea.

A hunched-up witch of a servant arrived with wine. Christopher refused it. He needed his wits about him and he had no faith in the cleanliness of the down-at-heel place. She departed, muttering under her breath.

Two buxom females slouched into the room followed by the *madame*, her eyes greedy.

'This is Berthé,' the woman announced, pointing to the one with rouged lips and straw-coloured hair. She wore a tawdry red velvet gown that skimmed her nipples and knees.

'And this is Yvette.' A slighter and younger version of Berthé with light brown hair and brown eyes had on a black lacy corset and filmy yellow skirt. The women flaunted their attributes and batted their eyelashes. Worn and tired, neither of them were Sylvia.

He shook his head at the fat woman. 'Nice enough in their way. But I want something fresher, more innocent in appearance, younger.'

Avaricious eyes gleamed from between rolls of fat. 'A virgin, *monsieur*?'

'A virgin would be a special treat,' he replied, trying to hide his disgust. 'But younger, smaller and…' he curled his lip as his gaze ran over the two women who postured before him '…a true blonde.'

The woman licked her red lips. 'If I had such a girl, she would be very expensive.'

Christopher pulled out a handful of gold. 'But, *madame*,' he said in an icy voice, 'do not presume to think to cheat me.' His hand moved suggestively to the cane at his side. 'I am as accomplished with one sword as I am with the other.'

She eyed his crotch and then his swordstick. She nodded as if coming to a decision. 'I have a girl who might suit you. I would as soon let you be her first as some fat merchant. You will teach her well, I think.'

'If I'm to be her tutor, perhaps you should pay me?'

Her fat face reddened.

Christopher put up a placating hand and smiled. 'I jest, *madame*.'

'Ah, a jest,' she said. 'So English to jest about business.' A suspicious expression crossed her face. 'Your name, *monsieur*?'

'Lord Albert, at your service.' He inclined his head. The name of the obnoxious dandy had jumped into his mind and the woman seemed satisfied. Christopher breathed a sigh of relief when she didn't ask for his calling card.

The pudgy hands slapped together. 'Yvette, go. Berthé, make sure *mon petit chou* is ready for milor'.'

'Surely the gentleman would prefer a more experienced woman?' Berthé said in surly tones.

The *madame* glared. 'Do as I tell you.'

With dragging steps, Berthé left the room. Jealous rivalry amongst whores seemed ludicrous.

'Where is she?' Christopher asked. 'Am I to approve of her first?'

'This one is special. You will see. But first we must conclude our business.'

The exorbitant price to which he agreed seemed all the worse since he strongly suspected he wouldn't get his money's worth. Deep in his heart, he wouldn't believe Sylvia had stooped to this.

Cane swinging, he followed the wheezing *madame* out to the dingy hall and up the staircase.

At the end of the second-floor passage she flung open a door and ushered him in.

Christopher froze at the sight of the naked woman on the bed.

Chapter Eleven

The scene, lit by one candle on a rickety nightstand, burned indelibly into his mind. The wanton Sylvia of his dreams waiting for him, naked, creamy skin on a silky white sheet, slender legs sprawled wide.

Each slow breath lifted her tawny-tipped perfect breasts. Fascinated, he imagined them hardening, responding to his tongue, peaking beneath his palms. A mental image of his hands on her body tingled his fingers and his gaze followed the lines of her tiny waist, the flare of her gently curved thighs crested by the fine, pale blonde curls of her mound and the hint of what lay beneath.

Roses perfumed the air. A vision of loveliness filled his gaze. He didn't want to believe she was here, waiting for him like this, but she was truly lovely and completely irresistible, when he had done nothing but imagine her like this for days.

His loins grew hard and heavy with need. Hunger ached deep in his bones. Never had he felt such driving, urgent need. He slipped out of his coat and waistcoat and pulled his shirt free of his waistband. One taste and he'd leave. He dragged off his shirt and stared at Sylvia.

Her eyes remained closed.

The abbess caught his questioning glance. 'A little laudanum laced with cantharides,' she whispered. 'You will find her most grateful for your gift.' She gestured at Christopher's groin, where his erection strained against the tight fabric of his pantaloons.

Drugged? Was she then not here of her own free will? He needed to get rid of the *madame* to find out.

His body burned to lie down beside her, to cover her, flesh to flesh, to feel her heat against his skin, explore her depths, join with her. Ruthlessly, he stamped out the fire. He bit back a groan and glared at the *madame*. 'I don't want an audience.'

Regret twisted her mouth. 'Too bad.' She wagged a finger. 'Teach her well, milor'. If she gives you trouble, call me and she will be punished. She is a wilful girl, but she will learn.'

The thought of Sylvia servicing men to this woman's command dampened his ardour. He stared pointedly at the door, hiding his revulsion, and she waddled out.

He listened to her heavy tread on the stairs. Certain she had gone, he placed a chair against the door in case she returned and set his swordstick alongside.

Forcing himself not to look at the tempting sight on the bed, he pulled the sheet from its foot up to her neck. He shook her shoulder. 'Sylvia. Wake up.'

After several repeated shakings, her eyelids fluttered open. She stared at him without comprehension, then smiled the blindingly beautiful smile he had seen at Dover and once for Garth.

'Christopher,' she murmured huskily, her French accent more pronounced than usual.

The pulse in his groin beat a wild tattoo at the sultry sound of his name on her lips.

Languidly, she snaked out a hand, reaching for him. The sheet slipped, revealing the rise of her breasts. Her fingertips dragged across his naked chest. 'Ummm. Soft,' she murmured. 'I wondered if you had hair there.' She giggled.

He shuddered on an indrawn breath. How much of the sultry seduction in her gaze was Sylvia and how much the drugs? She'd tormented him like this once before, in Dover. Clearly she wanted him and not for the first time.

Her gaze slid from his chest to his face like a hot caress. A frown furrowed her brow. Confusion darkened her eyes. 'Please. I need…'

Beneath the sheet, her hands caressed her body, over her breast, hardening her nipples to points against the sheer fabric. A flush blossomed on her delicate cheeks and travelled down her neck. Perspiration pearled on her upper lip and forehead. A picture of blatant sensuality.

Hard and ready, his blood a river of fire, he reached for the sheet, aching once more to fully feast his gaze on her glorious, slender body. He'd imagined this so often in his mind, he could taste her sweet flesh. He bit back a curse and stopped.

'Christopher,' she moaned. 'Help me.' She shifted restlessly.

There was only one thing that would ease her. Only a cur would take advantage of the situation 'They've given you drugs,' he rasped in a last-ditch battle for control.

With a moan deep in her throat, she arched towards him, rose up and wrapped her arms around his waist, then drew back with a gasp. 'So hot. I want…'

He closed his eyes. The torment of denial ached in every nerve. His chest shuddered on a breath. 'Where are your clothes?'

He flung open the wardrobe in the far corner of the room. A blue creation, like those the girls downstairs had worn, tumbled out. Useless. What had they done with the clothes she arrived in? He tried the lid of the press at the end of the bed. Padlocked. Damn them.

Again she stretched out her slender white arms. 'I want you to hold me,' she murmured, her accented voice husky.

His erection jerked to full attention at the raw need in her voice. He hauled in a deep breath, seeking control. He had to get her dressed and away, then he'd find a way to help her recover. He laid the flimsy garment on the bed—even with his coat over the top, it wouldn't cover much, but it was better than nothing.

Forcing a snake into a stocking presented an easier task than squeezing the wiggling Sylvia into the snug garment. While he pulled the gown over her head, she pressed her slim length against his body, begging for his help.

Once he had her vaguely inside it, he rolled her on to her stomach and knelt astride her. Pinned beneath his thighs, she moaned and struggled to turn over, her legs grazing the insides of his thighs. His breath hitched. The fires in his blood raged higher. Fingers trembling, he worked at the strings of the ridiculous froth of blue.

'Lie still and let me lace you.'

She lifted her hips and circled her plump *derrière* against him. 'I don't want a dress. I want you.'

Sweet agony. Desire built to raging proportion, a flaming conflagration, pushing him to the edges of reason, where lust warred for supremacy. His blood pulsed and his breath rasped in his ears. He hung to sanity by a thread. Sweat rolled off his forehead and down his cheek. With a groan he pressed her back to the bed with his knee.

She arched her back, her gaze desperate when she

looked over her shoulder. 'Christopher. Can't you…? I need…you.'

The appeal in her eyes snapped the rope of hard-fought resistance. The pressure of her hips at his groin poured sweet agony through every nerve. She wanted this. Nay, she needed it, desperately. And God help him, so did he.

He groaned and pressed a kiss to her nape. She shivered. He cupped her cheek with a hand that looked large and tanned on her pale complexion. Her soft skin burned his flesh. She turned her fiery mouth to kiss his palm. A lightning jolt of pleasure shot through his body. He hardened to rock.

She sighed. 'Love me, Christopher.'

When had an invitation ever been this sweet? He fumbled with the buttons and pushed his pantaloons over his hips. Stiff and pulsing, he pushed against her silken thigh. A glorious sensation.

She moaned her pleasure and her desire. Gently, with one hand under her stomach, he lifted her. The other cupped the swollen flesh of her. She rubbed against his palm, hot and moist. Ready for him.

Sweet heaven. It felt so good.

'Sylvia,' he whispered. 'Tell me you want me to do this.'

She whimpered.

'Sylvia, please. Tell me.'

'Yes,' she said. 'Oh yes.'

He massaged the delicate, hot female folds, slid a finger along her swollen heated cleft. She shuddered and moaned. His fingers sought her tiny nub of pleasure, circled and pressed. God, she was sweet and hot and slick with dew for him. He stroked her rhythmically, preparing her for his entry.

She cried out, shuddered and collapsed beneath him.

He almost howled his frustration. The cantharides had made her so ready, she had climaxed from his touch.

She lay still and limp beneath him. With a savage curse at the hell of unsatisfied lust, he hung above her, his chest heaving, and waited for his body to accept his will.

After what seemed like minutes of agony, he refastened his pantaloon over his rigid protesting flesh and scrambled back into his shirt and waistcoat. God knew how long it would take to cease its rampant demand for satisfaction, but cease it would. Once free of the slavery of the drug, she would remember this and then she would surely hate him for humbling her. He swallowed his regret. Better she hate him, than remain under this roof. What if it happened again? Bloody hell. They had to leave before the drugs took hold again, before he did something he would regret.

Regret? A wry smile twisted his lips. He regretted not having her. He took a deep breath and returned to the task of dressing her.

The chair scraped across the carpet.

He jerked his head around. The hunchback maid glowered at him from the doorway. In her hand, a wicked kitchen knife glinted. 'Get away from her, before I cut your balls off.'

Christopher glanced at his cane beside the chair. The maid stood between him and it, waving the knife. A trick to get more money? 'I paid my gold to your mistress. Get out.'

The old eyes raked his body. '*Cochon.*'

A hot flush rushed to his face at her scornful sneer.

Her gaze darted to the inert figure on the bed, her expression softening with sorrow. 'What filthy perversion are you forcing on her?'

'I haven't touched her.'

'Liar. You've had her. Bastard.'

She would understand the effects of the aphrodisiac, be aware that, without a climax, Sylvia would be all over him, trying to ease the effects of the drug. He deliberately kept his tone cool, all the while watching the knife. 'I caressed her and she came.'

The maid stole closer to the bedside, gazing down at Sylvia, while her knife pointed at the mismatched buttons of his pantaloons and his still-evident arousal. 'Poor little Sylvie. Damn all men. Taking, that's all you know.'

Her sorrow seemed genuine. Hope flickered in his breast. 'If you are any kind of friend to her, you'll help me. I need to get her away.' He gestured to the blue gown. 'There's nothing for her to wear but this.'

The old woman's eyes narrowed on his face. 'What is your name, *monsieur*?'

He hesitated. Instinct told him to trust the old Scot. 'Christopher Evernden.'

'I've heard of ye. I'm Jeannie. I served her mither. Are you her protector?'

'Her guardian. I am responsible for her safety.' And up to the moment, he'd made a damned fine mess of it.

Jeannie visibly relaxed. 'Sylvie trusts you. But it is too late. *Madame*, even now, arranges the move back to Paris. After today she will be rich.'

Christopher swallowed sour bile. He would have no hope of rescuing Sylvia from a Paris brothel. But rich? 'I didn't pay that much for the privilege of having her.'

With a short hard laugh, she laid a gentle hand on Sylvia's shoulder. ''Tis not you who makes *madame* rich, but her *cochon* of a father, the Duke. He paid *madame* to keep the mother, and now the daughter is back, he'll pay a fortune to keep her here too.'

'Why?'

She shrugged. 'He always has.'

What father would want to force his child, even an illegitimate one, into so abhorrent a trade when he could simply pay her off? 'It makes no sense.'

She smiled slyly. 'There's proof he's her father.'

A bastard daughter had no rights, and unless one was royal, the ignominy was better kept hidden by the child as well as the parent. 'It makes no difference.'

Her expression hardened. 'It does, else why would he pay all those years?' She made a cutting gesture across her throat and rolled her eyes. 'My poor Marguerite died after a journey from hell.'

She hobbled to the window and pulled back the curtain, letting in a long shaft of dusty light to reveal the filthy bed hangings and shabby furniture in squalid starkness. Christopher grimaced.

With light outlining her crooked form, she continued in a soft regretful voice, 'The *madame* blackmailed the Duke for years, threatening to expose him to the world. Madame Gilbert used to laugh about it behind Marguerite's back.'

'Why did the *madame* let Sylvia go in the first place?'

She dropped the curtain and swung around.

Christopher blinked, adjusting his vision to the candlelight.

'Your uncle came for the child the day before we fled Paris,' she said. 'Someone had a grudge against the *madame*. We left in such haste, she did not discover the child missing until we departed.'

With halting steps, she wandered to the bed and gazed down on the still-sleeping Sylvia. 'We hid here, barely making a living and with no means to contact the Duke during the war with England.'

She lifted her sad brown gaze to meet his. 'Until a year

ago. The noble pig sent his Irishman. He almost killed *madame* for letting the girl go to England.' Jeannie's glance shifted to Christopher. 'He promised to pay a fortune for the paper. The *madame* insisted he bring Sylvia back as part of the price. The hard-eyed Irish boggert found her and brought her back.' A smile of triumph curved her corrugated lips. 'But they don't have the paper. I stole it back, to buy my way to Scotland.'

Bitterness turned the smile to a wry grimace. 'Rafter'll kill Sylvie if he learns it's missing. The scandal, if it gets out, will ruin the Duke.' Her face crumpled. 'I'll have to give it to him. I'll no have the bairn killed.'

Bile churned in his gut. What sort of man would do this to his child? 'Who is this Duke?'

Jeannie shook her head and stared at Sylvia. 'The secret is the only thing keepin' her alive.'

Clearly, the old woman believed it, and it really didn't matter. 'You have to help me get her away from here.'

Jeannie shivered. '*Madame* will punish me if she found out I helped you.'

Christopher stifled his impatience. One cry from this woman and the game would be up. He gave her an encouraging smile. 'No one will know if we act quickly.'

Sylvia flung out an arm and Jeannie tenderly replaced the sheet. She put her knife on the table and prowled around the room.

Christopher judged the distance to the knife. It would be an easy thing to snatch it up and turn the tables on the old woman. But the noise might alert Madame Gilbert or, worse yet, the doorkeeper. He held himself ready in case Jeannie decided to betray him.

'Are ye not just like her father? Will ye throw her to the dogs when you tire of her?' Jeannie muttered.

Christopher winced. He had just about done that already. He'd been prepared to see her enslaved to some ghastly matron with a brood of spoiled children just to get rid of her. He squared his shoulders. 'I give you my word, I will care for her for the rest of her life. She will do nothing that is not of her own free will. I swear it on my honour.'

Jeannie stopped her restless walking and gazed into his eyes.

Sylvia moaned and Christopher glanced at her. Please God, she wasn't going to start that again.

'Her father broke his word of honour to Marguerite.' She stared hard at Christopher. 'I think you are different. You are like your uncle. If only Marguerite had loved him instead of being blinded by the glory of her precious Duke. The lying divil.' She drew in a deep breath. 'I will help you.'

Dare he trust her? Something told him he should. 'Help me finish dressing her.'

He rolled Sylvia on her stomach, trying to ignore the expanse of beautiful back above the lacy gown as the old maid worked. She tugged on the laces. 'How will ye get out of here? There is nae much time afore they come to tell ye your time is up.'

'The way I came in, I presume.'

The old woman straightened. She pulled something from her pocket with a smug smile. A small iron key. 'Then ye'll be needing this.' Quickly she unlocked the press to reveal Sylvia's clothes.

He rolled his eyes. 'Why didn't you say anything before?'

Jeannie shrugged.

'Never mind. Help me get her out of this costume and into her own gown.'

'There's no time. *Madame* will return soon. We must pull her gown over the top.'

The old woman was right. He held Sylvia up and the maid dropped the gown over her head. Between them they got her into her shoes and pulled her to her feet.

Jeannie shook Sylvia. 'Wake up, little one. You must leave here.'

Sylvia opened her eyes. She smiled and hugged the bent old shoulders. 'Jeannie. I never thought I would see you again.'

Christopher frowned at the thought of what might happen to Jeannie when they left. 'If I can get to my horse, you could come with us.'

Regret filled Jeannie's expression. 'I'll just keep ye back. And besides, you will have to fight Alphonse to leave here. They must not know I helped you.'

Alphonse, the dwarf doorman. Christopher knew the type, fists like iron and a head to match, a street fighter. His swordstick would be of no use in close quarters. He needed a pistol. He just hadn't thought to bring one.

He strode to the window. The room overlooked a weedy patch of garden at the back of the house. 'What lies below this room?'

Her brow wrinkled. 'The kitchen.'

'Who works there?'

'Only me.'

He pushed open the window and stuck his head out. Ivy grew around this window, just as it had at the front of the house. A thick stem clung to the wall just below the ledge. A nearby lead rainwater pipe went from the roof to the ground. Many a time he had followed Garth out of their bedroom window at their grandparents' country house on some mad adventure or other. Why not now? As long as Sylvia held on and provided the pipe and the ivy held both of their weights, it should be easy. 'We'll climb down.'

Jeannie pushed him aside and leaned out. 'Ye'll fall for sure.'

'No. I won't.' Hurriedly, aware of time passing, he stripped the sheets off the bed and knotted them together. He tied one end to the leg of the sturdy four-poster. 'We'll use this to slow our descent,' he said at Jeannie's questioning look.

Sylvia giggled. 'What are you two doing?'

He repressed the vision of two broken bodies at the mercy of Madame Gilbert and Alphonse. 'Jeannie, remake the bed when we are gone and close the window. It might keep them confused for a while.'

She nodded, then glanced at Sylvia leaning against the wall with a dreamy expression on her face. 'She canna climb down.'

'I have a solution to that.' Using Jeannie's discarded knife, he rent the pillowcase into strips.

Sylvia smiled mistily as he tied her wrists. He placed her arms around his neck and she leaned against him, nuzzling below his ear. Cold shivers of hot pleasure ripped through his body. He hardened.

Hell. She had no idea what she was doing. It meant nothing. He picked her up. She wrapped her legs around his hips. God, it felt so damn good.

He tossed his cane out of the window into a rosemary bush, then perched on the windowsill. Grasping the knotted sheet, he swung his legs out. Sylvia slipped from his waist and hung like a dead weight, apparently asleep. As long as she didn't fight him, he could hold her. He twisted the sheet around one arm, and leaned out. The muscles in his back screamed as he stretched across the distance. There. He had it. He scrabbled with his fingertips, then gripped the drainpipe. Using the ivy as a ladder, he clambered down.

As his feet touched *terra firma*, he let go a long breath. Swiftly, he lowered the sleeping Sylvia to the ground, behind a rosemary bush, then glanced up, seeking signs of pursuit. Instead, Jeannie stuck her grizzled head out of the window and beckoned him closer.

Blast. She should be closing the window and hiding the evidence.

Gesturing to her to hurry, he ran beneath the window.

'There's an abandoned farmhouse off the Calais road, if ye need a place to rest,' she whispered. 'About ten miles on.'

He waved his thanks.

She glanced over her shoulder. 'Wait a moment.'

Damn it. They did not have time for this.

She disappeared for an instant then returned with a bundle, which she dropped down to him. His driving coat and hat. He bowed his thanks and she pulled in the sheet and closed the casement.

He collected his sword and took a quick look at the sleeping Sylvia. Quiet for the moment, at least. He crept to the front of the house. His heart sank. While his horse was happily chomping on the weeds by the front door, Alphonse stood a few feet away on the portico, smoking a pipe, the pungent tabacco drifting on the breeze.

He cursed silently. There was no help for it, he would have to walk and he would have to carry Sylvia.

He ran back, and gathered her into his arms, and ran for the back gate. Rusty and half off its hinges, it creaked open at a nudge. With a quick glance at the house, he dashed across the lane and through a gap in the hedge. According to his reckoning, they were about twenty miles from the outskirts of Calais. The hue and cry would start the moment the *madame* realised her customer had not emerged satisfied and sated by her exquisite new girl. At most, he had an hour before they discovered him missing.

The rough terrain alongside the lane slowed his progress to a crawl. Sweat trickled down his back. Some thirty minutes later, he set Sylvia down on the ground and took stock of the distance he'd covered. A mile?

He glanced around. Too damned bad he hadn't been able to retrieve his horse. They would have been back to Calais and on the next packet to Dover long before dark. At this pace, so close to the lane, they risked imminent discovery. He had to cut across country.

Sylvia moaned as he picked her up.

Bloody hell. When she woke, he would have to contend with her needs again. *Don't think about it.* His body howled a protest.

Chapter Twelve

The rhythmic jolt of Sylvia's body matched the steady drumbeat in her ear. She inhaled the spicy scent of sandalwood and shaving soap and heated man. One particular man.

She opened her eyes. The world tilted, then righted.

Against a backdrop of grey sky, a firm stubble-lined jaw appeared inches from her gaze. A trickle of moisture coursed from his temple, over his cheek and down the strong column of his neck into his collar.

Christopher. A snaking desire to follow the trail of moisture with her tongue stilled her heart.

With a slight grunt deep in his chest, his strong arms flexed around her waist and beneath her knees, shifting her weight. Why was he carrying her?

An urge to press her lips against his warm skin flashed, torrid, through her body.

He stumbled and his grip tightened, squeezing the air from her lungs.

'Ouch,' she gasped and pushed at his shoulder.

'Damn it. Hold still.'

Gripping her, he sank to his knees and lowered her

on to the prickly grass. Brown flecked with green stared into her eyes.

'How do you feel?' His chest rose and fell in time to his harsh breathing.

Confused, Sylvia stared across an open field, trees in the distance a dark shadow against a horizon of black clouds edged with gold. The last thing she remembered was arriving in Calais. 'Where am I?'

'Still too close to Madame Gilbert's, I'm afraid.'

What did he mean? She tried to stand up. Her head spun and dry heaves wrenched her stomach. Bent double, she crouched on the grass, clutching at the rough stalks. She must have *mal de mer*.

'Are you all right?' he asked.

She would never be all right again.

A comforting pressure squeezed her shoulder. 'It's the drugs, I expect.'

Miserable and weak, she made no sense of his words, but the dizziness eased and she looked up into his concerned face. 'Drugs?'

'The *madame* drugged you.' His voice sounded strained.

What was he talking about? She glanced around. 'What are you doing here?' Where was here?

His stiffened. 'I might ask you the same question.'

Flashes of recollection tumbled through her mind. Rafter, Madame Gilbert. Oh God, she was going to throw up.

She retched, her empty stomach aching.

He held her hair back from her shoulders and patted her back. 'Relax. You'll feel better soon.'

A picture of Christopher, rippling muscles outlined in flickering candlelight, danced through her mind. 'What have I done?' she moaned.

'You haven't done anything.'

As the nausea subsided, she managed to sit up.

'Are you feeling better?' he asked and handed her a handkerchief.

She wiped her face and her eyes. 'Why are you here?'

His jaw tightened and he looked off into the distance. 'You left in rather a hurry. I followed you, to make sure you were all right. When I saw you with that man, I wasn't sure what to think.'

'I… Rafter. He forced me to go with him.'

He leaned forward and peeled a damp strand of hair from her forehead. 'I know.'

The fleeting touch of his fingers brought back other memories. Warm hands on her body, doing things, pleasurable, wonderful things. Shame swallowed her whole. She turned her face away, staring at the clods of earth and matted grass. 'How you must despise me.'

Fingers gripped her chin, warm and strong. He turned her face towards him. 'You have no reason to be ashamed. They drugged you. You could not help what happened.'

She remembered how she had clung to him. 'But you—'

He shook his head. 'I did not take advantage of you, Sylvia. Much as I wanted to. Jeannie saw to that.'

'Jeannie was there?'

He nodded.

In spite of what little she remembered of her wantonness, his hand touching her in intimate places and the terrible overpowering need followed by hot waves of pleasure, she believed him. He'd never once lied to her. 'I'm so ashamed.'

'You must not be. That wasn't you back there.'

Her heart tumbled over. She trusted him. A strange and wonderful feeling. 'Thank you,' she whispered.

The corners of his eyes crinkled as he smiled down at her. 'Do you think you can walk? We have a long way to go.'

She took stock of her body. Her stomach felt as hollow as a drum, her mouth dry and sour. 'I'm hungry and thirsty.'

With a gentle hand under her arm, he helped her to her feet. 'Water we can do something about quite soon, but food will have to wait.' He brushed the dirt from his knees.

She gave a shaky laugh. 'Water would be welcome.'

'There's a stream over there.' He pointed in the direction of a stand of trees, willows and larches and long grass. 'You can drink and rest, but not for long, I fear.'

Unable to do more than lean on his arm and force her feet to move, she followed his lead. A small stream meandered through the field and she knelt on the bank and scooped up the clear water in her hands. Cold and pure, it settled her stomach. Her head began to clear. She washed her face and hands, but with nothing to tie or pin her hair, she had to leave it loose.

When she had drunk her fill, he led her to the shade of a small larch. Grateful for the respite, she leaned against the rough bark. Small insects darted around her head and she batted them away. She felt safe with Christopher. Safe and secure.

He leaned his forearm against the tree above her head and scanned the horizon.

'Do you expect Madame Gilbert to leap out of the bushes?' she asked.

He threw her an irritated glance. 'No. But your Irishman might.'

A cold rock landed in her stomach, driving away the peace. 'He is not my Irishman.'

His lip curled. 'Maybe not. But he'd like to be.'

Nothing could be further from the truth, but who would believe a woman like her? Not true. She wasn't like those women. *Your mother was*, the little voice of doubt whispered, *so why not you?* She squeezed her eyes against the fear she'd carried for years.

'When did you eat last?' His breath grazed her ear and sent a delicious shimmer to the depths of her feminine core and ignited her blood. Her mind whirled away.

The drugs must still hold her in their lascivious grip. She fought her wicked desires.

'When?' he asked again.

'When what?' He spoke of food. She blinked to clear her thoughts. 'This morning. Early. I was to catch the first *diligence* to Paris.'

'We have hours to go before we reach Calais and an inn. Do you think you can last?'

He looked so handsome, so fierce, like a chivalrous knight determined to protect his lady. The kind of man she had dreamed of as a child, until she realised that no honourable man would ever want someone of her birth.

'How did you get here?' she asked.

'On horseback. The damned horse is nicely locked up in the *madame*'s stable by now.'

'How far to Calais?'

'Fifteen or more miles. Maybe less straight across country.'

Fifteen miles? Lethargy invaded her limbs and she slid down the tree to the leafy ground. 'I don't think I can walk that far.'

His jaw thrust forward and green fire blazed in his eyes. 'We have to move on, even if I have to carry you every step of the way. I'm damned if I am going to risk them catching up with us.'

The thought of Madame Gilbert spurred her on. She

stretched out her hands and he pulled her to her feet. 'Let us go.'

Clumps of coarse long grass ambushed her legs; pebbles stabbed the soles of her feet through her shoes, while ahead of her Christopher, in his serviceable riding boots, set a gruelling pace. Every now and then, she had to half-run not to fall behind. Sweat trickled down her back beneath a gown that seemed too tight. It constricted every breath she took.

Each time the memory of the darkened room flashed through her mind, a hot flush accompanied a horrible sinking sensation in her stomach.

Forget about it. He does not blame you.

Hours had passed since they'd first stopped to drink. Whenever they crossed a stream, they swallowed another mouthful or two of clear water.

They kept to the strip-farmed fields and, where possible, small stands of trees. They crossed lanes only when they were sure they were clear of other travellers. They avoided farms and other signs of habitation.

Night drew in. Sylvia's feet and thighs ached and burned. All her years of long walks on the Kentish downs had given her endurance, but she doubted her ability to continue much further. Hunger gnawed at her insides.

As if he had read her mind, Christopher ceased walking. 'We have to find somewhere to rest for the night. Even if there is a moon later, it might be difficult to find our way. If I am right, we should be close to the main road between Calais and Paris.'

Legs, leaden only moments ago, felt light and airy at the thought of food and a soft feather bed. 'Is there an inn nearby, do you think?'

He frowned. 'We dare not risk it and unfortunately I gave all of my gold for…'

The strange tone in his voice gave her pause, then the truth slapped her in the face. He'd spent his money to buy her.

Shame writhed in her stomach. She took a deep breath. What was done was over. 'We have to eat something.'

'Not until we reach Calais and I can pawn my watch.'

'Then what do you suggest we do now?'

'We will look for a barn, some sort of shelter, where we can spend the night.'

She stared into the dusk. 'A barn will mean a farmhouse.' Saliva filled her mouth. 'And hens, and eggs.'

Christopher shook his head. 'I told you, I don't have any money. And besides, I am hoping for something unoccupied.'

A growl rumbled in her stomach. There was more than one way to relieve a farmer of his produce, only Christopher Evernden wouldn't know about that. He had never starved in his life.

'Come on, then,' she said. 'Let's find this barn of yours.'

'I think I saw smoke up ahead,' he said, keeping pace at her side, a large comforting presence in the dusk.

Less than a mile later, lights flickered ahead of them. Its round oasthouse like a church spire, a stone farmhouse sat at the end of a dirt track. A wall enclosed the single-storey building and the barn.

'Devil take it,' Christopher murmured. 'The barn is too close to the farmhouse. We'll have to move on.'

Not when she could smell cooking. She picked up her skirts and began to run.

Christopher grabbed her arm. 'Where are you going?'

'To the farm. They will have food.'

'I told you, I don't have any money.'

She grinned. 'I hadn't planned to pay for it.'

A heavy silence greeted her words. His expression turned frosty.

She pushed her hair back from her face. 'Whether you come with me or not, I am going to get something to eat.' She tugged her arm from his hand and trotted towards the twinkling yellow lights. His heavy breathing and booted steps followed her.

A cockerel crowed and dogs barked as they neared the farmyard. Close up, the high stone walls made the farm look impregnable. A wooden gate gave access to the courtyard.

'You go to the front door and keep them talking, while I go around the back to the kitchen. Act like a stupid Englishman, speak dreadful French and ask for directions,' she whispered.

'I won't let you do this.' His voice cut through the night in a low rumble.

Carefully, she eased off her shoes with her toes. 'I cannot walk to Calais on an empty stomach.'

'I do not want to finish my days in a French prison.'

She grinned, snatched up her shoes and darted away. 'Then you had better hurry up and knock on the door or they'll catch me and I'll tell them you put me up to it.'

He groaned. 'You little witch.'

The stones and dirt, cold and rough under her feet, reminded her of her childhood. She'd often gone barefoot in the cobbled Paris streets, wandering the markets looking for scraps. Ordure had trickled along the kennels in the centre of the medieval alleys. They built to foul torrents whenever it rained. Soldiers and revolutionaries had loitered on every street corner on the look-out for aristos. She'd been full of bravado in those days, a skilful shadow, and she'd fed them all when business was bad, her and Mother and Jeannie. Anything, her mother had said, was better than Sylvia working on her back.

Dropping her shoes by the gate, she inhaled the scent of hay and manure and musty earth, wholesome country smells. Whatever she risked, she would never go back to that old sordid life.

The gate opened without protest. Squares of warm light from a ground-floor window revealed a well-swept dirt yard. No sign of the dog. Carefully feeling ahead with her bare toes before trusting her weight on her foot, she eased along the wall in the murky shadows. Her heart thundered in her ears. It was a long time since she'd felt such a nervous thrill. She reached the window and risked a peek through the open casement.

An apple-cheeked woman picked up a ladle from the heavy plank table running the length of the room. She bustled to the hearth and lifted the lid of a black cauldron suspended over the fire. A wonderful aroma floated out of the window. Rabbit stew. Sylvia swallowed her saliva.

The dog barked frantically. But at the front, not the back.

'Who is it?' the farmer's wife shouted above the yelps.

A sigh of relief escaped Sylvia. Christopher had followed her instructions.

A man shouted something from beyond the kitchen.

'I'm coming, I'm coming,' the woman called back and slammed the lid down on the hearth. 'Men,' she muttered. 'Can never do anything.' She stomped out of the kitchen.

Her breath held, Sylvia tiptoed to the back door and lifted the latch. It opened without a sound. She crept inside and left it ajar.

'*Oui, monsieur,*' the woman said in the distance. 'Yes. *À droite.* To the right.'

Christopher's deep voice said something indistinct.

'Non,' the woman shouted, as if at a deaf person. *'À droite*. That way.'

A ginger cat leaped from a chair seat and shot under the table.

Sylvia's heart jumped into her throat.

Steady. The front door seemed to be at the other end of the house. She had time. She picked up the cloth the woman had used to lift the cauldron lid. Glancing around, she noticed a door to the right. The pantry. She nipped in and laid the cloth on the flagstone floor. She rescued a round of cheese from a shelf and half-a-dozen rolls from a bin.

Her hard breaths rasped in the small, dark room. *Hurry*. She placed the cheese and the rolls on the cloth, lifted the four corners to the centre and tied them. She darted back into the kitchen.

'Calais, it is zat way.' The woman sounded angry.

No time. The stew smelled wonderful. Her stomach growled. Sylvia couldn't resist. She snatched up the ladle and scooped up a mouthful of bubbling stew, blowing hard. With one eye on the door, she sipped the delicious gravy. She hooked out a lump of meat with her forefinger and thumb.

'Oui, oui, monsieur, zat way.' The door banged shut and two grumbling voices headed her way. A big black dog raced into the kitchen, its nails rattling on the stones.

Sylvia shoved the meat in her mouth and dashed for the door. The cat hissed and spat, claws slashing her bare ankle.

'Sacré,' she mouthed.

Her stomach tight, she slipped through the open door and forced herself to close it without a sound.

The dog snarled and snuffled through the gap at the floor.

Wings on her bare heels, she flew across the courtyard and out of the gate. She grabbed her shoes and bolted.

A black shape rose up in front of her. She stifled a scream with her fist.

Christopher caught her by the shoulders. 'Watch out.'

'What in God's name are you doing down there?' she whispered, her heart pounding. 'Did you fall?'

'No,' he said. He took the bundle. 'Let's go before they miss this.' He sounded thoroughly peeved. 'You, madam, are a hussy.'

And that surprised him?

A carefree laugh bubbled in up her throat.

Sylvia sighed with satisfaction and leaned back on her elbows. 'I'm full.'

The abandoned barn stood alongside the crumbling ruins of a farmhouse, destroyed in the war, Christopher had thought. He hadn't been at all surprised to find it. They had climbed a shaky ladder with missing rungs to the loft and agreed it would make a good hideout.

Christopher discovered a leaky wooden bucket beneath a pile of old straw and lugged water from a nearby pond. They'd washed their hands and faces before sitting down to eat.

The remains of the bread and cheese lay on the gleaming white square of cloth. Poking pale shiny fingers through the opening high in the gable end and the chinks in the rotting roof, the moon served as their candle.

Christopher leaned over and flicked a straw out of her loose hair. 'I'm glad you are satisfied. Perhaps now we can get some sleep. But first I want to check to see exactly where we are.'

'Do you think we are in any danger of discovery?'

He rose to his feet, ducking his head beneath the great wooden beams. 'I certainly hope not. I'd like to have a better sense of what lies around us, though. We could have two lots of people after our blood now.'

He meant the farmer as well as Rafter. 'They had plenty of food. They won't miss it.'

'Perhaps not.' His voice echoed around the dark cavern of a barn. 'However, I don't care for stealing.'

No doubt he thought she did. Well, what else could she expect? 'I will send them money when we get back to England.'

He strode to the ladder. 'I left them a note saying as much.'

So that was what he had been doing on his knees by the gate. She tossed him a grin. 'The Right Honourable Christopher Evernden promises to pay for five rolls and a round of cheese.' She didn't mention the mouthful of stew.

'Something like that.'

She lay back in the scratchy straw and stared at a star between the roof planks. 'Then everything is right with the world.'

He chuckled. 'You are overly optimistic.'

A feeling of well-being washed through her. She had felt safe the moment she had opened her eyes and saw Christopher in the field beyond Madame Gilbert's house of ill repute. Her heart swelled. She would trust him with her life. And as long as he never knew how she felt, where was the harm? 'Why should I not? We have tricked the *madame*, we have food in our belly, and tomorrow we will be in Calais.' She closed her eyes and stretched her arms above her head.

At his sharp breath she looked up.

'I'll be back in a while.' His voice sounded gruff.

She sat up as the top of his head disappeared below the edge of the loft. Now what maggot did the stuffy Englishman have in his head? Still angry with her for stealing no doubt.

She was what she was.

With the thought came a new sense of freedom.

No one expected her to be perfect, or good or respectable. She had imposed those strictures on herself and look where it had got her. Right back where she had started. There was no use in pretending anything any longer.

No sense at all.

And another thing, she was tired of not being able to breathe properly. Whatever the garment was under her gown, it had to go. She struggled out of her gown, then worked at the laces down her back. Short and slippery, the strange shift barely covered anything. She managed to free the laces from the first few hooks, then her fingers encountered a knot.

Blast. She would have to wait for Christopher to untie it for her. She glanced around the loft. The floor was scattered with the remains of old hay and straw, but if she gathered them together, they might provide more comfort than hard bare boards. She set to work pushing the straw into a heap against the wall. Dust flew up around her. She sneezed.

Persevering, she soon had a rough sort of bed. Now, if she covered it with his driving coat...

'What in thunder are you doing?'

She swung around. 'Christopher.'

'For goodness' sake, be quiet. We are not three feet from the road. You could spit on it from here. I saw lights and the sounds of a carriage passing. With you crashing around like a maddened cow, I'm surprised they didn't come to see what was amiss.'

'I certainly wasn't crashing around. I was trying to make a bed.'

He stared at the heap of straw in the corner, then gazed back at her. 'Why aren't you wearing your gown?'

'Because,' she said as if he were a simpleton, 'this thing is so tight I can't breathe. And why am I wearing it anyway?'

He swallowed audibly. 'There was nothing else in that room for you to wear. Jeannie found your clothes by the time I had already dressed you.'

'You dressed me?'

'Yes.'

Flickers of memory came back to her. Him bending over her. Delicious sensations ripping through her body in an endless tide of pleasure. Distant pleasure, unreal, unfocused, part of her, yet far away.

And through it all, he'd remained honourable.

Her heart turned a somersault. She smiled and turned her shoulder. 'It seems to be knotted. Do you think you can release it?'

'If you wish.'

'I do.'

He stepped over the top of the ladder, bending to avoid the low beams.

Warm fingers brushed her skin. Tingles skittered across her back. Her insides tightened like an overtuned violin, reminding her of the delicious feelings he'd created in the dark bedroom at Madame Gilbert's. The desire she'd been ignoring for days unfurled deep in her body, wicked and urgent.

She bit her bottom lip, hard. Anything to take her mind off the sensation of his hands on her flesh.

After a few moments of fumbling, he cursed. 'Give me a moment.' He picked up his cane and pulled out a sliver of flashing blade.

Seconds later, the strings lay at her feet and she clutched the scrap of fabric against her chest.

'I'll leave you to change,' he muttered and stomped off down the ladder.

Always the English gentleman, just like his uncle. And she owed him more than she could ever repay in a lifetime. Freedom from Madame Gilbert.

She let the gown fall to her feet.

His head popped back up, his face all shadows and moonlit angles. 'Damn,' he said and dropped out of sight as she stared open-mouthed.

'I'm sorry,' he called out, his voice hoarse. 'I came back to ask you to let me know when you are ready.'

He wanted her.

It had only been a moment, captured in moonbeams, but the hunger burning in his eyes had been unmistakable.

Her heart soared. The only thing she had to offer in repayment for her rescue, she'd gladly give.

Chapter Thirteen

'Sylvia. Miss Boisette?' His whisper echoed around the barn.

Her heart tumbled over. 'Yes.'

'Are you ready?'

She shivered. 'Yes.'

With her back turned to the ladder and one edge of his driving coat tucked close around her, she held her breath and listened to his steps. The rustle of cloth, a faint huff and a thump drew pictures in her mind as he removed his coat and boots. Pictures of Greek statues.

The driving coat beneath her pulled tight as he lay down beside her.

She turned over and touched his arm. 'Christopher?'

'Go to sleep.'

How did one do this? The only man she had ever talked to in any meaningful way was his uncle. 'I'm cold.'

He sighed, a long exhausted exhale of breath, and sat up. His shirt gleamed white and a heavy weight landed on her shoulders. 'Here, have my coat.'

So much for seduction. Perhaps she'd imagined what she saw in his eyes and he didn't want her at all. Some time during the long day, her cold wall of pride had melted. Without its protection, pain pierced her heart. A prickling sensation burned the backs of her eyes. She muffled a sniff.

His body tensed. 'What is the matter?'

'You don't want to make love to me because you despise me. That's it, isn't it?'

He groaned. 'Sylvia, don't do this. Not again.'

'Again?'

'It is the drug they gave you.' His voice thickened. 'It makes you wanton and I won't take advantage of you in this condition.'

Joy filled every corner of her mind, like beautiful music, dispelling her fears. Christopher would never deliberately harm her. She ran her hand across his cheek, along a jaw rough with a day's growth of beard, dragged her hand over his warm lips.

He captured her hand and pushed it away. 'Stop.' He rose to his knees. 'I'll sleep below.'

'Christopher, this has nothing to do with the drugs.' She flung back the driving coat, baring herself to his gaze. 'It is you who makes me this way.'

In utter silence, he gazed down on her. Not a breath.

'Hell fire,' he whispered and swept her up in his arms. The earthy, hay-scented smell of him filled her nose, his strong, encircling arms crushed her against his hard body. His lips, warm and moist, brushed against hers, a note of deep yearning rumbled up from his chest and she melted against him.

He raised his head and nuzzled her neck. 'I have never seen a woman as beautiful or as courageous as you,' he murmured into her hair.

Her hands ached to touch him. She ran her fingers through his hair, across his back, down his shoulders.

She had never touched a man like this. He was granite heated by the sun, solid, stable; her fingertips wanted to explore every inch of him.

He drew her close and recaptured her lips. His kiss was soft and warm and gentle. She opened to his questing tongue, revelling in the hard wall of him pressed to her breasts.

He sat up. She almost cried out in disappointment until she saw him pull his shirt over his head. Within moments he had discarded his breeches and was as naked as she, his long body hard and warm. He fondled her breasts with a roughened palm. 'Beautiful,' he whispered.

He kissed her again and she pressed into him.

He nudged his knee between hers and she stiffened, suddenly afraid, harsh memories intruding. 'Will it hurt?'

'Then you haven't…?'

She turned her face away. Of course he'd thought the worst.

He touched her shoulder. 'I'm sorry. I thought—'

'The customers grabbed at me. One of them caught me on the stairs, up against the wall, he squeezed me so hard, I had bruises everywhere. He almost…' She gulped in a breath. 'I kicked him between the legs. That's what Mother told me to do. But I knew what went on, what they did, and how the women hated it.'

'Sylvia, what they did was not making love.' Raw pain filled his voice and he enfolded her in a gentle embrace. 'And that man, to try to attack a child… Ah, sweet, to betray the trust…to harm such delicate beauty… The foul cur.'

'I have feared men ever since.'

'My sweet Sylvia, I promise it will not hurt more than you can bear.' He breathed warm air against her throat. 'Trust me.'

'I do.' Her voice caught. 'I can't quite believe it, but I do.'

He ran his hands down her back, over her ribs. Touching, feeling, teasing his fingers, leaving heat and chills in their wake. Fire and ice. His reverential exploration tortured her quivering skin. He grazed his thumb across her nipple and tweaked the sensitive bud until she cried out with wanting. His hand roamed across her stomach and his fingers played with the curls between her thighs.

Pleasure tightened to breaking point. Yet still he touched her gently with hands and mouth and tongue until she thought she would die if he did not take her to some far-off peak. She whimpered, a soft noise in the back of her throat.

A deep groan rumbled in his chest and sent the world spinning around her as she sensed the depths of his desire. Her hands found his slim hips, and the hard muscles of his round firm buttocks. She dug her fingers into him, wanting, needing him closer. His heart beat strong and loud in time to her own.

He lifted himself and hung above her. He pressed his knee between her thighs and she opened to him. He lay between her legs, his hard member pressed hot against her inner thigh.

He slid one finger inside her. Intrusive, yet wave after wave of sensuous pleasure rippled through her.

He stared into her face, concern rampant in his moonlit expression.

'Tell me, Sylvia,' he said, his voice harsh with need. 'Tell me you want me. Now. Like this.'

She wanted him so much, she would die if she waited any longer. 'Yes. Now.'

He sighed, a rush of warm breath in her ear. Her body shivered in anticipation.

He eased forward, pressing against her, sliding into her, a small pause, one swift thrust, a small stab of pain and he filled her, hard, hot and delicious.

'All right?' he whispered in her ear.

'Yes,' she managed on a sigh, and she heard his sigh of relief.

'Hold on, darling.' His back muscles bunched and flexed beneath her hands as he drove forward yet again.

He filled her.

Her body stretched, adjusted to his heat and size. A thrill tightened every nerve as he moved inside her, with her. Heat suffused her. His strokes were slow and sensuous. Each fraction of movement driving her need to a higher notch of unfulfilled desire.

'You like this, my darling?' he asked in tender concern.

'Oh, yes.'

He thrust harder, deeper, his intensity a promise of fulfilment.

She lifted her hips to meet him. 'Yes.'

All she was resided in their joining of the place where his flesh became at one with hers. She was him, his pleasure mingled with hers, his flesh throbbing within her. Yet she wanted something just out of reach.

She lifted her legs high around his waist and raised her hips to meet his powerful thrust, to receive him deep inside her.

'Sylvia,' he moaned. 'You're making me come.'

He held still for a moment, trembling with effort, the muscles in his muscular back and arms taut and slick with sweat. She arched her back, encouraging him.

He reached between their bodies and circled his thumb on her nub of pleasure. 'Now, Sylvia. Come to me, now,' he said, commanding and desperate all at once, pleasure and sweet pain in his voice.

Delicious waves rolled through her, peaking with crests of excitement. She crashed through the barrier that held her earthbound and soared with him.

She felt him shudder and pull away. Gasping, he spilled his seed on her stomach. Moments later, he rolled on his side and pulled her close.

She floated to earth. Heat radiated out from her core, leaving her limp, sated and strangely triumphant, as if she had achieved some great feat. She was delightfully weary.

'Ah, sweeting, you amaze me,' he murmured and kissed her eyelids, her lips, her throat.

Somehow she managed to drape her arms around his neck and kiss his shoulder, inhaling his scent as if she could somehow keep something of him inside her.

'A moment,' he said and leaned over to wipe her stomach with the edge of his coat. When he lay back, she snuggled into his welcoming arm, her cheek against his thundering chest.

She would remember this for the rest of her life. She would always have this memory of him, of them, no matter what came to pass. She nuzzled his damp flesh. 'Thank you.'

He squeezed her tight, then pulled his driving coat over the pair of them.

A smile tugged at her lips; always considerate. She drifted on a soft cloud of contented tiredness.

A sound, furtive and out of place, brought Christopher alert, the scent of woman and old straw pleasant in his nostrils.

He lay still, breath held, listening. It came again.

Muffled footsteps. An animal chomping. The ring of a bridle and bit, indicating at least one horse.

Someone had arrived below while they slept. He cursed softly. He should have kept guard, not slept the night away in dreamless bliss.

Sylvia stirred in the crook of his elbow, but did not wake. Her hair, guinea bright in a shaft of sunlight piercing the ancient roof, lay in wild disarray across his naked chest. Visible beneath the dirty straw, the silver head of his swordstick lay just out of reach. He eased his arm out from beneath her head.

Careful to make no sound, he pushed to his feet, picked up his swordstick, releasing the blade, and tiptoed to the window. The road twisted away from the barn, empty in both directions. Whoever lurked below, they had apparently not brought reinforcements.

He stared at his pile of clothes. Idiot. At least he could have put his shirt on before falling asleep. Hopefully it was a local farmer stopping to rest his horse, and not Alphonse or the Irishman who had discovered their refuge.

He crept towards the opening where the ladder poked through. At any moment, someone might stick a head up through the floor. Christopher wanted to be ready.

Sleepy and warm, Sylvia couldn't believe her eyes. Christopher, standing as still as a statue, staring down into the barn. Strong, well-formed calves and thighs sprinkled with dark, crisp hair, a heavier thatch circling his male member and running in a line up his ridged stomach. The early morning light cast the muscles of his chest and arms into sculpted bronze. Glorious in his nakedness, he was quite the most beautiful thing she had ever seen. Tingles tightened her breasts and she lifted her gaze to his intent expression. She smiled.

He must have sensed her gaze, because he glanced

at her, frowned and shook his head, then pointed down the hole.

Someone was down there? Dread filled her heart. They had found them after all. It was all her fault. If she had not stopped to rob the farm, they would never have spent the night here. They would have kept on going to Calais.

She got to her knees, grabbed up her gown and slipped it silently over her head. She rose to her feet, staring at Christopher, waiting for a signal, some sign of what to do next.

He pressed his fingers to his lips and lowered himself to lie flat on the floor.

Her mouth dried. Never had she seen a man laid out naked like a banquet. Her gaze lingered on round firm buttocks and lean flanks, drifted up his narrow waist to his broad shoulders. Beneath his dark coats and quiet demeanour, Christopher was one very beautiful male. And she wanted to taste him. All over.

Had she run mad? This was definitely the wrong time to discover her salacious side.

She drew in a deep steady breath and crept across the floor to lie down at his side, peering into the darkness below, the only patch of light directly below the open hatch to their loft.

She opened her mouth. He shook his head.

Then she heard the snorting, chewing sounds of an animal that must have attracted his attention. An animal enjoying breakfast? The thought made her stomach rumble. It might just be a cow who had wandered in and found the old hay. Another sound. Shuffling footsteps.

'Ach. I was sure I'd find them here, wee horsy,' a voice muttered.

Sylvia giggled and rose to her feet.

Christopher jumped up and slammed his hand over her mouth.

She tore his fingers lose. 'It's Jeannie,' she breathed in his ear. She rose to her feet and prepared to go down the ladder.

He grabbed her forearm. 'Let me go first,' he whispered. 'She may not be alone.'

She swallowed a laugh and gazed pointedly down his length.

He coloured and headed for his clothes. With his back to her, he slipped his breeches over his muscled thighs and hid his gorgeous rump from her view. The muscles in his arms and shoulders rippled as he reached down for his shirt.

She narrowed her eyes. If there was someone else down there, they had come for her, not him. She could not let him be harmed.

Sucking in a breath, she grasped the top of the ladder, and placed one foot on the ladder.

'Sylvia.' Christopher's frantic whisper echoed off the ancient beams.

She frowned and put a finger to her lips. 'Wait here,' she mouthed and climbed down.

'Oh, thank God,' Jeannie said, twisting her neck to look up at her. 'Rafter is expected at the whorehouse at any moment. There will be hell to pay when they see the horses are missing.'

Sylvia closed her eyes in thanks. Jeannie would come with them. And Sylvia would care for her, as she had been unable to care for her mother. The thought eased a little of the hollow place in her heart. 'Christopher, she's alone,' she called up. She turned to Jeannie. 'How ever did you find us?'

'I mentioned this place to yon gentleman of yourn.

I hoped to find ye here. Alphonse scoured the land around the house last night when they discovered ye were gone, but *madame* would not send him further afield until the Irishman came.'

Sword in hand, Christopher scrambled down the ladder. He glared at Jeannie. 'Did you tell them where to find us?'

Jeannie drew herself to her full height and stared at his waistcoat. 'Of course I didna'. I told them I thought you would continue on to Paris, to your friend. The *madame* is going to kill me when she finds out what I did.'

Christopher wasn't looking at her, he was looking behind her at the horses at the manger. 'My God. You brought both horses.'

Jeannie's face broke into a grin. 'That, too. Alphonse isna' going to be happy. It will sure slow him down.'

Christopher slid his blade back into its sheath. 'Well done, Jeannie. Come on, then, we best make haste for Calais.'

'Aye,' Jeannie said. 'We'll need to hurry. Yon Irishman is due back at the house this morn, and he's nae gonna be pleased, I think. An' he'll soon realise ye didna' take the Paris road. Now there's a man I dinna want to face when he's fashed.'

The thought of an angry Rafter sent a shudder down Sylvia's spine.

Jeannie's fingers dug into Sylvia's waist as Alphonse's ancient nag ambled along the road. Christopher dropped back to her side. 'Can you go any faster?'

Sylvia glanced over her shoulder at Jeannie's terrified face. 'No. We are doing our best.'

'We will miss the last packet to Dover if we don't hurry. I don't want to be in Calais when Rafter arrives.'

Nor did she, but they'd been forced to take a circuitous route to the coast, not daring to risk the main highway. How long would it be before Rafter realised he'd been sent on a wild goose chase? Probably not long enough.

'Leave me, Miss Sylvia,' Jeannie croaked.

Sylvia shook her head. She had lost too many people in her life. She would lose Christopher when they returned to England, but she would not lose Jeannie.

Hours later, they clattered into the town, their horses' hooves echoing off the silent, cobbled streets. She recognised the inn she'd slept in a few days ago. They were almost safe.

A stable-boy dawdled from somewhere at the back to retrieve their horses. Christopher's weariness showed in his slumped shoulders as he dismounted, but his hands were strong and firm around her waist when he lifted her down, before he assisted Jeannie out of the saddle.

Poor Jeannie looked as if she had been out in a violent storm. Thin strands of grey hair hung around her face and she'd lost her cap. Sylvia put a hand to her own stringy hair. She probably looked worse after her romp in the hay.

In low tones, Christopher arranged for the stabling of the horses. Though his posture indicated confidence, Sylvia saw the concern in his eyes as he spoke to the groom.

He strode back to her and Jeannie at the stable door. 'We've missed the last boat tonight. I'm going to see if I can find a local fisherman to take us across. If you ladies wouldn't mind waiting in the parlour, I will return as soon as may be.'

Sylvia caught his arm. 'Is it safe to stay here? What if Rafter should come?'

Christopher frowned. 'I'll rent a private room for

you and Jeannie. Stay in it and stay out of sight. That's all I can do.'

He put a hand to his pocket. 'Blast. I haven't a penny to my name.'

'Perhaps we should take shelter in the barn?' She sent him a saucy smile.

'God, no. My credit is good enough and, if not, there's always my watch.' He caught her look and grinned. 'Hussy. Wait here while I make the arrangements.'

He strode into the inn.

Sylvia rubbed her chilled hands together. 'We won't be long now, Jeannie.'

The hunted expression in Jeannie's eyes cut her to the quick and she gave the old woman a hug. 'Hold on. Everything will be well, I promise.'

A moment or two later Christopher returned with a thin little innkeeper trotting behind.

'This way, ladies,' the skinny man said with a bow low enough for the Queen, despite their dishevelled appearance. Clearly, Christopher had paved the way well. Sylvia inclined her head, hooked Jeannie's arm in her own and followed the innkeeper.

The private parlour at the back of the inn welcomed them with a warm fire and bright candles.

'What can I get for you, *mesdames*?' the innkeeper asked.

Jeannie and Sylvia looked at each other. 'A nice cup of tea,' they chorused and laughed.

'Ah, *les anglaises et le thé*,' he murmured and bowed himself out.

When Christopher entered the empty taproom, his hopes of finding a ship's captain plummeted.

'No fishermen tonight?' he asked the boy behind the bar washing glasses.

'It is late, *monsieur*,' the pot-boy said. 'All the local men are all down at the waterfront where the women are.' He winked lewdly. 'We cater to a different clientele and they left on this afternoon's packet. You are the only guests tonight.'

'If I needed to find a man with a boat, where would I go?'

'At the Sign of the Mermaid most likely, *monsieur*. Can I get you something to drink?'

The days were such a blur, he couldn't remember the last time he'd had a tankard of ale. He swallowed the dust in his throat. He didn't have time. He had to get the women to safety before Rafter came up with them. 'No, thank you. Just give me directions to the Mermaid.'

The pot-boy did so and, intent on getting there before everyone was too drunk to sail, he hurried to the door. A pair of broad shoulders clad in black blocked his path.

'Kit. Finally I run you to earth.'

Christopher reeled back. 'Garth. Bloody hell. What the devil are you doing here?'

Garth's dark eyebrow flicked up. 'Nice greeting, I must say. I'm looking for you, of course. I thought I'd better make sure you were all right.' He frowned. 'Except when I got here, it was as if you had disappeared into thin air.' His usual devil-may-care expression turned grave. 'You are all right, aren't you? You look a bit pale.'

For Garth to notice that kind of detail meant he looked a perfect scarecrow. 'I'm passable.'

Garth stared at him. 'You've been involved in some sort of scrape without me to get you out of trouble. Devil a bit.'

Christopher gave a shout of laughter. 'Doing it a bit too brown, brother. It's usually the other way around.

I'll tell you all about it later. Right now, I have to get Sylvia and her maid back to England.' A thought occurred to him. 'You didn't by any chance sail over in the *Witch* did you?'

Garth grinned. 'I did. Thought you might need her and knew you'd never think of taking her yourself.'

Christopher stiffened. 'Why would I? She belongs to you now.'

Garth clapped him on the shoulder. 'You know how I feel about that. We always shared her when Father was alive. You're just too damned stiff-necked to accept anything from me.'

Christopher raised a hand. It was an old argument and the wrong occasion. 'The thing is, she's here. Can we get off tonight?'

'I'll have to ask Porter.'

'If anyone can do it, he can,' Christopher said.

'Right,' Garth replied with a nod and a big grin. 'Let's ask him.'

Chapter Fourteen

Luxurious indeed. Glowing from her sponge bath, Sylvia wandered around the *Sea Witch*'s well-appointed stateroom. So well appointed she'd found a nightgown to fit her in the sea chest, and, best of all, a sailor had brought jugs of hot water for bathing. Over Jeannie's protests that she ought to help, Sylvia had sent the poor old woman to bed. This luxury she needed no help to enjoy.

Absent-mindedly, she pulled a comb through her wet hair as she investigated the room. The polished mahogany fittings with brass hinges and handles gleamed in the swinging lamplight. An ivory-backed hairbrush rested in a cunning rack on the dressing table fixed to the wall. She picked it up and turned it over. Everything had a place and everything was small and neat, like a doll's house. Except the bed.

The blatant, opulent monstrosity had a midnight-blue canopy and pale blue satin sheets embroidered in gold with the Stanford crest. 'I'll join you in a while,' Christopher had said before he left her to bathe. Expectation blazed in his eyes and her heart had quickened.

After she had bedded him willingly, he assumed she

was his. Sadly, she was. Her body was his, but had she given him her heart? She wasn't sure. But she would not become his plaything, to be discarded at will. The thought of waiting for that dreadful day tore a hole in her chest. Better to get it over with before she became too attached.

She set the hairbrush back in its place and continued her roaming. This was Lord Stanford's room, she guessed. Or rather the room where he entertained his ladies. Fleetingly, she wondered where he would sleep tonight.

A cosy armchair behind the door looked inviting. Tucking her bare feet up under the hem of her gown, she curled up in it. She glanced at the bed again. Whatever would she would say to Christopher when he returned?

Anticipation simmered in her blood like water over hot coals. She wanted him. Just once more, she promised herself. Back in England, back to reality, she would insist they go their separate ways. Tonight would be their last together.

She turned her head at the sound of the opening door and smiled as Christopher entered. He had also bathed and was wearing a short blue-silk dressing gown. His or Lord Stanford's. Not that it mattered. His attention focused on the bed and she caught his disappointed expression in the dressing-table mirror when he saw it was vacant.

She laughed and opened her arms to him. 'I was waiting for you.'

In three short strides, he reached her and knelt at her side. 'You look beautiful,' he whispered. For a moment his large, warm hands cupped her cheeks and he brushed his lips against her mouth, a seductive invitation. She parted her lips.

'Ah, not yet,' he murmured against her mouth, his

breath moist against her skin. 'This time we use the bed.' He picked up a strand of her hair and ran it across his palm. 'I love your hair down. Like spun gold, yet soft as silk.'

She ran her fingertips across his jaw. 'You shaved.'

'Mmm. Garth lent me his gear.'

'You talked to your brother about us?'

'A little.'

'And?'

'Garth doesn't judge.'

Sylvia's gaze wandered to the bed. Of course Garth didn't judge.

'Come, sweet.' Christopher's soft tone turned husky. She'd never heard him sound so intense. He caught her up in his arms.

Spicy cologne filled her nostrils. 'Mmm,' she hummed against his neck. His indrawn hiss of breath in response set up a drumming in her pulse.

Without effort, he carried her to their own blue ocean of desire. Triumph gushed through her. For this brief moment he belonged to her.

Later, as she lay in his arms, sated, languid and content, she clung to the sense of belonging. If they could only stay here, rocked by the gentle motion of the waves, like innocent babes.

Her fingers traced the sculpted muscles of his arms and chest, circling its flat nipples and raking through the smattering of light brown curls.

'Mmm,' he murmured and she smiled and gave his shoulder a gentle nip.

She wanted to remember for ever the way he looked and tasted and felt beneath her hands. She placed her palm against the strong firm line of his jaw.

He turned his head and kissed the inside of her wrist.

From beneath his lashes, he glanced down at her, emerald fire in forest green. He smiled. Open, frank and youthful. The rare smile he seemed to save exclusively for her and for Garth, his brother.

He petted her hair where it lay over her breast. 'Pretty.'

'Why did you come chasing after me?' she asked. 'I assumed you would be happy to see me gone.' Her breath seemed to catch in her throat as she waited for the answer.

He looked puzzled. 'It was my duty. My uncle charged me with the responsibility of making sure you were settled.'

The reply didn't surprise her, but it sounded cold, unfeeling, and a chill ran over her skin as if a stray gust of sea breeze had found its way into their cosy nest.

She let go a little sigh, desperately trying not to mind. She could not expect him to feel as she did. While her parentage might be as noble as his, her bastardy put her beyond the pale.

His large warm hand closed around hers and she realised she had clutched at her locket. She glanced up and found him watching her.

'What did I say?' he asked.

'Nothing. I was thinking how lucky I was that it was you who…' Her face grew hot. Yet the time for blushes had long passed. She was a woman in truth. A well-bedded one. She chuckled. 'That it was you who came first to Madame Gilbert's. I just wish I remembered more about what happened.'

His shaft hardened against her thigh. Her own centre pulsed in reply. Interesting. Thoughts and words seemed just as sensual as touches. Something she had not learned as a child.

'I would sooner forget,' he growled.

She gasped. Hot prickles stabbed at the back of her nose and eyes; she sniffed to clear them away.

He tipped her chin with his clenched fist. 'Tears, Sylvia?'

'No, of course not.'

'Well, you might not remember all that happened, but it was torture for me. There you were, one of creation's most beautiful creatures, laid out like a dream, and you had no inkling of who was in the room.'

Others had said she was beautiful. She'd heard it all her life, with admiration or with envy, but never had it touched a chord in her heart as it did now. She wanted to throw her arms around him, bury her face in his neck, to ask him to keep her close for ever.

She couldn't. She didn't have the right to ask him to ruin his life, to bring his mother's wrath down on his head, to be excluded from his world.

'Why didn't you also take your pleasure?' She knew different words for the act of copulation, crude, disgusting words used by the whores. But what she and Christopher had done together was so much more. Blissful.

'I could have been anyone,' he said. 'Even though you said my name. How could I take advantage of a woman suffering under the influence of drugs?'

'Some men would have,' she murmured.

'They might,' he replied. His voice sounded harsh, as if just thinking about it made him angry.

'Then why not, when it was you I wanted?'

He drew in a deep breath and rolled on his side to face her, one heavy thigh splayed across hers. He picked up a lock of her hair and stroked the ends around the swell of her breast.

Suddenly she couldn't breathe. A thrum started low in her belly. A tickle between her thighs made her squirm.

'You are very responsive,' he murmured, leaning over to lick the tightly furled bud at the peak, before swirling the lock of hair around the other breast.

She swallowed. 'Why not, Christopher? I want to know.'

'Single-minded female.'

She bashed his shoulder with her fist. Not hard. Enough so he would know she meant business.

He sighed. 'Because it would have been wrong.' He bent his head and kissed the tip of her nose. 'To be honest, I almost succumbed. You were so ready, you did not give me time to get inside you before you came. But I was glad. I never would have forgiven myself for taking advantage of someone who could not say no.'

She traced his mouth with a fingertip, loving the fullness at the bottom and the fine sculpted upper lip. He caught her finger between his teeth, nibbled it, then sucked it into his hot mouth.

Desire jolted deep in her core. She rocked her hip against his thigh, felt the sweet promise of pleasure. 'Are you always so dutiful, so noble?'

He grimaced and let her finger go. 'You make it sound like a fault.'

'Oh, no. Pardon me if I seemed rude. I am surprised, that is all, and pleased, naturally. Most men, men like your brother, Garth, for instance, never give a thought to what is right or good for a woman. I must thank you for that. After my experience as a child, I very much feared that I could never let a man get close, let alone touch me. I am grateful.'

He stared at her. 'How do you do that?'

'I'm sorry, I do not understand what you mean?'

'You unman me. These things you say, they choke me up inside.'

'Is that bad?'

'Yes. Just accept the fact that any man with honour would not have taken advantage of your situation.'

'But, Christopher, you don't understand. Because it was you, I would not have minded had you taken your ease.'

He rolled on his back. 'Women,' he muttered. 'There's no understanding them at all. If you were to tie my hands and take me whether I wished it or no, do you think I would like it?'

She gazed at his erection, proud and stiff, then peeped at his frowning face, with a hesitant smile. 'I am not so sure you would not.'

'Sylvia, this is serious. Honourable men do not do that sort of thing.'

'I am sorry if I insulted your honour,' she whispered. 'It is just that I have never met anyone like you before.'

'There,' he said, his voice husky, 'you are doing it again.'

Perhaps he was right. That only if they were equal partners would the loving be right. Yearning for the contact he'd broken, her hand wandered his magnificent body. As it slid down the flat plane of his stomach, she encountered his turgid hardness. He sucked in a short breath. His stomach ridged with hard muscle. She stilled. 'Oh.'

'Don't stop,' he said. There was agony in his tone.

With a tentative fingertip, she touched him. He took her hand in his. 'Like this,' he said, moving her grasping fingers in swift hard strokes. She glanced at his face and saw abandonment to pleasure.

She'd learned some things from listening to the *filles de joie* growing up. Perhaps now would be her only chance to try them. 'How about this?' She squeezed him and his breath hissed between clenched teeth.

'Oh, yes.'

She bent her head and kissed the tip and found it silken and smooth, then raised her head to gauge his reaction.

'Sweetheart, don't stop now,' he begged.

She opened her mouth and took all of him in. Hard, hot, male musk and salt on her tongue. He filled her mouth. She cupped him in her other hand. So soft.

'Gently, girl,' he groaned. 'God, yes. That's it.'

She licked his smooth hardness, turning her head to savour the length of him with her tongue. He grew thicker in her mouth. It was an instrument of pleasure. Her pleasure. It was now her joy to pleasure him, however he desired. She tightened her grip around his rigid length.

He groaned, and threw his head back, eyes squeezed shut in the agony of ecstasy. He looked so beautiful she wanted to cry. He raised his head and caught her smiling at him. He grasped her shoulders and rolled her on to her back.

'I have to be inside you,' he said. He hung above her, his gaze fixed on hers. 'This is what you want, isn't it? Me inside you.' The fierceness of his tone frightened her for a moment. Then she saw his need to please her.

'Yes, Christopher. I want you. Just you and no one else. Not ever.'

'My girl. My lovely Sylvia.'

He pressed his hard male member against her opening. His eyes never leaving her face, he drove his hips forward. Pleasure rippled through her in growing waves and his pleased expression told her he delighted in her arousal.

With each slow stroke in, she lifted her hips to meet him. The feel of his groin hard against her was sweet grinding torture after sliding pleasure. She lifted her legs around his waist and he probed deeper yet. He filled her, tightening the knot of need, stretching her nerves to breaking point. And yet she did not break. She soared and flew on a gale of pleasurable sensation.

She cried out. Begged for the final flight to the stars.

'Yes, sweet. Soon,' he gasped. 'Hold on to me, stay with me, darling.'

He lowered his head to her breasts and laved each one with gentle strokes of his tongue that sent her mindless. Then he suckled. The cords that held her together were so tight, so fine, they thrummed in wild vibration. She shuddered.

His rhythm changed, harder, swifter, deeper. She could barely breathe, but still she matched him stroke for stroke.

The strands unravelled. Nerve endings shattered in a thousand points of light. She called his name. Somewhere inside her, she heard Christopher's groan of male triumph and her body surrendered to a river of hot bliss melting her bones.

She lay beneath him, smelling him, salt and sweat and musky man, feeling him stroke her hair, kiss her breasts, her lips, and listening to his soft murmured praise until she fell asleep. He was hers.

'Wake up, sleepy head.' Christopher's warm breath in her ear sent a shivery thrill to her core.

Stretching, full of contentment, she opened her eyes and smiled at a fully clothed Christopher.

A grin of pride beamed from Christopher's beloved, stubble-hazed face. 'We're here.'

'Here?'

'Dover.'

The word had the ring of a death knell, the ending to their interlude.

He took her hand and pressed it to his warm lips. He turned it over and, starting with her palm, trailed tantalising kisses up the delicate inside of her arm to its crook.

Her limbs turned to melted butter. She sighed and wiggled with pleasure beneath the covers. 'You are up early.'

He waggled his eyebrows. 'Definitely up.'

'I don't mean that,' she said, but couldn't resist a peek.

He chuckled. 'Garth has disembarked already, but I didn't want to wake you. You've been through hell these past few days.'

She sat up. Grey light from the window showed a new day. The ship barely rocked.

She flung back the covers. 'Goodness, I'm sorry to keep everyone waiting.'

Fire blazed in his hazel eyes as his gazed travelled her naked length. He leaned forward and kissed the rise of her breast.

Sun-gilded hair tickled her skin. She ran her fingers through the silky waves. 'Are you sure you want me to get up?'

A groan rolled up from his chest. He raised his head and looked down at her with a rueful grin. 'No, I don't. Unfortunately, Captain Porter has to get the *Sea Witch* berthed further down the coast. So, milady, you needs must arise.'

Placing her palms either side of his wonderful face, his lean cheeks rough against her palms, she kissed him soundly on the lips. Sandalwood and soap filled her nose. She loved the male smell of him. Clean and musky at the same time. She licked his bottom lip. 'Then you must leave and send Jeannie to help me dress.'

He chuckled. 'Then you must let me go.'

A sweet pang squeezed her heart. She never wanted

to let him go. Moisture blurred her sight. She gave a shaky laugh and released him.

His expression turned serious, his eyes the colour of mysterious northern forests. 'Don't worry. I will take care of everything.'

She nodded, unable to speak for tears. What a mix, happiness that she'd found him, tears of losses to come. She flashed him a brilliant smile and hoped he didn't notice.

With a last yearning glance, he got to his feet and strode for the door. 'Do you think you can be ready in half an hour?'

'If you want me to be,' she murmured with an eyebrow raised.

'Sylvia,' he said, his warning voice full of laughter. 'Be good.'

If she was good, she wouldn't be here.

A half-hour later, she and Jeannie met him up on the gleaming mahogany-and-brass-fitted deck of the *Sea Witch*. She raised her eyes to the white cliffs guarding the English Channel. Somewhere up there, Cliff House clung to its rocky perch. The house where she had grown up and learned the truth about her life.

Captain Porter touched his hat. 'Mr Evernden, a pleasure to have you on board again.' A knowing look crossed his face as his gaze rested on her. 'Ma'am.'

Inwardly, she squirmed. He knew, of course, what they'd done, what she was.

Christopher's protective hand touched the hollow of her back and he moved closer, claiming her. She relaxed.

'Thank you, Red,' Christopher said.

'Yes, sir. Good day.'

With Christopher's help she and Jeannie clambered into the small boat waiting to take them to the post-chaise at the dockside, where a yellow liveried post-boy sprang to attention and opened the door.

Once inside, Sylvia snuggled against Christopher, his strong arm around her shoulders pressing her into his hard wall of chest. It was as if all her childish dreams of a noble knight who would rescue her from the dragon of her fears had come true.

Jeannie, on the other side of the carriage, smiled and nodded.

Life suddenly seemed unbearably wonderful. Dare she hold on to it?

After a leisurely lunch at Cobham and several short stops to change horses, the chaise came to a stop outside a curving terrace of Palladian town houses. Sylvia frowned. This was not London.

'Why are we stopping here?' she asked.

'This is Blackheath. You are spending the night here.'

The house, fronted by a wrought-iron fence, looked over a green open space on the other side of the street.

'Surely we can reach London in another hour or so?'

Embarrassment filled his expression and he glanced at Jeannie. 'I thought you wouldn't mind staying here. It belongs to Garth. He doesn't actually live here, he… well, it's where he lives some of the time.'

Disappointment emptied her heart. 'It's where he keeps his mistress,' she uttered, her tone flat.

She couldn't help her reaction. For some foolish reason, a glimmer of hope had sprung to life that there really might be more than this in her future.

Christopher opened the door. 'Since there is no one living here at the moment, Garth is loaning it to us until we make other arrangements.'

Of course she couldn't return to his mother's house.

Not now they were lovers. She forced calmness into her voice. 'I see.'

'Rafter won't have a clue where to find you. If we go into town, there's the risk of him ferreting you out. He'll expect us to go to London.'

Christopher was carving out her future as surely as if it were set in stone and this the final lettering in the block.

The thought of parting with him tugged at her newly discovered heart. Why not accept? She could stay with him for a while, a month, a year. They'd make some happy memories together.

A nagging doubt, a memory of her mother, skittered across her mind like a spider scuttling out of a dark corner. She pushed it aside. If she wanted him, this was her only option.

With Jeannie trailing behind her, she alighted and followed Christopher up the two steps and in through the front door held open by the butler.

They were obviously expected.

On the outside, the town house looked unremarkable. Inside told a different story. Appalled, Sylvia gazed at the opulent marble staircase with its Turkey runner. Marble and plaster statues of Greek gods and goddesses filled elegant niches; paintings of nude women adorned the walls. Frolicking nymphs leered down from the ceiling.

Disappointment washed through her and extinguished her hopes. She was a fool to expect something less garish, more genteel. After all she had become her mother.

It suddenly seemed difficult to breathe.

'If you would step in to the drawing room, Mr Evernden, I'll arrange for tea,' the butler said.

'No tea for me, thank you, Bates,' Christopher said.

She followed Christopher into the drawing room, while Jeannie disappeared into the nether regions of the house with Bates. A sense of unreality numbed her.

She glanced around the room, at the rose-coloured walls and gilt furniture, at the satisfied expression on Christopher's face.

'At least Delia didn't get started on this room,' he said.

'Delia?'

'Garth's last lady. She had a thing about decorating. The entrance hall was her handiwork. It was as far as she got before she was handed her *congé*.'

The ease with which he accepted the departure of a woman who had made this place her home sent a chill down Sylvia's spine. 'Oh.'

'Eventually, we will go to my house in Kent. I haven't been there since my grandmother left it to me, so it will take a couple of days to make it ready for us. This will be perfect until then.'

'Perfect.' Her lips felt stiff.

He pulled her into his arms and pressed his lips against hers, firm and warm and so tempting. He ran his fingers through her hair and deepened the kiss.

The feel of him, his large body hard against her, his passion, his heat, his strength, drove her thoughts and fears into the far reaches of her mind. She melted into him. She wanted this with him.

She reached up and curled her hand around his strong column of neck, arching into him. She nibbled at his lower lip, felt his desire rise, a hard ridge of arousal pressed against her stomach.

Desire flooded her, rushing through her veins in hot rivers. She ground her hips against him and revelled in his sharp indrawn breath.

She never imagined wanting a man like this. It went

against everything she thought she knew about herself, everything she believed.

He groaned and pulled away. 'I'll be back first thing tomorrow.'

Panic gripped her. 'You aren't staying?'

'I have business requiring my attention, people relying on me.'

She couldn't stay in this place without him. 'Don't go.' She hated the begging note in her voice. 'Or take me with you.'

He smiled down at her and gave her a squeeze. 'I can't. My ships can't sail until I sign the manifest, and I have nowhere to take you in London except a hotel, and it would be too easy to find you.'

Pain pierced her heart. It was starting already. Him leaving her for his other world. His real world. A world to which she could never belong. 'Can you not go tomorrow?'

'I wish I could.' He nuzzled her neck, sending a delicious shiver all the way to her core. 'But I have already delayed this sailing by several days. We will start to lose our crew.'

Releasing her, he took her hands. 'Come, sit with me a moment.' He led her to the sofa and drew her down, his arm around her shoulder. 'Everything will be all right, you will see.'

She desperately wanted to believe him, but the spider crawled out of the dark and completed a web of doubt in her mind. Doubt about Christopher and, worst of all, about herself. She sought escape. 'What if Rafter comes looking for me again? Perhaps it would be better if I disappeared, went somewhere alone.'

His mouth flattened. 'Where else can you go where you will be safe? Not to London or France. This is the perfect solution.' He tipped her chin with one finger and gazed into her eyes. 'Don't you want to be with me?'

Every particle in her body and her heart said yes, but her mind knew better. 'How long must I remain in hiding?'

His expression darkened. He sighed. 'I don't really have the time to discuss this now. Bates will see to your needs until I get back. You don't have to worry, he's very discreet.'

He would have to be. She drew in a breath. Without Christopher to tempt her, to overcome her reason, she would be able to think. Perhaps it was better if he left. She fought the tears threatening to spill over and nodded.

He smiled and kissed her forehead. 'That's better. Rest now. You've been through a lot. We will talk tomorrow.'

She flung her arms around his neck, abandoning her lips to the pleasure of his for an all-too-brief moment.

Tomorrow she might not be here.

Unease churned in Christopher's gut as he took his hat and coat from the imperturbable Bates. Beneath Sylvia's impassioned kiss, he'd sensed tension.

Fear of her father? He stepped outside. Not fear, she was too full of courage for that, yet he sensed a brittleness, like a delicate vessel ready to break at a touch, the way she'd been the first day he had met her at Cliff House.

Something prodded him to turn back.

Bates raised his brows.

'Please see that Miss Boisette has everything she needs.' Christopher flicked the man one of the guineas he'd borrowed from Garth.

'As you wish, sir.'

A tension gripped him. Twice now she'd tipped him the double. He didn't want to risk her leaving again.

'Bates, I would prefer it if Miss Boisette did not leave the house. Not for any reason.'

The door hesitated in its swing. A frown puckered Bates's forehead, then smoothed. 'As you wish, Mr Evernden.'

Christopher turned and strode to the waiting post-chaise.

Chapter Fifteen

Light blazed from every window at the Mount Street house. A carriage disgorged a couple in evening attire. Christopher frowned. It seemed that Mother had gone all out for this birthday party. Damn lucky he'd remembered once he arrived in town. His brain still wasn't working right. Anxiety about Sylvia had haunted him all the way to London and through most of his meeting with his man of business. Something about his leave-taking felt wrong.

With a roll of his shoulders, he handed his rumpled driving coat to the butler on his way past. He headed for the stairs. Garth cast a laconic glance at him through the open drawing-room door, then looked pointedly at his watch. Things really had gone to hell if Garth needed to remind him about the time.

Studiously ignoring Reeves's darkling glances and tongue-clickings over the state of his raiment, he bathed, shaved and changed at breakneck speed and went downstairs. He joined a bored-looking Garth.

'I didn't think you'd leave her,' Garth murmured out of the side of his mouth.

His sly wink added to Christopher's sense of unease.
'I must have more control than you.'

Garth laughed.

'Christopher, darling.'

His mother bore down on him like a frigate about to
deliver a broadside. He gave Garth a don't-you-dare-
say-a-word stare and went to greet her.

'Here you are at last, dear,' Lady Stanford announced,
clearly in high spirits and her best looks. 'I was beginning to think you had forgotten.'

Somehow she made him feel guilty even when he
wasn't. Perhaps Garth was right to be so offhand. 'I'm
sorry I'm late. I was delayed on the road.'

'Blackheath, wasn't it?' Garth put in with a grin.

His mother fluttered her handkerchief in question.

'It doesn't matter where,' Christopher said.

'No, indeed,' his mother said. 'You are here now and
that is what is important.' In a swirl of silk and a waft
of lavender, she sailed away to greet the Molesbys. Even
from here Christopher could hear Aunt Imogene protesting about the rudeness of the hackney driver who had
brought them from their friend's house in Golden
Square and grossly overcharged them.

Over her shoulder, George Molesby raised an
eyebrow. Christopher could guess the question on his
mind. Sylvia. Damn the man. Still, he was glad to have
his mother's attention diverted. He glowered at Garth.
'Can't you be serious for a moment?'

Garth's brow shot up, but a smile lurked in his eyes.
'Apparently not.'

Christopher took a good look at him. 'You're foxed.'

'Not yet,' Garth replied with utter good cheer.
'Soon, I hope.'

The gentlemen gathered around their ladies, who

reclined on sofas or perched on chairs. The butler circulated with glasses of madeira.

Garth stepped forward and raised his glass. 'To Mother.'

'Lady Stanford,' the company chorused.

With a gracious incline of her head, Mother accepted their good wishes. It warmed Christopher's heart to see her so happy, something that had not occurred when their father lived. Christopher's earlier irritation dissipated.

He grinned when he saw Garth's thunderstruck expression as first one guest, then another presented a gift: handkerchiefs from the Molesbys, a miniature from Lord Angleforth, her latest flirt, some perfume from one of the other couples. Garth had obviously only just realised gifts were expected.

Christopher took pity on him and sauntered to his side. 'I bought something from both of us when I first learned she planned this party.' It seemed like aeons ago. Before he had gone chasing off to Dover, when his life had been ordered and organised and totally in his control. Strangely he didn't miss it at all.

'I'm in your debt again,' Garth muttered under his breath. 'I will pay you back.'

Christopher slapped him on his broad shoulder. 'Indeed you will.'

He pulled a slender red velvet pouch from his pocket and placed it in his mother's lap. 'From your sons.' She squealed and fumbled with the ribbon around its throat.

A general gasp greeted the glittering diamond-and-emerald bracelet as it spilled into her hand.

'Gad, young Kit. Where'd you get the ready for a piece like that?' Garth asked.

'Investments.' Christopher couldn't keep the pride

out of his voice. It might not be quite the thing for a noble gentleman, but his head for business had its uses.

'I'll have to take some advice from you.'

The respect in Garth's face gave him a deep sense of satisfaction. 'Any time, brother.'

'Dinner is served, my lord,' the butler announced and opened the double doors to the dining room.

'Looks like we are on parade, old chap,' Garth murmured. 'Who has she got you tied to this evening?'

Christopher groaned. 'The old Fanshawe trout.'

'Hah. Well, as head of the family, I've got Mama.' He didn't sound any more pleased than Christopher. Whatever lay between Garth and their mother, it ran deep and always left Christopher with a vague sadness.

But as always, they presented a united front and turned to their respective duties. It was not until dinner was over and the ladies had withdrawn, leaving the gentlemen to their port and cigars, that Christopher contrived a quiet moment alone with Garth on the dining-room balcony. While the other men lingered at the table over their wine, they ignited their cigars in the comfortable dark.

'So, did you get your little ladybird all nicely set up?' Garth asked, blowing a ring of smoke at the sky.

It sounded so bloody tawdry. 'Miss Boisette is not my ladybird.'

'You could have fooled me, dear boy. The *Sea Witch* practically keeled over after you went to the stateroom, not to mention the cries of delight. There I was, thinking of you enjoying yourself.'

Palms moist and cheeks heated, he held off from strangling Garth. 'Take a damper. I'll have her out of your house in a day or so.'

'What a bloody hypocrite you are.' Deceptively lazy,

the mocking tone lashed Christopher in a place he had not known was sensitive. 'She's a lovely armful. Keep her there as long as you want.'

'The house is too close to London and, with all the traffic buzzing down to visit Princess Charlotte, someone is sure to recognise me.'

The cigar glowed in the dark and Garth leaned one elbow on the balustrade. 'The truth now. What is this all about? What happened in France?'

'I don't think I should discuss it. It's bad enough that I'm embroiled in it. It seems Miss Boisette has powerful enemies.'

'Her father?'

'Likely. Anyway, I am taking her to my house in Kent, just as soon as I can make the necessary arrangements with my man of business.'

A low whistle emanated from the dark. 'You're inviting a scandal. Even I wouldn't install a woman like that in a family home.'

The hot rush of anger in defence of Sylvia surprised him. 'She's not *a woman like that*.'

'Good God. Have you lost your mind? She was Uncle John's paramour. Everyone said so.'

'I can assure you, she was no such thing.' He tossed his cigar on the stone floor and ground it out with his heel. 'I'm taking her out of sight for a while.'

'Take it from one who really knows women,' Garth said with a harsh laugh, 'she'll bleed you dry and move on to the next victim. Don't risk your precious reputation for a tumble in the hay.'

Christopher glanced over his shoulder. 'Sylvia would never do that.'

'You are a fool if you think so.'

'Your cynicism is ill founded.' Christopher reached

for the door handle. He knew Sylvia, and she was nothing like the women Garth favoured. Just a few more hours, his business finished, and he would be back in her welcoming arms. 'What is more,' Christopher said. 'I don't give a damn what you or anyone thinks.'

The realisation burst like champagne bubbles in his blood, lifting him to dizzying happiness. He strode out of the room and left Garth to think whatever he pleased.

Sylvia pulled back the rose-coloured damask curtain from the window. The fading daylight revealed only a sky threatening rain, a few passers-by on the pavement beyond the wrought-iron railings and the open common, where a small boy attempted to fly a yellow kite. No sign of Christopher.

With a sigh, she dropped the curtain and strode to the fireplace. A swift tug on the bell brought the butler within moments. She pressed her lips together, quelling the urge to say something cutting about him lurking outside the door.

Since it was Christopher who had earned her wrath, he would hear her opinions, not his instrument. 'Tea, please, Bates.'

'Yes, miss. Cook has prepared an early dinner for you. It is set out in the dining room, if you would care to partake?'

The thought of food nauseated her already churning stomach. Where was Christopher? She wanted to advise him of her decision to leave for Harrogate immediately.

The answer had come to her at dawn. She would not stay here or anywhere else as his mistress, always anticipating her *congé*. She'd steel herself and make the break, right away, before she became accustomed to having him near. No one would ever look for her in a so unfashionably remote northern watering place.

The butler remained in the doorway, awaiting her answer. If her plan was to be successful, she didn't need to faint from lack of nourishment. 'Thank you. Something light would be most welcome.'

She followed him into the dining room. This household's idea of a light repast exceeded expectations. A silver tureen filled the centre of the round walnut table. On the sideboard, several meat pies were set out along with a roast fowl, a large bowl of fruit and an assortment of cheeses and breads. Sparkling silverware on the white linen cloth, adjacent and intimate, waited for two people.

'Are you expecting Mr Evernden?' she asked.

The butler's expression remained wooden. 'The table is always set for two. Lord Stanford's orders, miss.'

She winced, stung by the butler's assumption she was the same as all the other females who inhabited this house under Lord Stanford's protection. What else would he think, since she had arrived here on Christopher's arm? She clenched her jaw. She had to leave here while she still had a shred of self-esteem.

He pulled out one of the Sheraton chairs. 'Please be seated.'

He filled the bowl in front of her with cream of mushroom soup. The delicate, delicious aroma filled her nostrils. He set a slice of wild pigeon pie on a plate beside it. When she refused his offer of burgundy, he filled her goblet with water.

'Will there be anything else, miss?'

'Just the tea, please.'

He bowed and left her in solitary state.

The soup was delicious, hot and creamy with a peppery tang. Lord Stanford employed an excellent chef for his *filles de joie.* Everything in this house was of the finest quality. He treated his women well. No doubt Christopher would follow his example. Her heart squeezed.

One mouthful of soup and her appetite fled. She poked at the pie with her fork, suddenly indecisive. This elegant existence would be hers with Christopher. A strange twist of fate had brought them together. Perhaps she should not fight it.

But she had always sworn she would not make her mother's mistakes. If only he would offer more. Marriage? How could she ask him to stoop to her level? In the end, he would hate her and abandon her.

No. She had made the right decision. She had to disappear from his life. She would control her own destiny.

But would Christopher let her go right at this moment?

She set the fork down. Her heart ached too much to allow food to pass down her throat.

Behind her, the door opened with a creak.

'Leave the tea on the sideboard. I'll help myself,' she said.

An amused chuckle made her swivel in her seat. 'Lord Stanford.'

Hands raised and a wicked smile on his lips, he bowed. 'Sorry. No tea.'

'I beg your pardon. I thought you were the butler.'

'Really? I told Weston this jacket fit me not at all well.'

She couldn't resist a smile at his barb against one of London's most fashionable tailors.

As lithe as a predator on the hunt, he sauntered to the sideboard and poured himself a glass of red wine. He spoke casually over his shoulder. 'No Kit today?'

'Mr Evernden has not yet returned. He had some business in town.'

A dark eyebrow winged up as he turned to face her.

'Mr Evernden, is it?' The appraising gaze that travelled from the top of her head to her bosom expressed his opinion. Once more, she felt the heat of embarrassment in her face and fought to remain calm.

'I am expecting your brother soon, my lord.'

'Please, call me Garth.'

He slid into the other chair. Beneath the table, his knee touched hers and she jerked away.

His mouth curled in a sardonic smile. 'I expected him to dash straight back here to your welcoming arms last night. I can't think why he would stay in town.'

He was trying to bedevil her for some reason. Beneath his insouciance, he seemed to care about his brother. But did he care enough to try to extract him from an unfortunate alliance? 'He is making arrangements for us.'

'Us?' For once, his face reflected his serious tone of voice. 'Just what sort of arrangements are you expecting, Miss Boisette?'

It took all her self-control not to throw his suspicions back in his face. Instead she curved her lips in a smile. 'Your brother is an honourable man. I am sure he will provide everything I ask.'

'And what will you request?'

She cocked her head to one side, tapping a finger against her lips. His eyes followed the movement. 'A very permanent arrangement, I think.'

His eyes darkened and his brows drew together. 'Christopher is not such a fool.'

This man despised her.

'Your tea, miss.' The butler had entered silently.

Garth rose to his feet, towering over her. 'Miss Boisette will take it in the rose room. And,' he said, leaning close and murmuring into her ear, 'then you will tell me everything.'

This might be her only chance for escape. She rose to her feet and placed a trembling hand on his arm. She allowed him to escort her into the drawing room.

They chatted idly as the butler set the tea tray on the table in front of the sofa. Sylvia kept up a flow of bright chatter, anything to hide the rapid beating of her heart as she prepared to play her role in what she hoped was the final scene.

'No interruptions, Bates,' Garth said.

Her stomach tightened.

The butler bowed and closed the door behind him.

Seated next to her on the sofa, Garth laid one arm along the back. With only a slight tremor in her hand, she poured tea for herself. She recalled the first time she had played this part with Christopher. She hadn't felt nearly so nervous. Despite his sternness, he hadn't frightened her. This man emanated darkness.

Garth twisted the stem of his wineglass in long strong fingers, gazing into the depths of the ruby liquid as if it were a crystal ball. She had never seen him quite so serious.

'Now, Miss Boisette. Tell me your story.'

Sylvia assembled her thoughts. 'I don't know how much Christopher, Mr Evernden, told you about my… my history.'

He sent her a sharp glance. 'He told me enough. I know you are in some kind of danger from your father, who is not interested in claiming parentage. I also know that you have my brother firmly in your toils.' He hesitated, pausing as if to select his words with care. 'Christopher is not like me, Miss Boisette. He led a sheltered life as a boy. Practically cloistered.' Garth's lips twisted in a mirthless smile. 'He's no fool, but he's always been too softhearted when it comes to a sad story.'

The chill, so recently gone from her heart, spread through her chest. His suspicions wounded far more than she expected. Even this unmitigated rake realised a woman with her past didn't deserve an honourable man like Christopher. He was right.

She took a deep breath and slanted him a glance through her lashes. 'How *much* do you want to rescue your brother?'

A slow, lazy smile curved his lips. His arm dropped from the sofa back and slid around her shoulders. 'How *much* would it cost and what else would I get in return?' He trailed a finger suggestively up her neck, along her jaw and brushed across her lips. His warm breath tickled her ear. A predator on the prowl.

Emptiness engulfed her. Christopher would never forgive her for this piece of work.

She leaned back and turned on a brilliant smile.

Garth drew in a sharp breath.

'One hundred guineas,' she said. 'And you get the satisfaction of knowing your brother is out of my toils.'

The easy, confident smile disappeared. 'I would offer you much more to stay here with me.' He stared at her mouth and leaned forward. His voice thickened. 'Jewels, clothes, whatever you desire.' The scent of his cologne, acid lemon mingled with musty bay, stifled her.

She forced herself not to flee the room. The fine line between coquette and harlot might drive him past the bounds of reason. A man with lust on his mind rarely behaved rationally, as she knew to her cost. Pinpricks raced down her spine.

The teacup her only barrier against his overpowering presence, she smiled. 'I don't think Mr Evernden would appreciate that.'

He shrugged. 'No, he wouldn't. It would be a pity to waste your talents, however.'

She sipped thoughtfully. 'I prefer not to become a bone of contention between two brothers who seem fond of each other.'

His lips thinned. 'That's awfully kind of you, *mademoiselle*.'

He took the cup from her hand, set it on the table and drew her to her feet. He placed his hands on her shoulders, hot and heavy, a weight almost too great to suffer. She held her ground and stared boldly into his intent, dark eyes.

'Christopher is a good man,' he said. 'Far better than I could ever hope to be. I suspect he'll give you his heart if you want it. Don't trample it in the dirt, if this is only about money.'

How long would she keep his heart before he tired of her? She couldn't bear to find out.

Keeping her voice flat and distant, she selected her words with care. 'Your brother feels obligated to provide for me. Like his uncle, he seeks to secrete me away like an unpleasant truth, to hide my scandalous past in case it besmirches the good name of Evernden. I prefer to go my own way.'

Doubt filled his expression.

Desperate, she played the last card in her hand. 'If you help me, I will disappear from his life. Otherwise, I shall do my utmost to convince him to marry me and I promise you I will lead my life as I see fit. Quiet isolation and discretion are not words in my vocabulary.'

The lines beside his mouth deepened. 'By God, you're a cold-hearted bitch.' A wolfish grin lit his face and he pulled her hard against him, breast to chest. He forced her chin up with his fist. 'I thought you were a scheming little slut when I saw you first. You certainly have Christopher fooled and I almost let him convince me otherwise. But truth will out, Miss Boisette. Your true colours are revealed.'

She allowed a sultry smile to dawn on her lips. 'And will you pay me to haul down my colours?'

He moistened his lips. 'I might be persuaded.'

'I have one request.'

'And that is?'

'That you say nothing about our arrangement to Christopher until I am long gone.'

A chuckle rumbled in his chest and vibrated through her. 'One kiss and you shall have your money and be on your way.'

He lowered his mouth to hers. Lemon and bay, the scent of betrayal.

Bile rose in her throat. She couldn't do it. She couldn't kiss Christopher's brother. She ducked his seeking mouth.

'What the devil is going on?'

They jerked apart.

Shaken, Sylvia turned to face the door and Christopher.

As bright with truth and honour as his brother was dark with deceit, he stared at them. Broad and solid. She wanted to fold herself within his strong arms. She cringed at the hurt in his eyes as he looked from one to the other.

With an awkward laugh, Garth raised his hands in a helpless gesture of appeal. 'Sorry.'

'Damn you, Garth. I'll see you in the study. First I want a word with Miss Boisette.'

Rigid, he glared at Garth, who sauntered out. He turned his smouldering gaze on Sylvia. 'Damn him. He's incorrigible. I'll make him apologise if I have to call him out.'

Mentally, Sylvia winced. 'I—'

'Never mind him now. I'll deal with him.' He strode to her side and took her hand in his, gentle and kind, warm and strong. The creases at the corners of his eyes begged for her touch. Control almost escaped her.

He guided her to sit and rubbed his thumb over her knuckles. Heat trailed from his touch all the way to her core. Her breasts tightened. She wanted to feel his hands on her body, his lips against her mouth. It was too late.

'Everything is arranged,' he said. 'I will take you to Kent the day after tomorrow.'

It took all her will-power to speak. 'I'm not going to Kent.'

His eyes widened. 'Don't be a fool. If Rafter discovers your whereabouts, he might do more than spirit you away to some ghastly brothel. You really don't have a choice.'

The choice lingered in the study. Her heart ached. 'I have plans of my own.'

His hazel eyes blazed, then his face hardened. 'I won't let you face Rafter or your father alone. Be realistic, Sylvia. You can't do this without help and you're penniless. Or have you forgotten that I have been keeping you for weeks?'

She was stung and heat rose to her cheeks. He'd turned something beautiful into a tawdry exchange of money for human flesh. 'I have the money from the sale of Cliff House.'

'There was no money. It was all mine, along with the gold I paid for you at Madame Gilbert's.'

She sagged into the sofa back, the size of her indebtedness weighing heavy on her shoulders. And she intended to repay him with a lie.

Anger at being forced into a corner sharpened her tongue. 'I will not continue as your dependant. I have my own life to live.'

He scrubbed at the back of his neck. 'Frankly, whether you wish it or not, it is my duty to my uncle to protect you.'

Desperate, she clung hard to her decision. She kept her voice flat and cold. 'Damn your duty, Christopher Evernden.'

When Garth told him what she had done, Christopher would recall this conversation and he would despise her. The thought of parting on such bad terms tore at her soul. Hot prickles burned behind her eyes and clogged the back of her throat.

Swallowing hard, she rose to her feet and, too cowardly to face him, glanced out of the window at grey clouds scudding across a watery blue sky. 'My mind is made up.' She strode out of the room and dashed up the stairs.

His angry words followed her. 'Damn it, Sylvia. You will be ready to leave two days from now.'

She slammed the door of her room and turned the key.

Christopher clenched his fists. He didn't know who he wanted to strangle first. Sylvia for her stubborn refusal to let him look after her, or Garth.

A picture of Garth with his hands on Sylvia rose up to choke him. Garth had frightened her. That was why she was behaving so strangely. Well, that was one problem he would resolve.

As Christopher entered the study, Garth leaned back in the chair behind his desk and lifted his booted feet on to one corner of the battered oak. He waved his glass towards the decanter in front of him. 'Brandy, Kit?'

'No. And you shouldn't be drinking, either, since you will be driving your curricle back to town tonight.'

Garth grinned. 'I drive better when I'm foxed, sobersides.'

'That's nonsense and don't change the subject. What the deuce were you doing with Sylvia?'

'Ah. The beautiful Miss Boisette.' He raised his glass in a silent salute.

What the hell was the matter with him? He'd always been wild, but never suicidal. 'Well?'

'A momentary lapse, Kit. An aberrant feeling of affection that I don't believe was returned.'

'You don't believe it was returned?' A red haze filled his vision. 'She was fighting you off, you idiot. Are you so foxed you can't tell the difference between one of your whores and a decent woman?'

Garth sneered. 'Are you?'

Garth must be sotted. It was the only possible explanation. Christopher stamped on his urge to smash his brother in the mouth. 'You drunken, lecherous bugger. I'll talk to you when you sober up.'

'You may wait a very long time.'

Unable to contain his fury, Christopher swept Garth's feet off the desk.

Garth lurched forward and spilled his brandy in his lap as his feet hit the floor. He cursed.

Christopher grabbed his coat front and, nose to nose, glared into his brother's sullen eyes. 'I'll only tell you this once. If you get within three feet of Sylvia again, I will call you out and I will kill you.'

Garth knocked Christopher's hands away and staggered to his feet, his lip curled in a snarl. 'You don't have a chance in hell.'

The stupid arrogant bugger. 'Try me.'

Garth's cynical sneer shifted to haughty. For a moment, Christopher thought Garth would take the challenge, then he laughed. The hard-edged sound was as unlike Garth as anything he could imagine. 'Not today, little brother. You have as much on your hands as you can manage.' He slumped back into his seat. He looked as if he wanted to say more.

Christopher scowled. 'Wait here and I will drive you back to London.'

Anxiety gnawing at his gut as he thought about the possibility of Rafter finding Sylvia, he took the stairs two at a time. Damn it, she would go to Kent.

He knocked on her chamber door.

'Who is it?'

Her voice sounded husky and thick. He winced. Was she crying in there? A pang tightened his chest. He was doing this for her own good. 'It's me. Christopher.'

'Go away.'

Not an auspicious response. He stared at the closed door. 'We need to finish our conversation.'

Silence.

He knocked again. 'Garth is an idiot. He is foxed. I am taking him back to town so you need not concern yourself about him any longer.'

'As you wish.' A sort of hopelessness filled her voice.

He wanted to hold her in his arms, comfort her, feel the silk of her hair against his cheek. 'I'll come tomorrow. Be packed and ready to leave.'

'I am not going.'

Christopher rattled the door handle. 'You are being unreasonable.' He eyed the doorframe. He could easily break the lock, if he thought it would do any good. 'Very well. We'll talk tomorrow.'

Besides, he'd have plenty of time on the drive to Kent to convince Sylvia he was right.

The door remained firmly closed and he regarded it with regret. He'd hoped to stay the night, but had he no intention of sleeping on the sofa like an out-of-favour husband. Besides, he needed to ensure Garth got safely back to London and he still had to finalise things with his man of business before he left for an extended stay in the country.

There would be many other nights in their future. But by God, he hated to leave.

On the other side of the door, Sylvia pressed her forehead against the cool wood. It was the closest she could come to Christopher without opening it. She willed herself not to throw the door open, not to fling herself at his feet, not to beg forgiveness.

Swift and light, his tread descended the stairs. She forced herself not to call him back. The sound of male voices in the hall and the sharp click of the front door closing released her from her trance. She would never see him again.

Heavy-hearted, she moved away from the door. The stiff leather pouch in the centre of the bed dinted the blue counterpane. Bates had delivered it while Christopher wrangled with Garth in the study. She picked it up. It weighed heavy on her palm. One hundred guineas—it felt like thirty pieces of silver. Her price for betrayal. Blood money. Somehow, some day, she would repay Lord Stanford every penny. Perhaps that would wash away her guilt.

Dispirited, she turned to the task at hand. She sat down at the delicately inlaid rosewood escritoire. The cold little note she had written lay on its polished surface.

Thank you, it said. Not, I'll die a little every day I don't see your beloved face.

I wish you future happiness, it said. Not, I hope that in some corner of your heart you will always remember me.

Goodbye, it said. Not, I'll miss your touch all the days of my life.

Cordially yours, it said. Not, *Je t'aime, je t'aime, je t'aime.*

Sylvia folded the note precisely, careful to ensure that none of her foolish tears marred its pristine surface. Slowly, lovingly, she wrote his name, *Christopher Evernden*.

Je t'aime, her heart replied.

Resolute, she propped it up against the glass inkwell where he would be sure to see it when he came the next day.

Chapter Sixteen

In the chill blast of the early morning air, Sylvia hugged the cloak she had found in the bedroom wardrobe tighter around her shoulders, then quietly pulled the side door of the town house closed behind her. Bates had left it unbolted just as he promised.

Her quick steps tapped on the flagstones as she made her way past the front of the house to the street. The iron gate, cold under her hand, swung open silently on well-oiled hinges. Grey clouds blushed rosy in the eastern sky. The air smelled of wet grass and the first coal fires of the day.

Also as promised by Bates on behalf of his master, a post-chaise waited at the curb. Sylvia forced herself to concentrate on the future, not the past, and definitely not on Christopher's likely reaction when he returned to find her gone.

Up at the second-storey window, Jeannie's pale face peered through the glass. Sylvia had given Jeannie enough funds to take her to her relatives in Glasgow, promising to send for her once she found a home for them both.

Taking a deep breath, Sylvia climbed into the carriage.

* * *

Anticipation hummed in Christopher's veins on his way into Evernden Place. It had taken him all morning to finalise his business; this afternoon he'd kicked his heels in Doctor's Commons for hours. He couldn't wait to get back to Blackheath and Sylvia. Why the hell had it taken him this long to decide?

He dashed past the butler, who had opened the door for him, and made for the stairs.

'Excuse me, Mr Evernden.'

Christopher swung around, knowing he had a grin on his face and not giving a damn. 'Yes, Merreck?'

'Lady Stanford asked to see you the moment you returned. She is waiting in the drawing room.'

Mother. Damnation. He'd hoped to avoid her. She was not going to be pleased at his decision. His hand strayed to the breast pocket wherein nestled a small velvet-covered box and a special licence. A pang of the old guilt stirred in his chest. He didn't want to be yet another disappointment in her life. What with his father's temper and Garth's dissolute lifestyle, she hadn't had an easy time of it. Surely when she realised this was right for him, she would come around? No matter what anyone thought, he was going to ask Sylvia for her hand in marriage.

At least Garth wouldn't turn his back. Some of his warmth dissipated as he recalled Garth's hands on Sylvia and his mocking comments. He pushed his unease aside. Garth would be surprised to know it was the sight of him mauling Sylvia that had finally tipped the scales. Unable to stand the thought of another man touching her, Christopher had known exactly how to solve the problem.

His grin broadened at the thought of her happiness. God. His happiness too.

Squaring his shoulders, he strode to the drawing

room and found Mother reclined on the sofa idly turning the pages of the *Ladies' Magazine*. He raised her hand and pressed a brief kiss to her knuckles. 'Mother. You were looking for me?'

She fluttered her handkerchief and the scent of lavender wafted around him. 'Christopher, darling. Where have you been all day?'

'I had urgent business matters in need of attention.'

'You are taking me to Lady Wallace's tonight, are you not?'

Wallace's rout. Damn. He'd forgotten all about it. 'I'm sorry. Something came up. I have to go out of town.'

She pouted. 'You're becoming just like Garth. You never have time for me any more.'

He grinned. 'Mother, you don't need me to escort you. You always end up abandoning me for one of your many admirers before the end of the evening.'

Her face brightened and her handkerchief stilled. 'I'll send a note around to Angleforth. He's always most obliging.'

'Good grief, Angleforth? He's nothing but a dashed Bond Street beau. And he's becoming far too marked in his attentions.'

'Your language, Christopher, is quite deplorable. The Marquess of Angleforth is one of my oldest and most faithful friends.' A pretty pink suffused her cheeks and Christopher hid his smile.

He dropped into the chair next to her. 'Mother, you do want me to be happy, don't you?'

A surprised expression met his change of topic. 'Of course. I want the best for both of my sons.'

'If I were to become involved with a person you weren't entirely pleased with, would you cast me off?' Coward. He should have said marry.

Wide-eyed, she sat up, her air of languor disappearing. 'Oh, Christopher. What can you mean?'

'You wouldn't, would you?'

Silent for a moment, she stared at him. 'If it's about that female…'

He frowned. 'Mother.'

She sighed and leaned back against the damask cushions. 'You are far too precious for me to deny you my company. But I would strongly advise you to proceed with care. The *ton* is unforgiving. No one knows that as well as I.'

A faraway expression crossed her face and Christopher was not sure what to make of it. She must mean Garth. He didn't want this day spoiled by recriminations about his brother. He would tell her of his own plans later, when it was too late for arguments. He got up. 'I have to go.'

'Think before you act, darling,' she murmured. 'Mistakes remain with you for the rest of your life.'

Half-forgotten memories tugged at his consciousness, bitter words and harsh voices. 'As with you and my father?' The words were out before he thought about them.

A glaze of tears softened her blue eyes and provided the answer. He left her to her regrets and her memories.

When he entered his chamber, he found Reeves laying out his evening wear. Still sour about being left behind on Christopher's last two excursions, the valet went about his duties in heavy silence. Christopher ignored him. His mood was far too high to be pulled down by Reeves's sulks and, as the valet assisted him to dress, he made no attempt to close the breach. He wanted to reach Blackheath for dinner.

Dressed and ready, Christopher claimed his hat from Reeves's outstretched hand.

'Mr Christopher.' Reeves glanced pointedly at his driving coat draped across the bed.

'I don't need it.' Then he softened at the misery etched on Reeves's face. The man couldn't help it. He'd spend most of his employed life worrying about Christopher. They all had since he had suffered one debilitating illness after another as a child. They seemed to forget he now stood six feet in his stocking feet and had gone several rounds with Gentleman Jackson at his boxing saloon.

'I'm not driving my curricle, so I won't need a coat.'

Reeves's expression lightened. 'Yes, sir.' Christopher picked up his discarded jacket, fished out the ring and licence and relocated them into the breast pocket of the one he wore.

Glad to be on his way, he whipped open the door. 'Don't wait up for me.'

He ignored Reeves's huff of disapproval.

Cold, soot-scented rain dampened Sylvia's cheeks and trickled down her neck. She shivered.

A smart town carriage clipped by at a fast pace. The horses' hooves rang on the wet cobbles as the wheels fractured the lamplit puddles and scattered them in showers of yellow diamonds.

Across the street, wrought-iron gates bearing a coat of arms of two fearsome-looking boars on an azure ground guarded the Duke of Huntingdon's mansion. A circular drive beyond the gate allowed for carriages to pull off the street. It was three times as big as the Evernden house on Mount Street.

The decision to confront her father with his crimes had seemed simple enough in Blackheath. Now, with rain running down her face and standing against the railing of the garden in the centre of the square, her feet felt as cold figuratively as they were literally.

She didn't belong here.

She had lost her right to belong anywhere because of the heartless and selfish man who lived in that great house. If she wanted to sleep at night, she needed to tell him what he had done to the woman who had loved him until the day she died.

A heavy weight rapped against her knee reminding her of the pistol she'd filched from Garth's study. Along with a deep breath, it bolstered her courage and before she could talk herself into running away, she darted across the road. A footman, the ducal badge on his navy coat and an expression as blank as the waiting front door, emerged from the gatehouse at her tug on the bell. He pushed back the pedestrian entrance in the huge gates.

Wordlessly, he opened his large black umbrella and escorted Sylvia to the massive front door. Rain drummed on the taut fabric. Dogs barked somewhere at the back of the house. A *frisson* of fear shimmered in her stomach. If any of them knew who she was, they'd set those dogs on her.

Beneath a lamplit columned portico fine enough to make a Greek god proud, he rang the bell and stepped back smartly.

As she clutched her cloak close to a throat as dry as three-day-old bread, her staccato heartbeat filled her ears. She suddenly felt like the child she'd been the day she had landed on England's shores, insignificant and out of her depth.

The door swung back and a middle-aged butler surveyed her from crown to heels. His expression changed from supercilious to puzzled. 'Yes, miss?'

'Miss Boisette, to see Lord Huntingdon,' she managed with barely a quaver.

'His Grace is not at home.'

Liar. She'd seen him arrive an hour ago.

The great wooden door swung ponderously closed. Sylvia thrust her foot in the gap. Pain shot through her toes, but she held her ground.

The butler peered down, then opened the door enough to allow his large silver-buckled shoe through the gap, ready to crush her foot like an earwig.

Sylvia shoved at the door. Off balance, the butler staggered back.

'It is to the Duke's advantage to see me,' she said.

'I told you. His Grace isn't receiving callers.'

'He'll see me,' she said with icy determination. 'Here's my calling card.' She dropped her mother's locket into his outstretched palm.

Indecision hovered in the butler's expression. Taking advantage of his momentary loss of aplomb, Sylvia pushed her way into the cavernous, circular entrance hall. On the floor, black-and-white marble tiles encircled the Huntingdon coat of arms. A double staircase swept up both sides of the hall to meet at an arched balcony beneath a portrait depicting medieval knights and their ladies.

'Look, miss. You can't just barge in here. His Grace is dining *en famille*. No one can see him.'

A wry smile curved her lips. Who better to join his cosy family evening than his daughter? 'Take him the locket. He'll see me.'

Apparently overborne by her confidence, he gestured to an upright gilt chair against the wall. 'Wait there.'

He disappeared down a corridor.

Either he intended to fetch reinforcements or in a

moment or two she would face her father. As the minutes
ticked away, Sylvia's tremors turned into earthquakes.
Her mind emptied second by second. Each carefully re-
hearsed word froze beneath the hard lump in her throat,
pressed down by the smell of beeswax and old money,
as if the weight of every ancestor rested on her chest.

She leaped out of the chair when the butler returned.
She was ready to leave.

'Follow me, miss.'

Her heart drummed with such force she felt sure the
butler must hear it. She swallowed and nodded.

They traversed the chequerboard marble and entered
a dark passageway beneath one of the staircases. She
followed him into a small room with a warm fire. He
gestured to the sofa in front of it. 'Wait here, miss. His
Grace will attend you shortly.'

The overstuffed sofa in front of the hearth looked comfortable, a walnut console stood beside the window
holding an assortment of brandy and wine and at the other
end of the room sat a huge desk. An untidy pile of newspapers occupied one end of the desk, a pipe rack the other.
Behind it stood a glassed-in bookcase. The Duke's private
study, his inner sanctum, bared to her curious gaze.

She moved around the room as if by touching its
contents she could breathe some life into the vague and
shadowy figure from her past. Her father.

Nothing about the room seemed threatening. A couple
of pictures of horses and hounds hung on the panelled
walls. A portrait of a rather haughty lady with a child on
her knee graced the wall above the hearth. The Duchess?

An ordinary study.

Drawn to the warmth of the fire, Sylvia sat down to
wait. She touched her throat, stilled, then remembered.
She'd given the locket to the butler.

A clock chimed nine somewhere outside. Feet scurried back and forth in the passageway beyond the door, the rattle of dishes indicating the progression of dinner. His Grace apparently intended for her to wait until after dessert.

She slipped her damp cloak from her shoulders and sat back, hands in her lap. Another hour or two in a lifetime of waiting to set eyes on him made little difference.

The door opened. Expectations bowstring tight, Sylvia looked up.

'Well, well. 'Tis a wet night to be out wandering the streets of London, to be sure, colleen.'

Rafter.

Her heart sank and she dragged the pistol from her pocket.

'You better know how to use that,' he said.

'Gone? What do you mean, gone?'

Christopher knew he was shouting at Bates, but he didn't care. The idiot. He had told him categorically that she wasn't to leave the house. Damn it all. Surely she understood the risk?

With so little money, where would she go? He closed his eyes as he imagined her wandering the highways and byways of England. Or worse yet, the streets of London. Why the hell hadn't he told her what he was going to do before he left? Because he hadn't known it himself.

He took a deep breath and got hold of his temper. She wouldn't be alone. She would have taken Jeannie. 'She took her maid, of course.'

'No, sir.'

'Blast.' His mind churning, Christopher sat down on the hall chair. 'Does the maid know where she went?'

'She says not, sir. She's all set to leave for Scotland.

I'm to take her to the stage in the morning. His lordship's orders.'

Suspicion stirred in his gut. 'Garth's here?'

'In the study, sir. The young lady left this for you.'

Christopher stared at the small white square of paper. She'd left him another damned note.

He breathed a sigh of relief. Now he would know where she'd gone. 'Why the hell didn't you say so right away?'

He snatched it up and read it through.

Nothing. He felt his jaw tighten. Not a bloody word about where she was going. Just goodbye and good fortune. And thank you. He felt like a flag deprived of breeze, deflated and limp. She hadn't cared for him one jot.

And Garth was here. He narrowed his eyes, remembering the scene he had interrupted. This was Garth's fault. He'd scared her away with his lecherous pawing.

'Send Jeannie to the study,' he said, marching down the hall. For once Garth would pay for his idiocy.

The door crashed against the wall and Garth raised his head slowly. He had that stupid, distant expression of a man in his cups. 'Hello, Kit, old boy. Drink?'

'You lousy, rotten bastard.' Christopher lunged across the room and hauled Garth to his feet by his shirtfront. He raised his fist.

Garth made no move to defend himself. Guilt shadowed his eyes.

'Blackguard,' Christopher said. 'You know where she is.' Disgusted, he shoved him away.

Garth staggered back and landed in the seat. He made a feeble attempt to straighten his cravat. 'I don't. I gave her the money to go.'

Christopher couldn't think or breathe. A cold numbness enveloped him. 'You gave her money?' His stomach crashed to the floor, leaving him nauseous. She'd taken money from Garth. For what? His fists clenched.

A small china bowl on the shelf at eye level filled his vision. He picked it up and flung it at Garth's head.

Garth ducked. The bowl hit the wall with a crash. He brushed the dusting of porcelain shards from his shoulders. 'I never did like that bowl.'

'You gave her money?' Christopher wouldn't believe it. His heart felt like the ornament, shattered in a million pieces. But he had to know. He had to let Garth give him the *coup de grâce*. 'For services rendered, no doubt.'

Garth's expression turned wary. 'No. I paid her to leave you alone. She's a scheming little bitch. She planned to wed you. She as good as admitted she planned to have a fine time at your expense. I wouldn't have believed it if she hadn't told me herself.'

The contents in the pocket over his heart burned a hole in his chest. His throat filled, clogged with a solid lump. He took a long slow breath, blinking away the hot sensation behind his eyes. He hauled in a shaky breath. 'What the hell happened?'

Garth shrugged. 'I asked her how much she wanted to buy her off.'

He had to know. Had to hear it. 'How much was I worth?'

'A hundred guineas.'

The world seemed to stop spinning. He felt empty. He hadn't for a moment thought she wanted money. It didn't make any sense. Hell, he could have bought her off the day after the will was read. He'd been taken for a fool. A short laugh scraped his throat raw. He'd been ready to marry her, a girl from the stews, the daughter of a prostitute, a bastard.

Somehow he'd been bewitched by her beautiful face

and luscious body. But by God, he wished Garth hadn't spoiled the dream. It took a moment, but finally he managed to speak. He kept his voice flat. 'You had no right to interfere.'

'Head of the family. Duty and all that.'

'Utter rot.'

They turned towards the opening door.

Jeannie, more bowed than ever, crept into the room. She had a firm grip on the butler's sleeve and a dog-eared paper clutched in her hand.

She glowered at Garth from beneath her bushy brows, then twisted her neck to look up at Christopher, holding out the scrap of parchment. 'She niver told me what she planned to do or I would have given her this.' She twisted her neck to glare up at Bates. 'All right, cully. Tell 'em where she's gone.'

Bates sputtered and pulled his arm out of her clawed fingers.

She wiped her eyes on her sleeve. 'Mr Evernden, I'm that worried about my wee lass.'

Chapter Seventeen

The pistol in Rafter's hand waggled and Sylvia stepped back as a fair-haired man, with distinguished grey at his temples and vivid blue eyes snapping anger, strode into the room. He halted in front of the desk and leaned against it.

This must be the Duke of Huntingdon, her father. An ache spread through her chest, so painful her ribs hurt when she drew breath. Her mother had adored this man. She had died, knowing he didn't care one snap of his fingers for her.

He couldn't be more duke-like. Regal and straight shouldered, his demeanour spoke of privilege and command, but his mottled red complexion warned of a volatile temper or some disorder of the blood. She'd waited all her life to look him in the eye. She took a deep steadying breath.

Rafter tightened his grasp on her arm. She winced.

The Duke swept back his black evening coat and set his hands on his hips. 'What is going on here, Rafter?'

'This woman pushed her way in, demanding to see you, your Grace. Bradford came and got me instead.'

'I heard a shot,' the Duke said.

'Yes, your Grace. She fired at me.'

Trust Rafter to tell only half the story. Sylvia glared at him. 'He grabbed at the gun and it went off.'

The Duke turned his haughty gaze on her. 'When I ask you a question, young woman, you will answer. Until then, be silent.'

Damn his arrogance. This was not the civilised conversation she had envisaged holding with him, the one where she held the gun.

'Your Grace,' Rafter said in dulcet tones, 'allow me to introduce Mademoiselle Sylvia Boisette.'

Sylvia forced herself not to curtsy. Instead, she acknowledged the introduction with a slight nod.

Huntingdon's cheeks turned a darker shade of red. 'Good God. What the hell is she doing here? I am surrounded by incompetence. I thought you said you could handle this problem.'

That was all she was to him, a problem to be swept under the carpet liked so much unwanted dust, or locked in the closet like a skeleton. She shivered. The truth of that thought came closer to reality than she cared to admit. She kept her gaze locked on his face. 'I came here to talk to you.'

The Duke seemed nonplussed. 'Damn it all, Rafter. You told me I'd heard the last of her. How much more will it take to be rid of you?' He curled his lip in distaste. 'Between you and your mother, you'll see me ruined.'

His scornful words and expression gouged into Sylvia's soul like the claws of a raging beast. 'Do you have any idea what my mother suffered when you abandoned her?'

A flash of pain flickered in his eyes, then his expression hardened. 'Give her what she wants, but get rid of her, Rafter. This is the last time I give her money and to hell with the consequences.'

What was he talking about? She'd never asked him for a penny and never would. 'I don't want your money. I want an apology for what you did to me and my mother.'

Scarlet-faced, he jerked his gaze to her. 'Apology?' The word choked him. 'Apologise to a woman who's been bleeding me dry for years? A woman who sells herself to the highest bidder just like her mother did? Never.'

Damn his arrogance. Her mother had given up her pride and her body so this man's child could survive. '*Cochon!* She had no choice because you never came back, you heartless cur.'

'I'm afraid we have another little problem, your Grace,' Rafter said.

Huntingdon stilled. 'What now?'

'This little ladybird has a friend. A Mr Evernden has taken her under his wing.'

Heat branded Sylvia's cheeks. Rafter had turned something beautiful into filth.

Huntingdon shrugged. 'Pay him off. Anything. Surely he'll see reason.' He glowered. 'Warn him of the trouble it could cause for him and his family. God knows I've seen enough of it.'

'Ah, your Grace,' Rafter said, his hoarse voice full of warm congratulation, 'that's the way of it. Threaten them into submission.'

The Duke brushed Rafter's words away with a sharp gesture. 'I don't care what it costs, get her and her false claims out of England. Buy Evernden's silence.'

Outrage boiled in her blood. She hated her father for what he had done to her mother. Now he wanted to do the same to her and make Christopher his accomplice.

She looked longingly at Rafter's weapon, the one

he'd pulled from his pocket after hers fired harmlessly into the wall. She wanted to put a bullet in the Duke of Huntingdon so badly she pictured the blood staining the pristine white of his shirtfront. She'd hang to feel the satisfaction it would bring.

Sylvia wrenched her arm from Rafter's grip. Ignoring the pistol aimed at her back, she crossed the thick patterned rug and glared into Huntingdon's face. 'Leave Christopher Evernden out of this game of yours. He has nothing to do with you or my mother. As far as I am concerned, I don't want to remember I have you for a father.'

His blue eyes blazed anger. 'You are no daughter of mine.'

'Liar. Why are you trying so hard to get rid of me, then?'

The Duke recoiled as if struck. 'Don't play me for a fool, my girl.' He lowered his voice. 'Look. I've paid you more than enough to set up your own establishment in Paris, much as the thought disgusts me. You've got what you want. Now go away and leave me in peace.'

Nothing he said made any sense.

Rafter crossed to her side, grinning like some insane Celtic pixie. For once, his usually implacable grey eyes danced with unholy amusement.

'I don't think it's going to be that easy, your Grace.'

The rain had eased into a fine drizzle. Moving swiftly through the garden at the back of Huntingdon's house, Christopher slipped and slid on sodden grass. He cursed the wet creeping up his legs from where he had landed in the shrubbery when he had jumped down from the back wall. He ducked as an ornamental willow slapped wet fingers in his face.

'Bugger,' Garth mumbled.

Christopher glanced behind him.

The light of a wall lantern caught Garth hopping on one foot. Deep barks issued from the back of a building the waft of manure and hay identified as the mews.

'Quiet,' Christopher whispered, wishing he'd made him stay behind. 'They will set the dogs on us.'

They skirted the patch of light spilling out on to the drive and strode up the alley beside the house as if they belonged there. At the side door, Garth grasped Christopher's shoulder. 'What if she's not here? We are going to look like a pair of fools.'

Christopher shook him off. 'Bates said she asked for a carriage to bring her here.' He had no doubts. He knew her only too well. She went after what she wanted with solid determination and she was in danger.

Christopher pulled his pistol from his pocket and pushed the door open.

A footman leaped up from his seat beside the door. 'You can't come in here…' He fell silent at the sight of Christopher's weapon aimed at his chest.

'Tie him up,' Christopher said to Garth.

With the footman's neckcloth as a rope and his handkerchief as a gag, Garth bound the servant to his chair.

'Which way now?' Christopher asked.

Duelling pistol in hand, Garth jerked his head towards the passageway. 'The formal rooms are that way. Lord knows where we'll find the Duke.'

They crept along the hall. A bustling figure, the butler by his dress, almost ran headlong into them. 'What the deuce?'

'Just the man we need.' Christopher pressed his pistol against the man's neck. 'One sound and you are a dead man, understand?'

The butler nodded.

'Where is his Grace?' Christopher muttered.

'In his study with Mr Rafter and a woman,' the butler croaked.

Now they were getting somewhere. He swung the man around and grasped his shoulder. 'Lead the way.'

The door opened unannounced. The butler, framed in the doorway, opened and closed his mouth like a landed carp.

'Get out,' Huntingdon said.

The butler lurched forward.

The room filled with broad shoulders and simmering male rage. Christopher shoved the butler aside and aimed his pistol at Huntingdon's chest. Garth stumbled towards Rafter.

Cold metal, hard and unforgiving, nudged Sylvia's temple.

Garth halted in his tracks.

'As I was saying, your Grace,' Rafter said.

Sylvia caught Christopher's glance in hers. No emerald fire, no smile, just a cool stare. Garth had told him, of course, and now he scorned her. She steeled herself to bear his hatred despite her longing to throw herself at his feet, tell him what she had said to Garth wasn't true. She must not. For his sake. She held her head high.

'Who the devil are you? And what are you doing in my house?' the Duke asked.

Garth flashed a charming smile and bowed with courtly grace as if this were some chance meeting in the park, or a morning call. 'Stanford, at your service, your Grace. We met at Lady Elphinstone's last month, you might recall. This is my brother, Christopher Evernden.' He raised an eyebrow at Rafter. 'I don't believe we've met.'

Rafter gave him a sharp nod. 'Seamus Rafter.'

Sylvia blinked as Garth swayed on his feet. Good heavens, he was his usual three sheets to the wind.

Stunned silence filled the room while the men took stock of each other. The fire popped. Everyone jumped except Rafter.

The Duke scrubbed a hand over his chin. 'Will someone tell me why you are invading my house?'

'I should have thought that was obvious, your Grace,' Christopher said. 'We are here to make sure no *more* harm comes to Miss Boisette.'

The protective words and the anger in his voice draped Sylvia like a warm blanket for all his impassive expression. He should not have come here, but even so her heart swelled with joy.

Then, at the thought of what could happen to him as a result, her mouth dried. 'Thank you, Mr Evernden, Lord Stanford, but I believe the Duke and I were about to come to a mutually satisfactory arrangement.'

Christopher's gaze flicked to Garth. 'Another one?'

Heat scalded her face. She couldn't blame him for his thoughts. The rage she glimpsed in his eyes seemed to twist the knife that resided in her chest. Clearly she'd burned her bridges.

Turning to Huntingdon, she forced herself to continue. 'Mr Evernden is an innocent bystander caught in your web. Let him go.'

Rafter chuckled. 'Too bad he didn't think of that earlier. Now, if you don't want the young lady dead at your feet, you *gentlemen* will drop your weapons.'

Christopher cursed and let his pistol fall.

Rafter narrowed his gaze on Garth. 'And you.'

Garth tossed his on the sofa. 'Now what, Kit?'

Everyone swung around as the door opened and a fresh-faced youth of about thirteen strolled in. His brilliant blue eyes immediately settled on Huntingdon. 'Are you coming, Father? I have set the chess board up in the library.' His voice faltered as he caught sight of Rafter's pistol. 'What is it, Papa? Who are these men? Shall I call the footmen?'

'Welcome to the play, Lord Basingstoke,' Rafter said with a grin. 'It's the final act.'

The lad frowned. 'Rafter, what is going on?'

'Allow me to do the introductions,' Garth cut in.

Sylvia gaped at him. He was definitely in his cups.

'This is your half-sister, Sylvia.' Garth nodded at the others as he went round the room. 'Mr Rafter you know. Behind your father is my brother, Christopher Evernden, and I am Stanford. Sylvia, this is your brother, David Woods, the Earl of Basingstoke. Oh, and shrinking in the corner over there is your butler.' He grinned with obvious delight at his own humor.

'Stow it, Garth,' Christopher muttered.

The young earl frowned at Sylvia. 'I don't have a sister.'

'Oh, but indeed you do, my lord,' Rafter said with smug satisfaction.

'Silence, Rafter,' Huntingdon roared. 'I'll not have my personal business bandied about in this fashion.' He pulled at his cravat, his complexion heightened with a nasty purple tinge.

Sylvia pulled her arm free of Rafter's hand. She didn't want to do this any more. Too many people had become involved in this confrontation with her father. 'There is nothing more to discuss. Give me your word you will not follow me and nothing spoken of tonight will leave this room.'

'You think I can trust a blackmailer?' the Duke asked.

'I don't understand,' the young Basingstoke said.

'You are right, David,' Huntingdon said. 'You don't

understand. She's not your sister, no matter what she says. Please leave this to me to sort out.'

'No one is going anywhere,' Rafter said, menace clinging to him like creeping sea fog. He shifted his weapon's aim to the boy. The lad's jaw dropped as Rafter continued. 'It's time your son knows what kind of a bastard you really are, your Grace. Or is it the other way around?'

Clearly distressed, Sylvia rubbed at her temple.

There was a red mark where Rafter had dug the metal barrel against her delicate skin. Christopher wanted to ram the pistol down Rafter's throat and make him swallow it.

'No,' the Duke's voice choked out in a whisper. He clutched at his chest, pushed Rafter aside and collapsed on the sofa.

David crouched beside his father, fingers fumbling at his neckcloth.

Garth stiffened to attention, his wide-eyed gaze fixed on Rafter. 'Dear God, no.'

Rafter's chilling laugh rippled around the room. He drew himself up straight, like a soldier on parade, and glanced in contempt at the Duke's anguished expression. 'It's time, your Grace.'

Sylvia knelt at Huntingdon's side and chafed his hands. 'Stop talking riddles. Someone send for a doctor. This man needs medical attention.'

Christopher couldn't believe it. She should be strangling Huntingdon, not helping him. He deserved to die.

Garth went to the console by the window and poured a snifter of brandy. He returned and handed it to Sylvia. 'Give him this.'

Sylvia coaxed the glass into Huntingdon's hand and guided the glass to his mouth. He took a swallow and gradually his colour reduced and his breathing became less ragged.

'Look out,' Garth cried.

Out of the corner of his eye, Christopher caught Rafter's swift movement. Too late. Rafter pressed the muzzle of his gun against the boy's neck while Garth stared at the lad as if he'd seen a ghost.

'Papa!' The boy's voice cracked with panic.

Christopher started forward, then stopped. Rafter would pull the trigger before he could knock the gun away.

'Let him go,' the Duke gasped. 'He's an innocent.'

Rafter shook his head. 'Wrong. He needs to know. Either you tell him the truth or he dies.'

'What truth?' Huntingdon asked.

'The truth about her mother,' Rafter said, malicious glee on his face.

Twin spots of colour stained Sylvia's cheeks. Her obvious distress sliced Christopher's heart. There was no need for this cruelty. 'The game is up, Rafter. If harm comes to Miss Boisette, I'll make sure you both pay.'

'It's not Miss Boisette, is it, your Grace?' Rafter tightened his finger on the trigger.

'Don't hurt my son.'

'It's all up to you.'

'You'll ruin us all,' Huntingdon whispered.

'You've run out of time,' Rafter said.

'All right. All right. Damn you. So I was married to her mother. It doesn't make any difference.'

Christopher glanced at Sylvia. Her expression was full of disbelief and shock and desperate hope.

A rush of gladness filled his veins.

'She's not my daughter.' The Duke's voice rose in a desperate plea. 'Tell them, Rafter. She's De Foucheville's.' His expression filled with anguish.

'God damn him for a whoring bastard and Marguerite for going to him.'

'It doesn't matter who sired her,' Christopher said. 'If you were married to her mother, she's your child.'

'Without a doubt,' Garth muttered.

What the hell had got into Garth? Christopher gave him a hard stare that told him to keep silent.

'For God's sake, Rafter,' Huntingdon pleaded, 'think what you are doing.'

Rafter sneered at Sylvia. 'You'd never believe it to look at him now, but your father and the Vicomte De Foucheville risked their lives for months, helping other aristos like them to leave France during the Terrors. Proper hero, he was.'

'Dear God,' Huntingdon said in a hoarse whisper, tears standing in his eyes as he stared into the past. 'De Foucheville got the poor sods out of Paris, then I took them to the coast and waiting fishing boats.'

'Then the Jacobins turned into rabid dogs,' Rafter said with a smirk. 'The Ambassador insisted that all the English leave. Your father had just arrived from the coast and sent me to collect your mother, while he reported in at the Embassy.'

The Duke bowed his head. 'It was hell. Women and children begging us to take them. We had to leave so many behind. It wasn't until we were on board that I discovered Marguerite missing.' He glared at Rafter. 'If I had known she hadn't boarded with the rest of the women, I would have gone back for her. I begged the captain to turn around. Later, when he returned to England, Rafter told me she had preferred to stay with De Foucheville.'

Huntingdon raised his head, his expression filled with dark hatred. 'Damn him. I thought he was my friend. And Marguerite. I never thought she'd betray me. Curse the pair of them.'

'No,' Sylvia said, standing up. 'De Foucheville was my mother's friend, nothing more. He tried to help her escape to England. He was arrested before he could get her out of Paris. Someone betrayed him.'

Rafter grinned. 'That would be me.'

The Duke swallowed. 'You said she was his mistress. That she was expecting his child. I loved her. I would have taken her, child or no, but you said she refused to come.'

'That I did, your Grace,' Rafter said. 'And I told her that you regretted marrying her and didn't want her any more.' Rafter shook his head. 'De Foucheville almost got her out and spoilt my plans. I had to turn him in.'

The Duke lunged at Rafter, halting only when Rafter tightened his grip on the boy. 'You betrayed De Foucheville?' He swore. 'Half the *émigrés* in England owe their lives to him.'

'Believe me, I regretted his death. I admired his courage. He had to die.'

'Because he got my wife with child? I never wanted that.'

'You fool.' Rafter pointed at Sylvia. 'Look at her. De Foucheville was as dark as a blackamoor. She's fair like her mother and you. She has your eyes. De Foucheville never touched Marguerite. He was your loyal friend to the last breath of his life. She is the child of your loins.'

Christopher's mind reeled. Rafter was like a puppet-master, manipulating lives for some dark purpose of his own.

A tentative smile on his lips, David glanced from his father to Sylvia. 'She's my sister?'

'Aye, spalpeen,' Rafter said with a firm nod, the boy

tight to his side. 'That she is. Your father's legitimate child, born in wedlock. Just as he's always known.'

'Oh, God,' the Duke said, his eyes wild. 'What have I done? I never meant them any harm. I believed Rafter.' He looked at the disapproving faces surrounding him, his eyes desperate and pleading. 'There's no proof of any of this.'

Christopher clenched his jaw at the sight of Sylvia's wounded expression. Damn him for being so stiff-necked.

'There's a room full of people who have just heard you admit you married her mother, Huntingdon.' Christopher couldn't bring himself to honour the man with his title. He pulled the document from his breast pocket. 'And this, I believe, is the missing proof.' Garth looked over his shoulder as he unfolded the note Jeannie had given him. The writing was blurred, but it had the signature of a Protestant cleric and the avowal that William Woods had married one Marguerite Seaton.

'But why the last name Boisette?' Garth asked.

'To hide her from the Jacobites,' Rafter said. 'Basingstoke, as he was then, was well known to the authorities.'

'Boisette,' Garth said. 'Little forest. A clumsy play on words, I presume.'

Sylvia pressed her hand to her mouth. 'It is the name my mother used in Paris.'

The Duke groaned. 'Madame Gilbert has been milking me dry for years with that document. Then *she* started sending letters.' He nodded at Sylvia.

Sylvia gasped. 'I did no such thing.'

'They are all there in that drawer.' Huntingdon jerked his chin at the desk. 'She wanted a king's ransom to set up a brothel in Paris, to follow in her mother's footsteps.'

'No,' Sylvia cried out.

'Ah, your Grace,' Rafter put in, 'did ye never wonder

how your trusted Irish factotum managed to buy a grand estate in Ireland and raise the best horseflesh this side of Arabia?'

'What?'

'It was never your wife or your daughter. 'Twas me that had most of your money once Evernden's uncle took the girl from Paris.'

'Papa, I don't understand.' David's eyes grew round. 'If she is my sister, why doesn't she live with us?'

'He just doesn't understand,' Garth murmured in Christopher's ear.

'Understand what?'

A wry smile twisted Garth's mouth.

'The reason is, my young buck,' Rafter said, 'if anyone ever learned the truth, there would be no heir and possibly no dukedom either. Right, your Grace?'

Bloody hell. Christopher had been so busy thinking about what all this meant for Sylvia, it hadn't dawned on him that if the Duke's second marriage was bigamous, therefore not valid, Sylvia became a legitimate daughter, and young David became a bastard, leaving the Duke with no heir at all. His revelation must have shown on his face.

'Exactly,' Garth said.

What the hell was wrong with Garth? He looked green about the gills. Any moment now, he would cast up his accounts. Christopher had never seen him look so strange.

Christopher concentrated on Rafter. Somehow they were going to have to put him out of action and Garth didn't look as if he'd be much help.

Rafter puffed with pride as the Duke crumbled into the sofa cushions, suddenly spineless. Huntingdon buried his face in his hands.

For some dire purpose, Rafter had deliberately set out to destroy the Duke, inch by painful inch.

Desperation ravaging his face, Huntingdon looked up at his tormentor. 'Don't do this, please.'

Rafter moved so he could look directly down into Huntingdon's eyes. 'I planned to reveal all this when your daughter was back in the brothel, a *bona fide* whore, used by every man in Paris. Unfortunately, the Right Honourable high-and-mighty Mr Evernden here has been nothing but a thorn in my flesh. Still, he did the job just as well as any other client of Madame Gilbert's, didn't you, mate?'

Christopher swore violently, but repressed the desire to smash his fist into Rafter's smiling face. He couldn't risk the life of the youth glued to Rafter's side. Christopher wouldn't let another innocent be harmed by this madman.

Forcing David to bend with him, Rafter thrust his face into the Duke's. 'How does it feel? Your wife died of the pox, your daughter is a whore and your son is a disinherited bastard.'

David gasped.

The Duke groaned. 'Why did you do this to me? First my wife and now my son. You've taken everything.'

'Why?' Rafter howled with glee. 'The sins of the father shall be visited upon the children. I did to you what your father did to me and mine.'

Sylvia sank to her knees and grasped Huntingdon's hand. She inched nearer to Rafter. Christopher frowned. What the hell was she doing so close to the lunatic? Her eyes brightened, she peeped from under her lashes at the pistol, then sent a quick glance at Christopher. Tension radiated from her body. He felt its vibration in his own.

Bloody hell. She was going to knock the man over or do something equally rash. But what other choice did they have? He tensed, ready to spring and gave her a slight nod of acknowledgement. He was ready.

Sylvia threw herself up and back and knocked the pistol away from David. Christopher snatched the gun out of Rafter's hand.

The Irishman backed away and raised his hands. 'Do your worst, Evernden. I've done mine.'

Eyes full of pain, Sylvia stared down at Huntingdon as he hugged his son close to his chest, his shoulders shaking with suppressed sobs. Anguish formed a shield around her stiff body and Christopher feared she might shatter if he spoke one word.

He reached out and touched her arm. She thrust his hand away, her eyes glittering bright. 'I don't care about all this.' She swung her arm wide. 'I hate you. I always have. Keep your precious heir. I'll not tell anyone the truth. I'm leaving.'

Plain Mr David No-Name, with set jaw and tears drying on his downless cheeks, pulled himself out of his father's arms. 'It doesn't work that way, my lady.'

Chapter Eighteen

A glimmer of hope lifted Huntingdon's expression. 'If that is what she wants, perhaps it is for the best. No one regrets what happened more than I, but to ruin so many lives... Think of your mother, son.'

David's young face flushed. 'Think of the dishonour.'

Huntingdon's tongue flickered over his lips and he glanced at Sylvia. 'I never meant Marguerite or her daughter any harm. I truly loved her. When Rafter told me you wanted to be a courtesan like your mother, I let anger rule my head. I was wrong. I promise to do my duty by you.'

Pain filled Sylvia's eyes; it cut into Christopher like a whip.

Hades. What a dilemma. In one fell blow the Duke had lost his heir, his whole future, but for the man to let his own daughter sacrifice herself was pitiful. He wanted to take Huntingdon by the throat and force him to apologise.

He clenched his fists at his sides. Sylvia had made it clear she would not welcome his interference.

David drew himself up straight, his child's face mirroring his father's earlier haughty expression. 'No, Father. You taught me better. I will not dishonour my name…' he swallowed '…your name, by adding further crimes to Rafter's misdeeds against my half-sister. She has her place and I have mine.'

'Well said,' Christopher murmured.

At Christopher's side, Garth looked as sick as a horse. 'The devil is in it now,' he muttered. 'Such bloody nobility and he's no more than a stripling. I'm going to lose my dinner.'

'The boy is right, your Grace,' Christopher said, his tone impartial. 'No matter how you try, you can never keep this hidden.'

'I'll make sure of it,' Rafter gloated.

'Silence,' Huntingdon and Christopher said in unison.

Sylvia frowned at Rafter. 'Why are you doing this now? You've made your fortune in blackmail.'

Rafter dropped on to the sofa across from Huntingdon, his weather-beaten face arrogant and insolent. 'Because the old duke forced all the tenants off his land in Ireland, so he could raise fecking sheep.' He curled his lip. 'My family lived on that fine estate, but I wanted more and went off for a soldier. When I came back, cock o' the walk at having made me way up through the ranks, the jingle of gold in me pocket, they were gone.'

His hands curled into fists on his knees, the sinews in his wrists corded tight. 'Not even the foundation of the old house remained to show where they had lived for generations, working the land for the betterment of Huntingdons. Nothing but grass and sheep.'

Seemingly unable to bear to look at the Duke any more, he gazed into the flames in the hearth. His voice dropped to a roughened whisper. 'Oh, I found them in Dublin, all right. Me da was dead of a broken heart. Me mother lay dying in a stinking hovel on the charity of her relatives and me little sister was selling her body for pennies.'

He drew a shaking hand across his eyes. 'That's why.'

Nothing but the ticking clock and the hiss of the fire filled the silence.

As angry as Christopher felt at Rafter's use of Sylvia to gain revenge, he couldn't prevent a surge of pity for the fellow's agony. Sylvia's eyes reflected a similar sympathy. Of all people, she should not feel sympathy.

'I knew nothing of this,' Huntingdon said, his voice hoarse. 'My father did it without my knowledge.'

Turning, Rafter straightened and arrowed a glance at the Duke. 'It was your obligation to know what happened to your people. Just as it was your responsibility to protect your wife and child. But ye left it to someone else. And it was not done.'

Huntingdon wrung his papery hands. 'If you had just told me—'

'You dashed off to France like the divil was after you. And he was.' He gave a sharp laugh. 'I'm satisfied. You'll get no more heirs off your old duchess, even if you marry her now, and your whore of a daughter is restored to the family, while your son wallows in bastardy.'

Garth drew in a sharp breath. He looked like he'd been cut to the quick.

But something about the story did not make sense. Christopher racked his brain for an elusive memory somewhere on the fringes of his mind. Slouched in his seat, Rafter's eyes shifted from Christopher's direct gaze.

Drawing herself to her full height, Sylvia fixed Rafter with a haughty stare, so like her half-brother's just moments before Christopher couldn't doubt their relationship. 'I won't be party to this revenge of yours.'

'You don't actually have a choice,' Garth muttered.

'Whether you like it or not, his second marriage is bigamous.' His mouth twisted in a bitter smile. 'Under the law, a man has to recognise another man's child born to his wife. Your half-brother has no claim to the dukedom. There is no heir.'

Young David stood unflinching beneath Garth's harsh words and stared his fate bravely in the face. Christopher could only admire his courage.

Sylvia reached out a hand to the lad. 'You've been bred and trained for this all your life. Surely something can be done?'

How could she be so selfless? She was the legitimate daughter of a duke, entitled to all of the privileges and rights that went with it. A cold fist bunched in Christopher's stomach as he realised the full implications of her new status. She was so high above him, so close to royalty, he normally wouldn't even be invited to the same functions, let alone be permitted to marry her.

A black pit opened up in front of him.

He shook the thought away. This was not about him, or Sylvia, this was about truth and justice. And by God, he would see justice done.

Rafter shifted on the sofa. His gaze devoured the duke's son as if the destruction of the boy satisfied some primal hunger. At thirteen, the innocent youth didn't fully comprehend the face of evil.

Whereas Sylvia had never had the chance to be truly innocent. Rafter and the Duke had seen to that. Christopher tasted ashes in his mouth. David was roughly the same age now as Sylvia had been when John Evernden had rescued her from a horrific future in the brothel.

The recollection clicked into place like tumblers in a well-oiled lock. 'What was the date of your mother's death, Lady Sylvia?' Christopher asked.

Rafter jerked in his seat.

Sylvia stared at Christopher as if he was mad. She blinked and shook her head as if trying to make sense of his question.

Christopher raised his voice. 'When did she die?'

'What does it matter?' Rafter shouted. 'Die she did. In the pain and agony of the pox. A whore.'

Sylvia recoiled, her face as white as parchment.

'Shut him up,' Christopher said savagely to Garth.

Garth, foiling Rafter's attempts to bite him, shoved his handkerchief in the Irishman's mouth.

The Duke, slumped in the chair, his skin as grey as the ashes in the hearth, raised his head. 'I heard from Rafter that she died in March 1805. I had married again the previous February, thinking she must be dead by then. I had heard nothing for years. My God. My poor Marguerite. I never wanted that for her. Never.' He covered his face with his hands. 'When Rafter brought the news that the marriage was invalid, I didn't know what to do. Cover it up, Rafter said. No one would know. I… When she—' he pointed at Sylvia '—started to blackmail me, I thought it served her right.'

Christopher kept his voice calm. 'Sylvia, think. This is important. Jeannie told us the date of your mother's death. It was three months after you left Paris. When was that?'

'I arrived in England in—'

Rafter struggled to his feet and threw himself at Sylvia.

Without thinking, Christopher shielded her with his back. He lifted her out of Rafter's path by her shoulders. Her sweet body pressed against his chest. Her rapidly beating heart matched the banging of his own. She softened, her warmth pulled to him, her lips curved in a smile as she glanced up at him. He forced himself to pretend it wasn't happening, this instant arousal between them.

Garth seized Rafter by the throat and flung him back on to the sofa.

Christopher set Sylvia down at arm's length, ignoring the overwhelming desire to hold her close, to shelter her from this room of raging storms. He locked her sapphire gaze with his. 'When?'

Comprehension sparked in her expression. 'It was the winter of 1804—January, I think.'

'Then she died before my parents were married,' David cried. Face flushed red, he leapt at Rafter, fists flying. 'You lied.'

Garth restrained David in a gentle hold. 'Relax, lad. He'll get his dues soon enough.'

The relief flooding Huntingdon's face told Christopher all he needed to know. Christopher rejoiced in Sylvia's good fortune, even as his own situation solidified with all the ugly twists of a churchyard gargoyle.

The legitimate daughter of a duke, an heiress, a beautiful, desirable woman with her pick of the most eligible bachelors of the *ton*, would never choose the second son of a baron. Nor would he expect it. Loss emptied his chest and left a hollow space.

He'd have to admit to ruining her and do the honourable thing and ask for her hand. For one blissful moment, he imagined Huntingdon accepting his offer, then despair rolled over him. If Huntingdon didn't laugh in his face, the old Duke would probably challenge him to a duel.

All he had ever offered her was a *carte blanche*. And now, right after he learned she was legitimate, he was going to offer her marriage. How bloody ironic. She'd never believe he'd already decided he didn't care about the misfortune of her birth. Not now.

He straightened his shoulders. No matter what, he'd do his duty.

* * *

'A Mr Christopher Evernden to see you, your Grace,' announced the Huntingdon butler.

Christopher. At last. After four long weeks since they'd seen each other, Sylvia couldn't prevent a smile from curving her lips or the rush of pleasure at the sound of his name. She threw her embroidery to one side and surged to her feet.

She caught the Duchess's raised eyebrows and subsided onto the sofa. Lady Huntingdon, with her tight bun and unusually severe style of dress for a member of the *ton*, had proved to be a welcoming angel to her long-lost stepdaughter.

The Duchess had accepted Huntingdon's explanation about his daughter's sudden emergence from an isolated convent in the French Alps. There had been stranger tales of lost family members during the French Revolution and the wars that followed.

The Duchess had thrown herself into the business of bringing Sylvia out with an energy that seemed to surprise even the Duke. Sylvia had begun to love her stepmother and she adored her half-brother, David. She'd even learned to forgive her father as she learned of the lengths to which Rafter had gone to destroy his belief in her mother.

Christopher paused in the doorway, his gaze sweeping the room and meeting hers. His forest-green eyes contained the haunted quality of a lonely mountain glen, all dark shadows. Had he missed her as much as she had missed him?

Not a hair out of place and his black coat and white cravat impeccably neat, he looked paler than when she had seen him last, thin and hollow-cheeked. She recognised his expression, reserved caution, the way it had

been at the reading of Monsieur Jean's will. But she had
seen the other side of him since then—anger, reckless-
ness, passion, tenderness. All the things she had grown
to love in him.

Christopher bowed low. 'Your Grace. Lady Sylvia.'

In the weeks since Rafter had made his dreadful reve-
lations, this was the first time Christopher had called.
She smiled and held out her hand. 'How lovely to see
you, Mr Evernden.'

He took it. His touch was fleeting, hesitant. 'I'm glad
to find you well, Lady Sylvia.'

'All the better for seeing you,' Sylvia said.

Christopher glanced at the Duchess, who watched
him with bright, expectant eyes in her severe countenance. 'I wonder if I might ask Lady Sylvia to take a
turn around the square with me, your Grace?'

She inclined her head. 'Of course, Mr Evernden. One
of the footmen will accompany you.'

Sylvia tamped down her impatience. This need for
constant attendance sparked her impatience at regular
intervals, but she tried to accept it with good grace.

Her heart fluttered with anticipation. How clever of
Christopher to think of it. Walking with a footman a
few steps behind would give them more privacy than
her stepmother's drawing room and she had so much
to tell him.

She hastened to her chamber to fetch her shawl and
hat. By the time she got downstairs, Christopher held his
hat and gloves in his hand.

He placed her hand on his arm and they stepped out
into the street and crossed the road to the small
deserted park in the centre of the elegant square.
Sylvia glanced up at the grey sky. No doubt the inter-
mittent rain had kept the nursemaids and governesses
indoors today.

Silently, they strolled beneath the overhanging branches and between the flowerbeds full of daisies and roses.

Sylvia revelled in Christopher's closeness, the heat of his body at her side, the firm strength of his arm beneath her fingers, and yet she sensed a distance in him.

'I'm so glad you came today,' she said. 'So much has happened these past few weeks. My head is spinning. You can't imagine. I have been introduced to so many people I can't remember them all.' She laughed. 'To tell you the truth, I am not sure if I am on my head or my heels, but I missed you.'

'I didn't get back into town until yesterday. I came as soon as I received your note.'

Disapproval coloured his tone, as if sending him a note were somehow improper.

'I met Lord Stanford at Almack's and he mentioned you would be back this week. I wanted to talk to you.'

'Well, here I am.'

There was brusqueness in his tone, a subtle impatience she had never heard before.

She stopped and turned, staring into his eyes, trying to see behind the greens and browns gazing back at her. 'What is wrong?'

His expression remained polite, formal, as if they were strangers. 'Nothing is wrong. I just didn't expect to receive a note requiring my presence, that is all.'

A dreadful sense of impending doom ran like a cold snake down the back of her neck and into her stomach. 'If I hadn't sent you a note, would you have come to see me at all?'

He shrugged and gestured that they should continue walking. He matched his steps to hers.

Fear sharpened her tone. 'Would you?'

'Lady Sylvia, I am sure you have realised by now that you are far above my touch. You are moving in circles to which I could never aspire.' He paused as if he were searching for words.

She glanced up at him from beneath the brim of her hat. His gaze was fixed on the distance, his mouth a thin straight line. 'I think it would be better if you do not contact me again.'

Her breath caught in her throat. It was as if someone had placed something heavy on her chest, a rock, or a mountain. Hot tears choked her throat. No wonder he hadn't been to see her. Here she was, assuming she was respectable enough for him at last, when all the time he wanted nothing to do with her.

Fool. He had never spoken of love. He had wanted her and she had given herself to him with all the abandon of a whore. He was telling her he had had his fill. And now, just like her mother, she would humble herself before him because she couldn't help it. Because she loved him. 'Why?'

At the centre of the park, four wrought-iron benches sat in military square formation. In front of them, an ornamental fountain played gentle water-tunes to a pool of reeds and water lilies.

'Please be seated, Lady Sylvia,' he said.

Boiling temper erupted from deep inside her. Rage at her own foolish heart. Anger at her belief in him and at his coldness when she needed his warmth. She plumped down on to the seat and glared up at him. 'Lady Sylvia this and Lady Sylvia that. Are you so impressed with titles then, Mr Evernden? And is it still not good enough for you? Or is it because you know the truth about my mother?'

A flash of pain glittered like splintered glass in his

eyes. He glanced away. 'You are talking nonsense.' His tone was harsh. 'My business demands a great deal of my time. In fact, I do not know how much longer I will be in England, since I have business interests abroad.'

A muscle flickered in his jaw, then he lowered himself to sit beside her. He flicked at a speck of dust on his boot with his glove. 'Your father has great plans for you, Lady Sylvia. He has an opportunity to make up for all the years he lost because of Rafter and his schemes. You should be happy.' His words were rational, his tone gentle, persuasive and patently false.

Aware of the rapid beating of her heart, Sylvia took slow, deep breaths. She'd controlled this pain before, this urge to cry hot tears. She'd been hurt many times by careless cruelty. But not like this, her heart cried.

He didn't love her.

It wasn't a mountain on her chest, squeezing out every bit of hope and joy she'd ever known, it was a whole continent.

She kept her gaze fixed on the footman, who gazed with blank concentration at a nearby rhododendron bush. Hands behind his back, he rocked on his heels and kept a wary eye on them. But for his presence, Sylvia might have thrown herself at Christopher, kissed him and taunted him to tell her that he didn't want her. It had worked last time.

She felt her need for him with every fibre of her being each time he glanced her way. Like the yearning note of a violin, it thrummed sensuously in the air between them, calling. Sickened by her weakness, she turned her face away.

'And what about you, Mr Evernden? Are you happy?'

'Of course.'

Two of the smallest words in the world, they were

rapier-sharp and accurate in the precision with which he used them.

Anger, fear and pain all disappeared at their cruel incision.

An icy calm filled her. A cold emptiness chilled her blood, her limbs and her sliced-to-ribbons heart. She had too much pride to let him see the effect of his carefully delivered *coup de grâce*.

She schooled her face into calm indifference. 'Thank you for coming to visit me today, Mr Evernden.' She rose to her feet. 'I appreciate you taking the time, since you obviously have so many more important matters demanding your attention. Now, if you will excuse me, I believe I have an imminent appointment with the *modiste*.'

Careful to avoid allowing her skirts to brush against any part of him and with a bare nod in his direction, she swept past him and strolled home, a home as meaningless as a prison.

Sylvia craned her neck to see around the gentlemen who hemmed her into the corner of Lady Dunfield's glittering ballroom. She had hoped Christopher would attend this last major ball of London's Season before everyone departed for the summer. It was two in the morning and no sign of him yet. Why would tonight be any different? She hadn't seen him once in all these weeks since he'd called on her.

She had no pride left, she realised sadly. Each morning she got up, hoping that today she would see him, and that his eyes would reveal his feelings and prove her heart wasn't broken, even if his lips would not speak the words. That, in spite of what he had said, in his heart he loved her.

Each night, she went to bed and cried into her pillow.

Before she had met Christopher Evernden, she had never cried. She dragged her mind from the memory of his beloved face to the eager young fop murmuring in her ear.

'Allow me to fetch you some lemonade, Lady Sylvia,' Colonel Nettle said.

Sylvia nodded, squinting against the dazzle of diamonds and staring past the flurry of pinks and lemons and whites of the débutantes swirling on the arms of their black-coated escorts in the last waltz of the night.

Lord Banbury on her left said something and Sylvia nodded absently as Lord Stanford, a full head taller than most of the men around him, threaded his way around the room. It wasn't so much that others blocked his path, he just seemed to be taking a highly circuitous route. The reason became clear as he hauled on the shoulder of a footman carrying a tray of drinks and nearly pulled the man over. Stanford was a positive drunkard and nothing like his brother.

She wanted to go home.

'Will you, Lady Sylvia?' Lord Banbury sounded insistent.

'Yes,' she said to be rid of him.

'Wonderful. I will call for you tomorrow at half-past four.'

Sylvia turned her full attention to the pimply Viscount. He was at least twenty-five, but from her observation of him at the dizzying number of balls and routs she had attended these past few weeks, he behaved more like an emerging adolescent. 'What?'

He pouted. 'You weren't listening. But you said you'd come. I'm driving you to the park tomorrow. You said yes.'

Sylvia took pity on him. It wasn't his fault he wasn't Christopher, that he didn't have hazel eyes with emerald fire in their depths or an intellect like a steel trap. 'Of course. But you will have to excuse me, I need to speak to my mother.'

'You lucky dog, Banbury,' Marchant said, a wisp of man who had stepped on her toes twice during the co-tillion. 'The Snow Queen never drives with anyone. She won't even waltz. We should try to distract her more often.'

A ripple of male ridicule lapped against her back at Banbury's discomfort. God, they were such a shallow lot. Sylvia walked towards her stepmother as swiftly as she could in her slender-fitting blue silk ballgown and matching slippers.

Broad shoulders collided with her and their owner turned to apologise.

'Good evening, my lady.'

Garth. *Merde.* She didn't want to speak to him. 'Excuse me, Lord Stanford,' she said and glided away.

He kept pace with her. 'Still the same cold-hearted bitch, I see,' he said low in her ear. 'I would have thought driving my brother out of England would have been enough to warm even your chilly little heart.'

The words penetrated her haze of misery. 'He's leaving the country soon?'

Garth's smile was a sardonic sneer. 'People in your exalted world don't hear much about the damage they do to the little people, do they?'

He referred to Rafter, no doubt. 'What about Christopher?'

He raised a slashing dark brow.

Heat climbed into her face. 'Mr Evernden, I mean.'

'He's taken your father at his word. He's leaving for America. You'll never have to suffer the embarrassment of his presence again.'

She recoiled at his venomous tone. 'My father?'

'Just so. At the request of the Duke and to avoid you further distress at the sight of lowly, unwanted Christopher, he sets sail on the *Free Spirit* out of Dover. She casts off at noon on Saturday. I can't imagine what he ever saw in a hardened cow like you, for all your beauty.'

With a flourish, he executed an unsteady bow. 'You, dear lady, will be happy to know you got your way. He's leaving England.'

As he strode away, several female heads turned to watch the dark and dangerous rake's progress. His imperceptible roll spoke volumes about his state of inebriation.

Christopher was leaving.

For a moment, Sylvia felt strangely dizzy. A hollow sinking sensation swirled in her stomach. It clawed its way into her chest and filled her mind with darkness. A rushing sound filled her ears. *Oh, God. Don't let me faint. Not here.*

'Are you all right, Lady Sylvia?' Nettle, with her lemonade, hovered at her elbow.

She took slow deep breaths. Christopher had never spoken of love. Never had he indicated anything beyond passion during their brief time together. She had convinced herself his omission was unintentional. Now she had her answer. She must have been mad to think anything else.

The wall of ice that had protected her all her life did nothing to shield her from the ache where her heart had once resided. Carelessly ripped out and discarded by a man who cared nothing for her, it lay crushed at her feet. She was just like her mother, waiting for a lover who would never return.

Incroyable. She was not her mother. She knew better.

She glanced at Nettle's anxious expression and gave a shaky laugh 'Yes. Thank you. I just...' Her eyes burned and she choked on her words. 'Excuse me,' she murmured and followed Garth into the card room.

'Goodbye, Kit.'

Dover's white cliffs towered above Christopher's head and seagulls screamed abuse at the stiff breeze supporting them aloft. He hunched into the collar of his thick woollen coat.

Dover. It seemed as if some of the most portentous moments in his life were somehow connected to this dirty port. He released his grip on the rail and turned to grasp Garth's outstretched hand.

'Look after yourself, brother.' Garth's voice hoarsened with unspoken emotion.

It wasn't like Garth to be so serious, so grave, almost lost. Christopher blinked away the mist blurring his brother and the clean lines of the *Free Spirit*. 'I'll miss you too. Take care of Mother. I know she acts as if she favours me over you, but if you'd be a little kinder to her, Garth, you and she might rub along better. I talked to her about it too. Yesterday.'

Garth took a step back, his mouth open. 'You did what?'

Christopher shrugged. 'I told her she could be a little less hard on you.'

'And what did she say to that, pray?'

She'd closed up like an oyster protecting a sharp grain of irritation. 'She changed the subject.'

Garth blinked. 'Kit...' His gaze dropped to the deck. He cleared his throat, tugged at his cravat. 'Kit, there's something you need to know.'

'What?'

'The devil. It's not really my secret to reveal, but, damn it it all, you are the only one who doesn't seem to realise...'

Never had Christopher seen Garth speechless. 'Spit it out, before you choke, or the ship sets sail.'

'I'm not an Evernden.'

Garth had something loose in his attic. The drink was finally ruining his mind. Christopher put a hand on his shoulder, prepared to suggest he visit a doctor.

'I'm not Father's seed,' Garth bit out. 'Mother... made a mistake. I'm sorry.'

The deck pitched beneath Christopher's feet, yet the sea remained calm. 'My God. That's why you acted so oddly at the Duke's. But why apologise to me?'

'You're not thinking, Kit. You should have been the heir. You are Father's first-born.'

'Bloody hell.' The realisation hit him like a hammer between the eyes.

Garth stared over the rail. 'I hope you aren't going to hate me, the way Father did. The way Mother does.'

'You numbskull. Is that why you've been such an idiot all these years? Look around you. I have everything I could possibly want.' Everything except Sylvia, and a minor title wouldn't have helped him in that quarter.

'Thank you, Kit. You don't know how much that means.' Garth's voice sounded hoarse.

'Please,' Christopher said, 'do something for me. Try to get along with Mother until I return?'

'God,' Garth drawled, suddenly his old insouciant self, 'Mother's hooks are so deep into Angleforth, she wouldn't notice if I dropped dead tomorrow.'

Christopher laughed just as Garth had wanted. He shook his head. 'She'd notice.'

'I wish you weren't going.'

'I'll be back before you know it. Five years is not so long.'

'Yes,' Garth choked out. 'It bloody well is.'

Christopher found himself crushed in Garth's bear-like hug, his nose pressed into the rough wool of his brother's coat. He squeezed back and patted Garth's shoulder. They parted and gazed past each other with embarrassed grins and watery eyes.

A bell rang. Whistles sounded. The ship strained against its creaking ropes as if anxious to be underway.

Christopher rubbed his chilled hands together and nodded to the waiting tender. 'If you don't go soon, you'll be on your way to America.'

'I wish.'

'Come with me.'

A cynical smile twisted Garth's mouth. 'Sounds too much like hard work.'

They walked together to the gangway where a boat waited to row Garth to shore. One last link, a flimsy wooden boat soon to sever the tie with England. Tarry-pigtailed sailors shouted back and forth at the capstan and released the hawsers holding the ship at anchor.

'I saw her,' Garth said, stepping through the gap in the rail.

His breath caught. He didn't have to ask who Garth meant. 'Don't,' he managed.

A strange rueful grin on his lips, Garth hesitated a moment before he plunged down the ladder, nodding at the sailor waiting, oars at the ready. A few strong pulls took him to shore, where his long stride carried him swiftly along the dock, past the sailors and fishermen and past the blowsy fishwives who followed his broad-shouldered figure with longing glances.

The *Free Spirit* slipped her moorings and eased out of her berth.

Christopher walked to the stern, keeping his gaze fixed on Garth's back, now just a black speck, until he could no longer discern him from the rest of the teeming ant-like masses scurrying along the shoreline.

Returning to the rail, he kept his gaze fixed on land, determined to see the last of England before he went below to his stateroom.

It was an over-luxurious apartment for a merchant-man, but this was his ship. He glanced around with pride at the gleaming decks and smartly turned-out crew. He acknowledged the captain's salute with a nod. He lacked the sense of excitement he'd once felt for this ship, yet his pride remained—after all, it belonged to him.

He returned his attention to the horizon. The wind picked up and the ship heeled over, making every yard of canvas count. The sun escaped the confines of billowing grey-and-silver clouds, making steely waves shimmer like pirate's treasure. Far off, the cliffs gleamed like brilliant sails, the ancient walls of Dover Castle a turreted crow's nest against the skyline. The great ship of England was departing, leaving him alone on an insignificant wooden platform, marooned in a vast ocean, perhaps never to see it again.

The clouds returned to gobble great bites out of the light and the coast became a faint smudge in the distance above sluggish grey-green water.

Somewhere along that smudge he had first set eyes on Sylvia. She had been so solitary at his uncle's funeral. Alone, but bright and hard-edged like a polished jewel. It wasn't until he'd looked deep beneath the glittering facets that he'd found the fire of her soul. But once found, there was no forgetting its heat.

As the ship drew further from shore, he realised no distance would be far enough to allow him to forget. He struck the rail with his fist. Shockwaves vibrated up his arm and jarred the hollow emptiness in his chest. He clenched his jaw. Nothing, not even sheer physical strength, could change what had happened.

He took a deep breath and forced himself to calmness. Sylvia deserved better. The Duke had put it succinctly the morning Christopher had gone to make his offer of marriage. All her life, she had been deprived of the privileges of her birth. It was Huntingdon's avowed intention to restore everything Rafter had stolen from her.

Everything. Including a brilliant marriage.

Forced to agree with Huntingdon, he hadn't flinched when the Duke had suggested it might be better if Christopher left London. He was a distraction and a possible cause of gossip. He'd made his plans to leave for America the same day.

Hell. He had always wanted to go to the New World. It was a land where men stood or fell by their own abilities, their wits, their physical strength, not by who their father was, or the order of their emergence from the womb.

His cabin was filled with books about the new country he was about to embrace. They would keep his mind off his regrets. He turned away from the sight of land.

A lone figure, slight, windblown, leaned against the mast.

Sylvia? Strands of gold hair lashed her rosy cheeks. Her bright blue gaze held steady on his face.

Half-expecting to find some kind of mystical sea beast had enchanted him, he gazed around the ship. He was dreaming, only now he was doing it in the daytime.

He shook his head to clear his vision. But this was no mirage. This was a living breathing Sylvia.

She braced one hand against the mast and cocked her head in question.

What the hell had she done? If word got out, she'd be ruined. His feet seemed glued in place.

* * *

Despite Garth's assurances, Sylvia hadn't been completely convinced Christopher would be happy to see her. At the sight of his shocked face, the deck began to crumble beneath her feet.

'What the hell are you doing here?' he shouted against the wind.

She forced herself to remain still, not to throw herself against his broad chest and beg him to let her stay. 'I'm going to America.'

He strode across the deck and grasped her shoulders, his eyes full of green fury. 'What are you talking about?'

She took a deep breath and flung herself trustingly over the edge of the precipice of her pride. 'I love you and I'm coming with you.'

Stark horror filled his expression. 'You can't.'

She was in a headlong fall and Christopher hadn't made a move to catch her. 'You don't have to marry me,' she gabbled. 'I'll leave whenever you get tired of me. But I won't spend my life waiting.'

He shook his head.

Oh, God. He was going to let her shatter in a million pieces at his feet.

He pushed his hair out of his eyes. 'You have to go back.'

Sharp rocks of despair rushed up to meet her. He didn't want her. He really didn't.

She began to pull away.

He caught her hand. 'Your father. He's only just found you. He'll be devastated.'

This was about them, her and Christopher. 'He knows. He doesn't like it, but he understands. Christopher, please.'

His lashes swept down, blocking his thoughts, deep lines etching the sides of his mouth.

The ship rolled and bucked beneath her feet; the sound of the wind reverberated like thunder in the sails and hummed in the rigging. Her hair whipped at her face, salty and damp. Each second crawled like an hour, while she waited for his denial.

He opened his eyes. Powerful yearning and fierce possessiveness burned deep in their gleaming emerald depths. 'Sylvia. My love.'

He pulled her tight against his warm, hard body. He bent his head and found her mouth with his. Crushed in his arms, his heart beating steadily against her chest, the pure delight in his voice ringing in her ears, her fear faded like sea mist.

She floated to the ground as light as thistledown, caught firmly in his arms.

'Oh, God,' he whispered against her mouth. 'I love you so much. I thought I'd come back and find you married to a bloody marquess or an earl.'

He tilted her chin until he could look into her eyes. 'You're absolutely sure about this?' Anxiety roughened his voice.

She didn't try to hide the tears of joy blurring her sight. She nodded.

His hand came up and freed her hair from its pins. It swirled around them, a shimmering veil of gold. 'I love you.' His mouth covered hers with infinite tenderness.

A boom thundered overhead and they looked up.

A red flare streaked above them. 'What the devil...?' Christopher muttered.

'*Sea Witch* on the port bow, sir,' the captain called.

Sylvia laughed at the ludicrous expression of surprise on Christopher's face when they went to the rail.

'How the hell did Garth get my mother on that ship?'

Sylvia felt the heat rise in her cheeks and looked down at the deck. Now he would know they were all in the plot.

'Bloody hell. And your father and brother. They're all on the *Witch*.'

Sylvia peeped over the rail at the madly waving crowd on the deck of Garth's yacht and waved back. A string of coloured flags climbed the mast.

'Message from the *Sea Witch*, sir.'

'Well?' Christopher said, his mouth quirking at the corners.

'It says "marry the girl", sir.'

Christopher fumbled at his neck, pulling at his neck-cloth.

Braced against the ship's rail, Sylvia held her breath, suddenly unsure. He pulled free a chain and opened the clasp. A gold circle encrusted with diamonds and sapphires lay on his palm. Christopher took her hand and went down on one knee.

'My lady, would you do me the very great honour of becoming my wife?'

A huge burning lump blocked her throat and made her eyes water.

He gripped her hand. 'Sylvia,' he said. 'For God's sake. Will you?'

'Yes.' She laughed through her tears. 'Oh, yes. I will.'

He leaped up, slipped the ring on her finger and crushed her to his chest.

'Sir,' the captain said. They turned to face him. He wore a huge grin and beside him stood a parson with a bible in his hand.

'Garth managed to find a cleric who wanted to travel to America,' Sylvia explained at his look of amazement.

More rockets burst overhead. Christopher glanced

over the rail at the upturned faces of the expectant, but distant, bridal party and raised a questioning brow.

'Shall I begin, sir?' the parson asked.

Christopher encircled Sylvia in the warmth of his strong arms and his chuckle reverberated through her body.

'What the hell are you waiting for, man? Begin. Time is wasting and we've some catching up to do.'

* * * * *

0609/04a

MILLS & BOON
Historical

On sale 3rd July 2009

Regency

THE NOTORIOUS MR HURST
by Louise Allen

Mr Eden Hurst is sexy, talented, intelligent – and resoundingly *in*eligible! It seems an impossible task, but Maude sets out to make cynical Eden realise he needs love…and her. Society is about to see she can be just as shocking as her Ravenhurst friends when she puts her mind to it!

The penultimate instalment of Louise Allen's
***Those Scandalous Ravenhursts** mini-series!*

RUNAWAY LADY
by Claire Thornton

With his curved Turkish sword and dark, brooding looks, Harry Ward is a formidable adversary. Lady Saskia van Buren's life is in danger, so she has fled to London and hired him as her protector. But Harry is torn between duty and desire, and will do whatever it takes to keep Saskia safe – even make her his convenient bride…

Available at WHSmith, Tesco, ASDA, and all good bookshops
www.millsandboon.co.uk

MILLS&BOON

Historical

On sale 3rd July 2009

Regency
THE WICKED LORD RASENBY
by Marguerite Kaye

The devastatingly attractive and wealthy Kit, Lord Rasenby, is bored, so the incurable womaniser is tempted by a most unusual offer. If he provides the intriguing Clarissa with the adventure of a lifetime, she will provide him with – herself! No self-respecting rake could turn such an offer down…

SURRENDER TO THE HIGHLANDER
by Terri Brisbin

Growing up in a convent, Margriet was entirely innocent in the ways of the world. Sent to escort her home, Rurik is shocked to be drawn to a sensual woman – wearing the habit of a nun!

THE RASCAL
by Lisa Plumley

No man would ever trap Grace Crabtree into wedlock – so why did the rugged, laconic, *infuriating* Jack Murphy keep flirting with her – and why did it make her feel so delicious inside…?

Available at WHSmith, Tesco, ASDA, and all good bookshops
www.millsandboon.co.uk

0709/10/MB227

The beautiful Fitzmanning sisters
are ready to scandalise the Ton

Three fabulous Regency stories in
one volume featuring:

Justine and the Noble Viscount by Diane Gaston

Annalise and the Scandalous Rake
by Deb Marlowe

Charlotte and the Wicked Lord
by Amanda McCabe

Available 19th June 2009

www.millsandboon.co.uk   M&B

0609/27/MB223

In the Sheikh's power

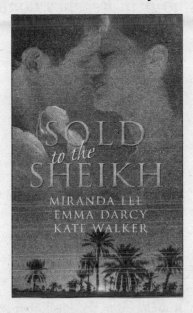

Be tempted by three seductive Sheikhs in:

Love–Slave to the Sheikh by Miranda Lee
Traded to the Sheikh by Emma Darcy
At the Sheikh's Command by Kate Walker

Available 5th June 2009

www.millsandboon.co.uk

Sparkling ballrooms and wealthy glamour in Regency London

Kidnapped in the small hours,
Miss Helen Walford was rescued by the
infamous rakehell, the Earl of Merton!

Her only defence lay in anonymity. But captured
by her beauty and bravery, the Earl of Merton
knew that he had to find his mysterious lady.
He'd move heaven and earth to track down the
woman he knew to be his destiny.

Available 19th June 2009

www.mirabooks.co.uk

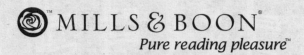

MILLS & BOON®

Pure reading pleasure™

www.millsandboon.co.uk

- All the latest titles
- Free online reads
- Irresistible special offers

And there's more...

- Missed a book? Buy from our huge discounted backlist
- Sign up to our FREE monthly eNewsletter
- eBooks available now
- More about your favourite authors
- Great competitions

Make sure you visit today!

www.millsandboon.co.uk

FREE!

2 Books
and a surprise gift!

We would like to take this opportunity to thank you for reading this Mills & Boon® book by offering you the chance to take TWO more specially selected titles from the Historical series absolutely FREE! We're also making this offer to introduce you to the benefits of the Mills & Boon® Book Club™—

- ★ **FREE home delivery**
- ★ **FREE gifts and competitions**
- ★ **FREE monthly Newsletter**
- ★ **Exclusive Mills & Boon Book Club offers**
- ★ **Books available before they're in the shops**

Accepting these FREE books and gift places you under no obligation to buy, you may cancel at any time, even after receiving your free shipment. Simply complete your details below and return the entire page to the address below. You don't even need a stamp!

YES! Please send me 2 free Historical books and a surprise gift. I understand that unless you hear from me, I will receive 4 superb new titles every month for just £3.79 each, postage and packing free. I am under no obligation to purchase any books and may cancel my subscription at any time. The free books and gift will be mine to keep in any case.

H9ZEF

Ms/Mrs/Miss/Mr ....Initials ....
BLOCK CAPITALS PLEASE

Surname ....

Address ....

....

....Postcode ....

Send this whole page to:
UK: FREEPOST CN81, Croydon, CR9 3WZ

Offer valid in UK only and is not available to current Mills & Boon Book Club subscribers to this series. Overseas and Eire please write for details. We reserve the right to refuse an application and applicants must be aged 18 years or over. Only one application per household. Terms and prices subject to change without notice. Offer expires 31st August 2009. As a result of this application, you may receive offers from Harlequin Mills & Boon and other carefully selected companies. If you would prefer not to share in this opportunity please write to The Data Manager, PO Box 676, Richmond, TW9 1WU.

Mills & Boon® is a registered trademark owned by Harlequin Mills & Boon Limited.
The Mills & Boon® Book Club™ is being used as a trademark.